GIDEON DRAKE

Realm Of Illusions

Copyright © 2024 by Gideon Drake

All rights reserved. No part of this publication may be reproduced, stored or transmitted in any form or by any means, electronic, mechanical, photocopying, recording, scanning, or otherwise without written permission from the publisher. It is illegal to copy this book, post it to a website, or distribute it by any other means without permission.

This novel is entirely a work of fiction. The names, characters and incidents portrayed in it are the work of the author's imagination. Any resemblance to actual persons, living or dead, events or localities is entirely coincidental.

First edition

ISBN: 9798285830726

This book was professionally typeset on Reedsy. Find out more at reedsy.com

To those who have ever questioned the line between dreams and reality,
To the ones who have battled their own illusions, facing fears that lurk in the quiet corners of the mind,
And to the dreamers who dare to step into the unknown—may you always find your way back.
This book is for you.

Acknowledgments

Writing *Realm of Illusions* has been a journey through the depths of fear, imagination, and the blurred line between reality and dreams. This book would not have been possible without the support, encouragement, and inspiration from so many along the way.

To my family and friends—your unwavering belief in me, even when I doubted myself, has been my anchor. Your patience as I disappeared into the world of nightmares and illusions means more than I can express.

To my fellow writers and readers—you are the fuel that keeps the fire of storytelling alive. Every discussion, critique, and word of encouragement has helped shape this story into what it is today.

To the creators of eerie stories, haunting dreams, and psychological thrillers—your works have inspired me to dive deeper into the mysteries of the mind.

And to you, the reader—thank you for stepping into this world, for allowing yourself to be swept into the dreamscape of *Realm of Illusions*. Without you, this story would remain a whisper in the void.

May you always find your way through the illusions.

Other books by Gideon Drake

"Awake In The Shadows"

Prologue

The light flowed across the twisted walls and undulating floors, creating shadows that defied comprehension. I stood at the center of a vast hall—or what felt like one—its walls bending inward at impossible angles, folding into themselves as though the architecture obeyed a logic not meant for human eyes. Overhead, untethered chandeliers floated in empty air, catching light from no discernible source and scattering it in fractured shards that danced across the curling surfaces.

The part of me trained to cling to evidence, physics, and reason whispered in protest. Angles did not bend like this. Light did not fracture and slither this way. But beneath that thin veneer of logic, something colder stirred—something that murmured, "Here, they do."

A melody drifted through the space, delicate and piercing, like music drawn from glass. It shifted ceaselessly, a fragile thread never weaving into a recognizable pattern, pricking at half-buried memories. It brought back the dissonant lullabies of childhood, the eerie tunes that left me sleepless, eyes pinned to the ceiling long after they should have coaxed me to rest. And beneath that melody, the whispers began—thin, silken murmurs at the edge of hearing, threading into my thoughts like cobwebs spun too fine to brush away.

They appeared without sound, without warning. One blink, and they were simply there, encircling me in perfect symmetry. They carved their masks into eternal expressions, sharpening joy into cruelty, bloating sorrow into grotesquerie, and polishing rage into something almost holy. Gold leaf traced the contours of jeweled eyes, catching the molten light and making the masks shimmer as if they breathed or watched.

"Welcome to our circle," a voice intoned—not through lips, but directly into my mind, bypassing the clumsy vehicle of sound.

One figure turned, pivoting with an unnatural fluidity toward its neighbor: a fox mask wrought of silver and rust. Before my eyes, its surface rippled, liquefying into the tender shape of a dove mid-flight, the shift so seamless it tore at the primitive part of my brain that still understood the boundary between what could and could not be. A knot tightened in my gut, twisting into that old, ancestral command: Run.

Their gowns and suits shimmered with an otherworldly sheen, the fabric sliding like water over hidden depths, whispering in a language I couldn't decipher. The air around them pulsed, each breath of silk suggesting folds that concealed endless, secret hollows. Then came the question, a voice of pearl and bone: "Are you here to watch—or to perform?"

The circle drew tighter. I saw no movement, yet the space around me constricted, the air itself closing in until each breath came sharp and shallow. Their expressions had changed—I hadn't seen them shift, but they had, and panic scraped up the brittle edges of my composure. I grasped at a mental lifeline, conjuring my office, its battered leather chair, the steady blink of monitors, and the clean, ordered world of sleep studies. I clung to that image, white-knuckled and desperate.

PROLOGUE

Raising trembling fingers to my face, I traced lips, cheeks, and nose. Bare skin. Human. For a moment, relief surged, bright and brittle—until my eyes caught the fractured reflection in a shard of light. My features stretched, twisted like taffy drawn across a funhouse mirror. And just like that, a childhood memory surged up—six years old, lost in the maze at the carnival, surrounded by bent mirrors that turned Mother into a stranger and self into a monster. For a breathless eternity, I had believed I'd never escape.

"What is this place?" My whisper fractured in the air, splintering back to me in layered echoes, each return deeper, more hollow, until it no longer sounded like my voice.

The masked figures began to sway, their movements rhythmic but wrong, limbs bending at impossible angles, folding and unfolding with an eerie grace. They moved like the sleep-trapped patients I had studied: beautiful, unsettling, lost in a realm neither waking nor dreaming. A hum rose among them, faint at first, coiling under the melody, insinuating itself not into my ears, but directly into my mind.

That old lullaby resurfaced—Sleep, little one, dream away—its sweetness curdling into something ancient, something predatory. Words flickered at the edge of comprehension, a language I shouldn't know but instinctively understood: promises of endless sleep and dreams that consumed the dreamer whole.

The dance spiraled inward, their bodies weaving shapes my mind strained to follow, patterns slipping through reason like water through cupped hands. Their masks remained fixed, even as their bodies melted into fluid, inhuman grace. My stomach clenched in revolt. I tried to close my eyes, but the knowledge that worse might wait in the dark kept them open.

The whispering swelled, the music knotting into a tangled, unbearable harmony. Each note seemed to warp the space around it, bending the walls, making the air viscous and heavy with memory. The weight of forgotten moments pressed against my skin, crushing breath from my chest. I fought to inhale as hands emerged from the tangle—too long, too pale, moving with a precision that defied life. Where they passed, they left afterimages burned into the air, brief flickers of vision stolen from sleep disorders and patient files—faces half-seen in sleep paralysis, shadows that straddled the worlds of dream and waking.

I tried to run. My body became immobile, paralyzed by terror, with my limbs frozen as if the very air had thickened into glass. Time slowed, thickened, each second dragging until it cracked, refracting the moment into a thousand splintered shards. The chanting surged to a fevered crescendo, a vibration that sank into teeth and into bones, a frequency that gnawed at the edges of reason.

And then the voice came. "Don't leave us, Dr. Sullivan." It threaded from every corner, layered, distorted—like the slurred recordings of patients muttering in sleep, multiplied and twisted into something unholy.

The masks rippled faster: gold to silver, flesh to mist, shadow to something raw and pulsing beneath. I recognized the faces beneath those masks. Mrs. Chen, from two floors down, her gentle smile curdled into hunger. David, my patient from that morning, his anxious features locked into a calm that chilled the marrow.

The hands inched closer, and I saw it all—translucent skin stretched over pulsing light, fingers too long, too knowing. My heart slammed once, twice—then faltered, each beat warping into an eternity. I opened my mouth to scream, but no sound emerged, only a silence as thick and suffocating as tar.

They danced, whirling faster, a nightmare ballet of shifting faces and bodies that bent through dimensions I couldn't name. And then, through the storm of motion, a figure emerged. The ancient, hollow-eyed face of my mother rose from the chaos like a pale moon. Her mouth opened in a soundless scream, a cavern of endless sorrow.

And then—my face.

Over and over.

Young. Old. Twisted. Broken. Each incarnation of myself, whether past or present, was more profound than the previous one. My knees buckled as the hands closed around me, fingers brushing skin, and in that instant, time shattered.

Chapter 1

Sunlight slanted through the blinds in thin, precise bands, carving the office into a checkerboard of light and shadow. Perfectly positioned were the DSM-5, patient files neatly stacked by appointment time, and pens arranged in a soldier's row beside the laptop. Behind me, my credentials hung in perfect formation, each frame meticulously leveled, the glass polished until it caught even the faintest glint of morning light. These credentials served as proof of years spent earning, striving, and mastering—but on some days, a hollow echo stirred beneath that perfection, a small voice questioning whether I had truly deserved them.

With a flick of my hand, I adjusted the tissue box on the side table, aligning it with the chair's corner until the symmetry calmed something tight in my chest. The faint lemon tang of disinfectant clung to the air, masking the traces of earlier sessions, a scent I found myself renewing more often of late. Scrubbing the room seemed to erase the strange tremors that ran through my patients' stories—their sleepless nights, their dreams of masked shapes.

The intercom crackled. "Dr. Sullivan? Mrs. Thompson is here for her nine o'clock."

"Send her in." My voice felt cool and steady. I smoothed

CHAPTER 1

my blazer, opened her file, and let the crisp whisper of paper ground me in its familiar ritual. Order. Routine. Control.

Sarah Thompson entered with hesitant steps, the deep crescents beneath her eyes speaking of long, unraveling nights. She collapsed into the chair, her movements weighed down by something invisible. "The nightmares are worse," she murmured.

A flicker stirred at the back of my mind, something cold and half-buried, but I shoved it aside.

"Tell me about your sleep hygiene," I said, pen poised above the page. "Are you keeping consistent hours?"

"Yes. Exactly as you told me." Her fingers twisted her wedding band, the skin reddened from the pressure. "But these shapes—they're always there. They wear masks, and—"

"Let's focus on quantifiable data first." The interruption came too quickly, but the numbers steadied me. I scanned her sleep log, which showed a decline in hours from six to four. A steep, clean drop. Something I could chart, graph, and contain.

My questions unfurled in their usual sequence, each one precise and practiced. I meticulously transcribed her chaotic state into concise bullet points. Folding her terror into clinical language. Her eyes blinked momentarily, causing a prickling sensation beneath my skin. But I pressed it down, adjusting my pen, aligning it square against the notepad's edge.

"Dr. Sullivan," she whispered, her voice splintering, "I'm scared to close my eyes."

My fingers reached for the prescription pad, the smooth paper a refuge. "A mild sedative, alongside cognitive behavioral protocols, often stabilizes circadian rhythms," I murmured, letting the ritual carry me forward. Clinical. Detached. Safe.

It had worked before. It had to keep working.

As Sarah left, her steps faded down the hallway, and the quiet stretched taut. Three knocks broke it—sharp, familiar.

Marcus Kim leaned in the doorway, lab coat slung over his arm, a smile playing at the corners of his mouth. "Still buried in paperwork?" His tone was teasing, but his eyes held the glimmer of concern. "A few of us are headed to Murphy's. You in?"

I kept my gaze fixed on Sarah's file, smoothing it closed. "Thanks, but I have more cases to review."

"Brooke, when's the last time you left before dark?" The casual warmth in his voice softened, a thread of real worry weaving through.

For a beat, I let myself imagine it—the hum of conversation, the clink of glasses, and laughter curling around dark wood and old stories. But the image felt dim, like something remembered from another life.

"I need to finish these." I stacked the files, creating a barrier, hands precise, movements small.

"Tomorrow, then," Marcus offered, his voice easy, though his smile slipped just a fraction before he turned away. "The offer's open."

When the door clicked shut, the room seemed to contract. The air grew still, the silence heavier, but this was safer. Work was safer. It had always been.

By four, my last patient arrived. Amy Park stumbled in, her hair mussed, eyes raw at the edges. She thrust her phone out, hands shaking. "I recorded it," she said, voice frayed. "The whispers. They're real."

I gestured calmly toward the chair, smoothing my face into neutral lines. "Let's begin with your sleep diary."

CHAPTER 1

"Please." Her voice broke at the word. "Just listen." Her eyes glistened, tears trembling at the edge. "Three nights. No sleep. I can't do this anymore."

For the first time that day, I set the notepad aside.

"Amy," I said softly, leaning in, letting the wall between us slip a little. "Look at me."

Her gaze lifted, hesitant, fragile.

"You're not alone in this," I told her. "Your fear, your exhaustion—they're real. We'll face it together."

The words came unbidden, surprising even me. They weren't clinical. They were true.

Amy's shoulders crumpled, a breath shuddering out of her as if the weight she carried had lessened by some small degree. Her sobs softened, falling into tremulous breaths.

"You believe me?" she whispered.

"I believe you're suffering," I said quietly. "And that's enough."

Without thinking, I reached out, the briefest touch on her hand. A contact I hadn't allowed myself in years. It was small and human, and it sent a fine crack through the armor I'd wrapped so tightly around myself.

When Amy left, the air in the room felt different, infused with an indescribable quality. I stayed there, in the quiet, the soft echo of her gratitude drifting like the faint scent of rain after a long drought. For once, I didn't straighten the desk or disinfect the space. For once, I let the feeling linger.

The drive home blurred past in a stream of headlights and traffic lights, the city peeling away like a half-remembered dream. I parked in B7, always B7, and rode the elevator up, watching the numbers rise in their smooth, mechanical precision. My apartment greeted me with its familiar symmetry:

white walls, sharp corners, and counters wiped to a polish. No photographs. No mess. No memory.

I hung up my coat with careful hands, brushed my teeth until the mint stung, and folded my clothes into perfect squares. The bed waited, its blankets smooth, edges tucked sharp.

But tonight, the darkness pressed heavier.

I lay beneath the ceiling fan, the soft churn of its blades casting restless shadows along the walls. The sound, once soothing, now pulsed in a strange cadence, murmuring against the edges of hearing. I squeezed my eyes shut.

Behind the lids, shapes bloomed.

Porcelain masks, their hollow eyes fixed on mine. Grinning. Weeping. Shifting. Melting into grotesque distortions that flickered in a terrible procession.

My eyes flew open. The fan spun, the shadows slid across the walls—but they no longer seemed like shadows.

They looked like fingers.

Reaching.

Grasping.

Tearing.

"No," I whispered, hands clenching over my eyes until pinpricks of light danced in the dark. "Just exhaustion. Just work stress." My fingers fumbled for the lamp, knocking it over with a sharp clatter. Light flooded the room, harsh and clinical, revealing furniture, clean lines, and the ordered quiet of an untouched space.

Nothing wrong. Nothing out of place.

But when my gaze flicked toward the darkened television, when my eyes caught its reflection, just for an instant—

I saw it.

It was a pale, glimmering mask.

CHAPTER 1

Smiling.
Watching.
Waiting.

Chapter 2

Casting thin bars of sterile white over my office walls, the overhead fluorescent lights pulsed with their customary low, electronic drone. The room maintained its usual perfect order, unaffected by the mayhem that inevitably befell anybody who stepped foot within.

As a little ritual that I held onto, I repositioned the patient file on my desk, this time making sure that its edge was flush with the grain of the polished wood. When I felt disoriented, I could rely on the mechanical rhythm of the wall clock to ground me. Every surface, every corner, reassured: the degrees lined up in black frames, the folders arranged by color-coded tabs, and the reference books sorted by size and subject. Order, I reminded myself, was a shield.

Lately, that shield felt thin.

A knock at the door pulled me from my thoughts. My hand, suspended over the pen, twitched at the sound.

"Come in," I called, my voice smoother than I felt.

Jason Matthews entered with the slow, burdened shuffle of someone carrying far too much. His shoulders hunched forward, his eyes ringed with dark circles, and his hands fidgeted in constant, restless motion. He scanned the office in quick, darting glances, as if the polished surfaces or neat

CHAPTER 2

stacks might conceal something waiting to lunge.

I recognized that look. I'd begun to catch glimpses of it in my mirror.

"Please, have a seat, Mr. Matthews." I gestured calmly toward the leather chair, watching it creak under his weight while he perched on the edge, jittering.

I opened his file, letting the act steady me as I flipped through the intake notes. "I understand you've been experiencing sleep disturbances," I said, careful to keep my tone measured and clinical, the voice I'd practiced over the years to help patients find ground when theirs was falling away.

Jason raised his gaze to mine, his eyes wide and glassy, akin to someone standing on a precipice. Sweat dotted his brow despite the office's cool air. "That's… that's one way to put it," he murmured, fingers knotting in the fabric of his jeans. "I haven't really slept in days. Every time I close my eyes…" He faltered, his throat working as if the words were too heavy.

The click of my pen broke the silence, sharp and deliberate. "Take your time," I said, though a flicker of something uneasy stirred beneath the surface of my voice. Even as I reassured him, I felt the nagging tug of doubt inside myself, the thin crack in my professional armor.

He exhaled shakily. "They watch you. All the time. Their faces…" His fingers pressed hard against his temples. "At first they look normal. And then—they shift. They transform into something else. Every time I blink, they're closer."

The chill that moved through me was instinctive, undeniable. I gripped my pen tightly, grounding myself against the rising pulse in my throat. Jason's description mirrored too closely the images from my own nights—the masked figures with too-long limbs, the crawling shapes that twisted in the periphery.

No, I thought sharply. This was a projection. I was the professional here.

Jason leaned forward, his voice low, ragged at the edges. "Sometimes… they wear faces I know. My wife. My kids. My parents. But wrong. Like someone's wearing them—like a costume." He shuddered, squeezing his eyes shut. "Like they're trying to fool me."

My stomach clenched. A bitter taste rose in my throat.

Pulling in a slow breath, I summoned the language that had been my armor for years. "These are common manifestations of stress and sleep deprivation, Mr. Matthews," I said, reaching for the practiced calm that had carried me through countless sessions. "The subconscious can distort familiar images under duress. We can address this with relaxation exercises and sleep hygiene techniques."

I reached for the prescription pad, the motion familiar, automatic—until a faint sound snagged at the edge of my hearing.

Music.

Soft, tinkling, childlike. The carousel tune of a carnival, circling in slow, warped loops.

I swallowed hard, forcing my gaze back to Jason. He didn't react—still rubbing his hands, lost in his storm.

But my eyes slid past him, to the wall.

There—a flicker, a poster I didn't remember hanging. Swirling reds and golds, masks frozen in grotesque dance, limbs stretched beyond anatomy. I blinked sharply, and the image dissolved, leaving only the clean white surface. But the echo of it burned behind my eyes.

"For sleep hygiene—" My voice caught, turned brittle.

CHAPTER 2

In the glass door of the bookcase, movement flickered. A pale figure. Porcelain mask. Lips too wide, crimson, smiling where no one stood.

My breath hitched as I turned, sharp and fast. Empty space. Shadows that stretched just a little too long.

The office door creaked open.

Dr. Edwards entered, his silver hair a slash of brightness under the fluorescents. "Sorry to interrupt," he murmured, his eyes brushing over Jason before landing on me. "Troubling dreams again?"

I offered a tight nod, closing Jason's file carefully, hands steadier than I felt.

Edwards lingered a moment longer than needed. "You know, Brooke," he said lightly, "sometimes, it's the things we avoid that bind us the tightest."

I pressed my pen hard to the paper, watching ink bloom into a spreading black stain. "Thank you, Dr. Edwards. We're just finishing."

He nodded once, then slipped out, the door clicking closed with a sound that felt too final.

I turned back to Jason, my shoulders stiff. The faint thread of carnival music had faded, but its imprint coiled through the air. I walked him to the door, the professional smile fixed in place, though my fingers trembled slightly against the cool metal handle.

"Remember to practice the exercises we discussed," I said softly. "And if the symptoms intensify, don't hesitate to call."

Jason hesitated at the threshold. His gaze flicked to the corner of the room, where I had seen the reflection, then slowly back to me.

"Dr. Sullivan," he murmured, voice thin, fraying. "Do

you ever feel like…" His words faltered. "Like something's watching you—even when you're awake?"

The music stirred again, barely a whisper, as though circling just beyond the walls.

I steadied my grip on the doorframe. "Anxiety can present in many forms," I told him, hearing the hollow echo of my reassurance. "What you're experiencing is a natural reaction to stress."

Jason gave a slow, uncertain nod, his gaze shadowed with doubt.

As he shuffled down the hallway, his footsteps echoed softly, his silhouette drawn out under the harsh light. Just before he turned the corner, he glanced back—and in that fleeting glance, I saw it.

The reflection of my fear, mirrored in his eyes.

That desperate, fragile hope that science could explain everything. And the deeper, unspoken dread that some things defied explanation altogether.

Chapter 3

Under the dim glow of the fluorescent lights, Jason's footsteps resounded as they made their way down the hall. Then there was complete stillness as I stood there, my hand still on the doorframe, and there was a slight aroma of antiseptic and old paper in the air.

For a moment, I imagined I could still hear the music. The warped melody, sweet and sharp like the tune from a broken music box, haunted the edges of my mind, not the piped-in lobby tunes or the distant shuffle of night staff.

By the time I turned back toward my desk, the room seemed smaller. The walls leaned inward, just a breath. The corners darkened, shadows gathering like a slow exhale. I told myself it was exhaustion, the weight of too many hours, too many patients, too many nights spent chasing order through the chaos of unraveling minds.

When I finally left the office, the night air bit at my skin, cool and metallic. By the time I reached home, routine had taken over—coat hung, shoes aligned, teeth brushed until the sting of mint chased away the lingering taste of nerves. Pillows fluffed, bedding tucked, and curtains pulled halfway against the streetlight outside created a sanctuary of harmony in the bedroom.

As I lay down, I took a deep breath in. The ceiling fan swung gently in the sky, its steady hum lulling me to sleep most nights. But this evening, the darkness seemed too thick, the silence too oppressive, as though the space were holding its breath.

I attempted to call upon the known by closing my eyes. Every detail was perfect: the pillow's coolness on my cheek, the sheets' plushness, and the faint sound of the floorboards creaking under the fan.

Instead, cold.

Air rushed past my skin in a sudden gust, and the soft weight of the blankets vanished. Beneath me, the bed dissolved. My stomach lurched, a sickening drop into open space, and when I opened my eyes, I was no longer in my room.

Mirrors.

A vast wall of them stretched into the darkness, swallowing every direction, reflecting faint light that seemed to come from nowhere at all. I stumbled forward, breath hitching. The reflections shivered and flickered, a thousand versions of myself—each one subtly wrong. One smiled when I frowned; another winced when I stepped closer.

Tentatively, I lifted a hand and laid it against the nearest glass. Ice shot up my fingertips. The surface rippled outward like water, and my reflection warped, mouth twisting, eyes stretching, body bending in on itself.

"This isn't real," I whispered, a desperate thread of sound.

A chorus of voices answered—not just mine, but dozens layered on top of each other, warping and slowing, curling around the words until they collapsed into nonsense.

Panic clawed its way into my chest. Spinning in place, I searched for an exit, but the mirrors offered only more

CHAPTER 3

distorted selves: the child I had been, curled tight in fear; the older woman I barely recognized, eyes hollowed by grief; the doctor in a stained coat, hands streaked with something dark and gleaming.

Each breath thickened the air, pressing inward. My pulse roared in my ears like fists beating against glass.

One mirror caught me—a figure not quite me, not quite other. It wore a porcelain mask, pale as bone, its surface painted with swirling gold that slithered at the corners of my vision.

"Hello?" My voice fractured across the space, a shattering echo.

The mirrors rippled, a tremor sliding through the maze. I reached again toward the glass, fingers trembling, and watched as a little girl appeared on the other side—my face from years ago, warped by terror, tears streaking down small cheeks, hands pressed to the glass.

I stumbled backward, heart hammering, only to crash into another mirror. My reflection there grinned—a stretched, glistening smile that bared teeth too sharp, too wide, eyes sunk into bottomless pits.

Every surface is now twisted with something worse: memories that have been dredged up from the deep places I had worked for years to bury.

"Let me out!" I screamed, fists slamming against the glass. The surface rippled, my voice swallowed and thrown back at me in ragged, mismatched laughter.

I ran. The floor pitched beneath each footfall, the maze shifting, folding. With every turn came more mirrors, more figures: myself and not myself, faces flickering from joy to grief to rage.

A hissing sound slithered through the space, like steam escaping from cracks just beneath the surface.

And then, the whispers.

"Brooke..."

I pressed my back to the nearest mirror, chest rising in shallow gasps. My name rustled through the dark like dry leaves, curling from every direction. Shadows shifted beyond the glass, cloaked figures emerging, masked faces gleaming.

"Come join us, Brooke..."

Their voices intertwined, a melody warped out of tune, brushing against every raw edge of my nerves. My heart thudded faster, a hollow, frantic rhythm.

More of them stepped forward, masks twisting from delighted grins to hollow-eyed frowns. "We've been waiting..."

I tried to speak, to push the words out, but my voice caught, crumbling in my throat. They inched closer, their movements smooth, their fingers too long, tapering into smoky tendrils that traced the air.

Frost laced across the mirrors as the temperature plummeted. My name—whispered, hissed, pleaded—filled every inch of space.

"Remember, Brooke... remember..."

One figure approached, mask shifting as it moved: smile, frown, hollow eyes. When it raised its hand, the darkness rippled. Fingers touched my cheek, and cold shot through my bones, threading into marrow, into memory.

It wore my face.

Not the one I showed the world, but the face I feared: brittle, practiced smile; hollow eyes that had learned to hide too much.

Every instinct screamed to run, to break away—but the

CHAPTER 3

weight of all I'd buried pinned me in place. The other figures circled, weaving their dance of longing, their whispers curling deeper under my skin.

The hand brushed closer, a final breath of cold—and then it touched me.

Pain lanced through my body. Cold, sharp, almost familiar.

I wrenched backward with a raw gasp—

And jolted upright in bed, heart hammering, skin damp with sweat, breath ragged in the stillness of my room.

White walls. Stacked papers. The soft glow of the streetlight pushed through the blinds.

But the dark was too deep, the silence too thick.

My hands flew to my face, fingers tracing skin, bone, familiar contours. Yet across the room, the mirror caught only blackness, its surface blank and waiting.

The doctor in me whispered: stress, exhaustion, nightmares spun from unraveling nerves.

But the knot in my stomach whispered back: no.

The masks. The whispers. The shifting, twisting faces.

They hadn't felt like dreams.

They had felt like invitations.

And some part of me understood—this was only the beginning.

Chapter 4

Sitting on the side of the bed, I gripped the cool leather frame with all my fingers as I struggled to draw breath into my lungs. Long, twisted shadows stretched over the floor, their forms distorted into grabbing fingers that clutched at the room's corners, cast by the amber light of the streetlights that slanted through the blinds. My pajamas clung to damp skin, the thin fabric chilled by sweat, and the red numbers of the digital clock burned in the dark, sharp and relentless. Time dragged, stretching thin as my pulse hammered in my ears, and I fought to anchor myself in the quiet sterility of the room, in the familiar weight of floorboards beneath bare feet, and in the faintly antiseptic scent that clung to the walls.

But the room tilted. The walls breathed.

I squeezed my eyes shut, hoping to drive the sensation away, only to see them—carnival masks, blooming like bruises across the dark behind my lids. My heart lurched, slamming against my ribs as I snapped my eyes open, the echoes of whispered voices still clinging to the air, curling through my mind, my name woven into their mocking chorus.

"Get it together," I muttered, pressing my fingertips into my temples until the ache blurred everything else. My gaze landed on the stack of medical journals beside the bed, their clean, ordered spines a silent promise of rationality, of science, of explanations. Despite my best efforts to construct a clinical defense, the images continued to consume me, evoking memories of shifting masks and twisted figures.

As the vehicle sped by, its headlights flashed across the wall, causing the shadows to writhe and twist into ragged patterns before disappearing into thin air and making the room go silent again. I jerked my gaze toward the floor, grounding myself in the tangible, in the solid weight of wood beneath my feet. I took a deep breath in, held it, and then exhaled slowly and methodically, going back to the breathing practice I had given countless patients, hoping that each irregular breath would eventually settle. The technique was robotic, and the motions were fragile and lifeless, yet I powered through them, one heartbeat at a time, until my hands stopped shaking and the darkness subsided.

As I gently turned the page of a worn journal, I could hear the spine breaking under my fingertips and inhaled the reassuring aroma of aged paper. The page was crammed with words: parasomnias, hypnagogic hallucinations, and sleep disorders. As I frantically scribbled notes onto a yellow pad, clutching onto the clinical jargon like a lost woman, each phrase served as a talisman against the burden of recollection. Chest pressure. Visual hallucinations. Masked figures, a known cultural manifestation of sleep paralysis. "Just sleep deprivation," I whispered to the dark screen across the room. "Stress-induced parasomnia."

Leaning back, I rubbed at tired eyes, the leather chair creaking as it shifted beneath me. This was my world—studies, symptoms, and explanations laid out in neat lines, immune to the chaos that lurked just beneath the surface. No shifting mirrors or carnivals were unfolding in the darkness. "Nightmares happen," I murmured, forcing the words out louder. "Sleep deprivation causes hallucinations." The reassurance resonated softly off the cabinets and the walls, yet it felt weightless, as thin as paper.

With practiced precision, I gathered my briefcase, smoothed the wrinkles from my jacket, and stepped into the raw hush of predawn. The street stretched wide and empty, the buildings still asleep, the air sharp with cold. There was no small talk to navigate or laughter to sidestep. Perfect.

At the office, I buried myself in research, pulling case files close like armor. Seven point six percent of the general population experiences sleep paralysis. The numbers steadied me, each statistic a small weight in my palm, each clinical detail a thread in the tapestry of order I was trying to stitch back together. Slowly, the chaos settled. My hands stilled.

"Morning, Dr. Sullivan!" Sarah called brightly from the front desk, her face peeking around the door. "We're grabbing coffee. You coming?"

"Thanks, but I have work," I replied, offering the polished smile that passed for connection these days.

"Come on, live a little!" She laughed, the sound light and effortless. "The paperwork will wait."

"Maybe next time," I murmured, already turning back, hands moving reflectively to realign the pen holder on my desk.

Later, Dr. Chen leaned into the doorway, easy and relaxed. "Tom's birthday party is tonight. You should come. The whole department's going."

"I'll think about it," I said smoothly, the lie slipping out like breath.

CHAPTER 4

The practiced smiles and deflections had become instinctive. Data didn't ask for vulnerability. Data didn't expect warmth; I no longer trusted myself to give it.

By late morning, my eyes blurred over Mrs. Henderson's file, words slipping into each other, refusing to stay still. A flicker stirred at the edge of my vision, a shadow stretching long against the wall. The overhead light stuttered once, twice, throwing shapes across my desk, shapes that coiled and unraveled in impossible ways. My screen went black, and for a breathless second, two hollow eyes gazed back—white porcelain, a grin stretched too wide, teeth bared in something that was not a smile.

I jolted backward, the chair squealing against the floor. A blink—and it was gone. The pale glow of my desktop patiently waited. My fingers trembled as they closed around the coffee cup.

"Dr. Sullivan?" Mr. Roberts stood hesitantly in the doorway, his face edged with concern.

"Fine," I heard myself say. "Just a migraine."

He nodded, settling into the chair across from me, eager to unpack his episodes.

As he spoke, a faint melody brushed the edges of the room—thin, discordant notes drifting like the memory of a carnival tune, scraping faintly at the back of my mind. I forced myself to focus, to listen, to root myself in the moment. "How often are the episodes occurring?" I asked, pen poised, hand steady.

"Three times last week…"

But his voice wavered at the edges, blurred beneath the music, beneath the ripple of movement just behind him. A shadow stretched long against the wall, arms unfurling in a dance that defied every rule of anatomy.

"Dr. Sullivan?"

I blinked. I forced a smile. "Please, continue."

Even as the shadows shifted, even as the music threaded tighter through the air, I stayed poised, scribbling notes with a steadiness that felt more brittle by the second. "Let's focus on your sleep hygiene," I said calmly, though the words tasted like ash. "An overtired mind can distort perception."

When Mr. Roberts left, I folded into the chair, pressing my palms hard against closed eyes, chasing the spark-flare of color in the dark. Just stress. Just exhaustion. I repeated it as if it were a ritual, a prayer, or a lifeline that I no longer trusted to support me.

Later, in the bathroom mirror, I confronted the woman staring back: drawn face, tight jaw, eyes shadowed but still clear. Still functional. I maintained my composure. I combed my hair, adjusted the collar of my jacket, and rehearsed the expression of competence.

"This is manageable," I murmured to the reflection. The light above flickered once, a sharp pulse across the mirror. I didn't flinch.

"I can control this," I whispered, fingers white-knuckled against porcelain.

"I will control this."

And beneath it, unspoken, something darker coiled—a silent promise I didn't dare name.

Chapter 5

The mirror in the bathroom had barely cleared when I left it behind, my reflection still etched into the back of my mind: hollow-eyed, trembling, a woman unrecognizable in the pale fluorescent light. By the time I stepped back into my office, the fragile sense of control I'd rehearsed so carefully was already splintering.

The clinical brilliance of the overhead fluorescent lights sliced through the fragile barriers I had built around me as they hummed their unrelenting rhythm. As I looked out the window, I saw my reflection staring back at me with limp, tattered strands of hair instead of the neat bun I'd styled that morning. The blouse I had smoothed with such care hours ago bore a careless coffee stain across one sleeve, the fabric creased and sagging like a deflated mask.

Dark rings clung to the skin beneath my eyes, bruising the shadows of my face until the woman looking back was both familiar and foreign. A shuffle at the edge of the desk sent several documents tumbling to the floor. As I bent to retrieve them, the room tilted sharply, the horizon of my office slipping sideways. My hand shot out, clutching the desk's edge, knuckles whitening as I fought to steady myself. With each shallow, harsh, and constricted breath, the antiseptic aroma that had before signaled order and security encircled my neck like a noose.

As if the room were leaning in on me, watching and waiting, the long, crooked shadows in the corners curled toward me like a pair of grabbing fingers. I straightened my collar in a gesture of pure habit, but the fabric cinched tight at my throat, a small choke of panic blooming at the edges of control. My eyes skated across the words on the open report, but they twisted and swam on the page, the lines bending into shapes that no longer made sense. The wall clock wavered in the corner of my vision—2:45, then 3:45, then flicking back to 2:45 again—numbers splitting and multiplying like cells dividing unchecked inside my pounding skull.

A soft knock cut through the thickening fog. Dr. Edwards stood framed in the doorway, his silver beard neatly trimmed, brows furrowed low in a line of quiet concern.

"Brooke? Staff meeting in fifteen. Quarterly review."

"Right," I murmured, pawing blindly at the scattered papers, unable to focus on a single word.

He lingered, fingers drumming lightly against the doorframe. "You seem... different lately. Everything okay?"

"Just tired," I replied, the words automatic, as natural now as breathing.

"It's only Tuesday," he said gently, his frown deepening.

"Fine," I snapped, sharper than I meant.

He lifted his hands in surrender, a small, cautious smile flickering at the corner of his mouth. "Room 204," he reminded me before slipping away.

The murmur of colleagues filled the hall, their voices soft and familiar as they drifted toward the meeting. However, beneath the sound of their voices was another noise—something thinner and sharper: the buzz of static coiling under their words. My eyes drifted closed, too heavy to keep lifted. Above, the fluorescent lights dimmed and flickered, and the air around me thickened, syrup-slow.

When I opened my eyes, I was no longer in my office.

The ceiling loomed close, sterile and white, the unmistakable ceiling of a hospital room. My body lay stiff and unyielding against the rigid bed, a thin gown clinging to my skin. Beep. Beep. Beep. The heart monitor at my side marked time with clinical indifference. An IV line stretched from my arm, cool liquid crawling through veins that felt distant, disconnected, no longer my own.

The room pulsed with emptiness. No flowers. No visitors. Only machines were present, standing guard over a body that had been completely emptied of its contents. In the window's darkened glass, I caught sight of myself—hollow, spectral, the faint outline of a woman drained of substance and light.

A voice seeped through the silence, soft yet omnipresent. "If you keep going like this, you will lose yourself entirely."

The monitor faltered; its steady beat was skipping and hesitating. I clawed at the bedrail, the cold metal biting deep into my palm as I tried to lift my head. My muscles quaked with the effort.

"No," I rasped, my voice barely a whisper. "I'm in control. I have to be."

The voice slid closer, oiled with certainty. "Are you? Look what you've become."

Tears blurred the edges of my vision as the reflection in the glass sharpened—sunken cheeks, hollow eyes, the collapse of a life built to be impenetrable. The walls I had spent years fortifying around myself had become a coffin, sealing me inside.

With a desperate gasp, I jerked upright, back in my chair, heart pounding, papers spilling to the floor like brittle leaves. The clock on the wall blinked back at me: 4:15 p.m. An hour has passed.

Muffled voices drifted from the hallway. "Has anyone seen Dr. Sullivan?" "She missed the entire quarterly review." "That's not like her."

My hands scrambled across the desk, trying to restore some semblance of order, but the fluorescent lights stabbed down, each flicker driving spikes of nausea into my skull. My phone buzzed once, twice, then settled into a silent thrum. There were fifteen missed calls. Twenty-three unread messages. Dr. Edwards. Sarah. Names I rarely spoke now circled me like distant satellites, tugging me back to earth.

I lurched to my feet, the room tilting in sickening circles. The afterimage of the hospital clung to the edges of vision, spectral monitors pulsing faintly against the sterile office walls. My hands closed around the edge of the desk, knuckles pale, breath tight in my chest.

A knock sounded, sharp and close. "Dr. Sullivan? Are you all right?" Sarah's voice, threaded with worry.

"Just... just a moment," I called back, my throat dry and raw.

In the darkened window, a woman watched me. Hair tangled, mascara smudged beneath exhausted eyes, skin pale and drawn—a stranger wearing the last remnants of my face.

The leather chair sagged beneath me as I collapsed back into it, heart pounding in my throat. Patient files littered the desk—Mrs. Thompson's climbing anxiety scores, Tommy's fragmented sleep study, and Jason's spiraling nightmares. Each folder a small, desperate plea for help. Each one was a

CHAPTER 5

quiet reminder of all the ways I was failing.

Sarah's silhouette filled the doorway, hesitant. "Dr. Edwards asked me to check on you," she said softly.

"I'm fine," I murmured, the lie dissolving on my tongue.

She lingered a moment longer. "The quarterly review... they reassigned your cases to Dr. Martinez."

The air left my lungs in a thin rush. Martinez was a young, untested, and eager individual. Unfamiliar with the nuances, the slow-earned trust I'd worked to build with these patients.

The voices in the hallway grew sharper now—concern, pity, the kind of well-meaning whispers that landed like arrows. The office, once my refuge, now felt foreign, the scent of coffee and paper souring into something jagged and wrong.

I picked up my phone again and scrolled through the names, noticing that each unanswered call represented another crack in the mask I had worn for too long. They knew. They all knew. The weight of it pressed in, crushing against my ribs, forcing the air from my lungs. These people had trusted me with their fears, their hopes, their shattered nights. And I had fallen asleep at my desk.

The darkened computer screen reflected a figure slouched in a chair—cheeks hollow, eyes sunken, lips pale. For a heartbeat, the image flickered: an office chair dissolving into a hospital bed, monitors blinking in the shadows, and a paper gown tugging at thin shoulders.

My fingers dug into my temples, pain spiking behind my eyes. When had I last slept? Truly slept—not just closed my eyes and waited for morning?

"You need to stop," I whispered to the trembling figure in the glass. "You can't keep going like this."

My hand reached for the cold coffee cup, trembling faintly.

The caffeine was no longer holding the darkness back; if anything, it was hastening the collapse, thinning the walls between what was real and what waited just beyond the edge of sight.

The hospital bed flickered again, the vision sharper this time—the figure inside still, silent, waiting.

Something had to change.

I straightened, meeting my own ravaged gaze. Behind the ruin, something stirred—not strength, not quite hope, but something rawer. Desperation, maybe. Or defiance.

Either way, it was time. It was time to confront whatever lurked in the shadows. Before it reached across the line—and took everything.

Chapter 6

The clock's ticking filled the office, each second dragging across my nerves like a stone scraping glass. My gaze drifted over the papers scattered across my desk, but the words refused to hold shape, blurring together into a haze of meaningless text. How had I let things slip this far? My patients depended on me to guide them through the shadows of their dreams, to steady them when they trembled on the edge—and yet here I sat, barely holding the seams of my unraveling mind together.

The memory of the hospital bed lingered in the back of my mind: the sterile sheets, the mechanical beeping, and the sickly green light that had felt too real to dismiss. It clashed sharply against the present moment, the flickering fluorescents overhead casting their pale sting into my aching eyes. I pressed my fingers into my temples, trying to ease the pulsing pain that had taken up permanent residence there. This wasn't how it was supposed to be. I was the one with the answers. I was the one meant to walk others out of their darkness, not be swallowed whole by mine.

A faint knock at the door snapped me upright, my heart jarring painfully in my chest. Dr. Edwards stood there, his expression a measured blend of sympathy and concern.

"Brooke, are you alright?" he asked softly, stepping just inside the doorway. "You missed the meeting. I just wanted to check in."

I forced a thin smile, though my throat burned around the words. "I'm fine. Just under the weather, that's all."

The lie left an acidic taste on my tongue. Edwards studied me a moment longer, his brow furrowing, his gaze heavy with quiet scrutiny. "You know," he said carefully, "if there's anything you need—"

"I said I'm fine." The words cut through the air more sharply than I had intended, revealing the raw edge of panic.

His shoulders shifted, the faint disappointment darkening his eyes. "Brooke," he murmured, "you can't keep going like this. You're exhausted. It's affecting your work. Maybe it's time to step back. Just for a little while."

"I don't need a break," I said tightly, my hands curling into fists beneath the desk. "I need to keep going. I can't abandon my patients now."

He exhaled, a soft, weathered sigh. "You can't pour from an empty cup, Brooke. If you don't take care of yourself, there's going to be nothing left to give."

His words sank deeply into my chest, exerting a crushing pressure. I wanted to argue, to insist he was mistaken, to push back with every ounce of stubbornness I had left—but the exhaustion clung to me like a wet cloth, dragging me under, holding me still.

"Just think about it," Edwards said gently, pausing once more at the door. "Your well-being matters too."

When he left, the silence settled thick around me, dread curling low in my gut. He was right. But the thought of stepping back, of admitting that I was slipping, made my

CHAPTER 6

pulse rattle with unease. I turned back to the files on my desk, the neat rows of labeled names staring up like quiet, relentless accusers. How could I walk away from them now? But beneath the weight of those lives lay the heavier burden of my collapse—the visions, the creeping fatigue, the hospital room that shouldn't have existed.

I closed my eyes and drew a shaky breath, the sound brittle in the stillness. I couldn't keep this up. I knew that. But surrender still felt, in some small but unshakable way, like a kind of death.

By the next morning, I arrived at the office early, determined to erase the stain of my failure from yesterday. Yet as sunlight poured through the office windows, the familiar space felt altered, stripped of its grounding. It was as though I had stepped onto a stage I no longer recognized.

I was still sorting through files when Dr. Edwards reappeared, two coffees in hand. "Got a minute?" he asked, offering me one.

I nodded, the warmth of the cup seeping into my fingers, chasing some of the cold from my bones.

"About yesterday—" I began, but he lifted a hand, stopping me with a quiet shake of his head.

"I wanted to talk about Jason Thompson's case."

The mention of Jason's name sent a sharp twist through my stomach. Faint, twisted strains of carnival music hovered at the edge of hearing, and I shoved the memory aside with practiced force.

"His description of those masked figures," Edwards continued, settling into the chair across from me. "It struck me. It was... unusually vivid."

I forced a neutral tone, reaching for the professional detachment that had once come so easily. "Many patients experience detailed hallucinations during sleep paralysis."

Edwards watched me carefully. "Sure. But this was different. He wasn't confused—he was terrified. Said they were watching. Reaching." His gaze held mine for a long beat. "When's the last time you spoke with him?"

"Three days ago," I murmured, pulling up my calendar. "He was scheduled for a session yesterday afternoon."

Edward's brows lifted slightly. "He missed it?"

I stared at the appointment block on the screen, cold creeping into my chest. I hadn't been there. I had been unconscious at my desk.

"I'll call him," I said quickly, my hand trembling as I reached for the phone. Each ring pulsed in my ear, sharp and loud. No answer. I tried calling again and again, my heart racing as each call went to voicemail. His emergency contact. His office. Nothing.

"Nothing," I whispered, more to myself than to Edwards. "He's never missed a session. Not once."

A weight pressed down on my lungs, squeezing the breath from them. What if he'd needed me? What if he had been in danger while I remained collapsed in my chair?

"We should notify—" Edwards began, but I cut him off.

"I'll handle it. He's my patient. My responsibility."

I dialed another number. On the fourth try, someone picked up.

"Hello?" The voice on the other end was tense, edged with quiet panic.

"This is Dr. Sullivan," I said quickly. "I'm Jason Thompson's sleep therapist. I've been trying to reach him."

"Mark here." The voice cracked. "I've been trying, too.

CHAPTER 6

Fifteen calls, no answer."

"When did you last speak with him?"

"Three days ago. He sounded... wrong. He said that he couldn't tell what was real anymore.

My hand tightened on the edge of the desk. "Any idea where he might have gone?"

"No. But I stopped by his place yesterday. His car's there. His phone's inside, still ringing." Mark's voice lowered. "I'm worried, Doc. This isn't like him."

The calliope melody pressed closer, warping at the edges of sound. I clenched my jaw, pushing it away. "Has he disappeared like this before?"

"Never. Even when he was struggling, he'd answer. He kept saying the faces were closer. That they were watching."

I scribbled Mark's number onto a notepad, my hand shaking. The masked figures that haunted my sleep were now tearing through Jason's.

"If you hear from him—"

"You'll be my first call," Mark promised. "Please. Find him. Something's wrong."

The police station was washed in a cold, institutional light, the fluorescents casting long, tired shadows across the linoleum floor. My heels clicked sharply as I crossed the lobby, radios crackling and murmuring around me.

At the front desk, a heavyset officer glanced up from his computer. "May I help you?"

"I need to report a missing person," I said, my voice tight. "Jason Thompson. My patient. No one's been able to reach him."

His fingers hovered over the keyboard. "When did you last see him?"

I gripped the counter to steady myself. Dates spun through my memory like loose papers in a storm. "Three days ago," I admitted softly. "He was experiencing severe hallucinations. Masked figures. Following him."

The officer's brow rose slightly. "Was he on medication?"

"No. It wasn't like that." I opened Jason's file, my fingers stiff and uncooperative. "He described everything in detail—carnival masks, movement in the shadows. Watching him. Closer every time."

The officer's eyes flicked up, studying me for a long, unsettling moment. His fingers hovered over the keys, but then his voice softened. "Now what, Dr. Sullivan?"

My breath caught.

I hadn't told him my name.

The fluorescent light overhead gave a brief, stuttering flicker. For a brief moment, the officer's face shimmered, warping like a reflection rippling in dark water. I blinked hard, heart hammering. The vision dissolved, and his face was calm again. Normal.

But something cold slipped down my spine.

"I think I made a mistake." The words barely scraped past my lips, a thin whisper swallowed by the low murmur of the station. "I should have listened more carefully. These weren't normal nightmares."

The officer at the desk began typing, each sharp click of the keyboard landing like a hammer blow against the taut quiet around us. "We'll look into it," he said briskly, sliding a form across the desk. "Fill this out."

I reached for the paper with fingers that trembled despite my best efforts to still them. The pen felt heavier than it should have, weighted with the unspoken truth behind every

CHAPTER 6

blank line. Last known location. Physical description. Recent behavioral changes. Each prompt dug deeper, carving into the brittle shell of competence I had so carefully constructed. By the time I reached the final box, it felt as though my chest was collapsing inward, the air thinning in the room.

The drive to Jason's apartment complex felt disjointed, as if I were moving through someone else's life. My hands clenched white-knuckled on the wheel as I trailed the police cruiser, the city around me folding into unfamiliar shapes despite the years I'd spent within its borders. Officer Martinez met me at the complex's entrance, his face tight and unreadable as he gestured toward the stairwell. "Third floor," he murmured. "Management gave us the key."

The echo of our footsteps on the concrete staircase filled the narrow space. On the third floor, the hallway stretched ahead, dim and silent, the air stale with disuse. We stopped in front of 3C. Years of use had dulled the tarnished brass numbers on the door to a faint glint, leaving the lock scratched. Martinez slid the key into place, the lock surrendering with a reluctant click.

"Jason?" My voice came out soft and hesitant as we crossed the threshold into the dark. Martinez flicked the light switch. Nothing. His flashlight snapped on, cutting a narrow beam through the shadow, and what it revealed made my breath hitch.

The apartment was empty. Not messy. Not in disarray. Just erased.

There was no couch, coffee table, scattered books, or abandoned clothes. There were only bare floors and walls, the faint sheen of dust untouched by a single footprint. I pulled out my phone, my fingers cold and clumsy as I double-checked the address. "This is the place," I murmured. "He described it to me… the blue couch by the window, his vinyl collection…"

Martinez's flashlight swept across the walls, the dust swirling in its wake. The stillness pressed in, a kind of quiet that felt less like absence and more like an echo of something deliberately removed.

"How long has he been your patient?" Martinez asked, his voice quiet.

"Six months," I said, stepping cautiously into the kitchen. My heels clicked sharply against the bare floor, the sound swallowed too quickly by the hollow space. The cupboards hung open, empty. There were no dishes, no crumbs, and there was no sign of life.

"He was just here," I whispered. "He had a life. A routine. This… this isn't possible." A cold draft slipped across my skin, raising goosebumps along my arms. Instinctively, I turned towards the window, only to find the panes tightly sealed. Still, the chill lingered, coiling at the edges of the room like an exhale from something unseen.

"Dr. Sullivan?" Martinez called from the bedroom. "You'll want to see this."

I found him standing at the open closet, holding a small object in his gloved hand. Wordlessly, he passed it to me—a faded carnival ticket. Realm of Illusions. Once beautiful, the delicate, swirling script suddenly struck with a force akin to a hammer.

Jason's hands trembled with fear. His voice was filled with panic. The masked figures creeping closer with each sleepless night. I had told myself it was exhaustion, stress, a mind besieged by its anxieties. I had disregarded my unraveling

CHAPTER 6

dreams.

"I failed him," I whispered, the words cracking in my throat, the sound of them raw and unsteady. "He came to me for help. And I—" My voice gave out, the silence answering back like a hollow echo.

Martinez's flashlight swept through the room, catching the dust in midair, the particles glinting like carnival confetti. The empty rooms felt like wounds, each one a hollow where memory had been scraped away. Where were the journals Jason mentioned? The photographs? The blue couch where it all began? I pressed my palm flat to the wall, willing myself to summon the memory of the floral wallpaper he'd described. But there was only a cold, unyielding surface.

"I made him doubt himself," I murmured, my voice shaking as the weight of the admission settled in. "He trusted me to see what he saw. And I dismissed it. Just like I've dismissed…" I trailed off, the words crumbling under their weight. "Some therapist I turned out to be."

The ticket crinkled sharply in my grasp, its edges biting into my skin. "I was so focused on clinical distance I couldn't hear what he was really saying. I couldn't see it."

The apartment wasn't just empty. It was hollow. A shell. It felt as if a force had hollowed him out of existence, slicing away his life piece by piece, and now that same void was tugging at the edges of mine.

Kneeling, I swept the flashlight's beam across the floor. Something glinted faintly beneath the grime. My fingers closed around it, trembling. A photograph. The photograph's edges frayed and its colors faded, yet the moment I touched it, the air caught in my throat.

Children clustered around a cotton candy stand, their

laughter frozen in the captured instant. Balloons bobbed above their heads, bright against a twilight sky. And there, half-concealed behind a striped tent pole—

A masked figure.

It was not a trick of light, nor a digital smear. A figure. Watching.

The figure's head sat at an unnatural angle.

My chest seized. I knew this place. I knew this moment.

Because I had been there.

"I was there," I breathed, brushing a trembling finger across the image. The paper felt fragile, ready to dissolve beneath the weight of memory. First came the scent—caramel apples, popcorn, spun sugar. Then the sound—twisted calliope music looping through the back of my mind like a warped lullaby. Then the taste—sweet cotton candy, turning to ash the moment my gaze fell on the figure watching me. No one else had seen it. Not my parents. Not the other children. Only me. Even as a child, I had felt its gaze burrow beneath my skin.

In the photograph, I stood at the edge of the frame, half-turned, my face caught between awareness and denial. Even then, I had known better than to look too long.

"Dr. Sullivan?" Martinez's voice broke through, hesitant. "What did you find?"

I couldn't answer, not right away. My eyes stayed fixed on the masked figure, its porcelain face too familiar to dismiss. The figure had the same empty eyes that Jason had described. The stillness remained constant. It was the same impossible presence that had haunted my dreams.

Tightening my grip on the photograph, I exhaled a shaky breath. "Evidence," I managed. "Evidence that I should have

CHAPTER 6

believed him."

The apartment seemed to pulse around me, the walls pressing in as though the space itself remembered. How many times had I labeled his visions as parasomnias, as hallucinations, as fragments of dream logic? How many times had I done the same to myself?

Tracing the outline of my younger self in the photo, I felt the years fold inward. Even as a child, I had turned away rather than face it. Jason hadn't disappeared. He hadn't run. He had been taken, just as he feared, just as I had once feared and been buried and forgotten.

Martinez's flashlight swept the room again, its glow flickering faintly, as though the dark itself had thickened. I focused on the masked figure, reaching for the echo of its presence, for the memory of its impossible gaze. This was no longer just Jason's story. It was mine. It had always been mine. And now, the thread running beneath it all was pulling tight.

Outside, sunlight struck my face with an almost violent clarity. I blinked hard against it, dazed, the photograph a heavy presence in my coat pocket, its edges sharp against my ribs. Martinez spoke into his radio, his voice flattened to static, while officers moved around us, their words clipped and efficient.

But none of them knew what they were dealing with. How could they? I barely understood it myself.

I reached for my car keys, the cold metal biting into my palm. The photograph. The ticket. Proof—or maybe warning. This was more than just a figment of my imagination. Perhaps I had already crossed the boundary.

A siren wailed in the distance, cutting through the afternoon like a blade. I flinched. Every sound felt sharpened, too loud, too immediate. The world around me—the cars, the passing voices, the distant bark of a dog—felt paper-thin, as though something darker waited just beneath the surface.

"Dr. Sullivan?" Martinez's voice called softly. "We'll need you to come in later. To give a statement."

I nodded, my throat dry, the sunlight cold on my skin. The chill wasn't from the air. It was something older, something coiled deep in my bones.

Jason was out there. Somewhere. Lost in the same place I had once wandered into—and somehow found my way back from. Maybe.

The weight of my failure followed me to my car, each step dragging like I was wading through some invisible tide. The roar in my ears drowned out the world. And beneath it all, curling at the edge of hearing, was the music.

And it was getting closer.

Chapter 7

Outside, the world blurred by as I drove home, the photograph heavy in my pocket, its edges pressing sharp reminders into my skin with every breath. The sunlight had felt thin against my shoulders, a warmth I couldn't carry with me into the car, into the house, into the walls of my life that now felt transparent and brittle. By the time I stepped into my office and locked the door behind me, the mask of the day had cracked. The city sounds faded, the last conversation with Martinez dissolved, and what remained was the restless hush of a room that had once made me feel safe. Now, every shadow seemed to pulse at the corners of my vision, every reflection a quiet invitation to look closer, to stop pretending I didn't know the shape of the thing drawing near.

I sat at the desk, the photograph trembling in my hand, and felt the edge of exhaustion coil through me like wire drawn too tight. As the computer screen flickered to life, spilling pale light across the cluttered surface, I knew this was the moment when denial ended. The last walls were crumbling. I had to follow where Jason had led me—into the dark, into the questions I had refused to ask.

As I fixated on the blinking search bar, the light from my computer screen cast pale blue shadows on the papers that were scattered about my desk. Feeling a twinge of fatigue course through my arms, I nervously dangled my fingertips over the keyboard. Next to the keyboard, Jason's photograph waited—edges frayed, colors faded, its surface worn soft from my touch. The masked figure in the corner of the image seemed to lean closer each time I looked; its presence hovered just out of reach, like in my dreams.

Rubbing my eyes, I fought against the creeping fatigue coiling in my chest, but the office around me had already shifted. Once, the sterile space had comforted me—the ordered files, the antiseptic scent, the soft buzz of the fluorescent lights overhead. Now, it all felt like a paper-thin disguise stretched over something more dangerous. Every corner seemed to cradle a deeper shadow, and every reflection in the glass cabinets felt like it was one heartbeat away from revealing a porcelain face, watching.

"I can't keep pretending," I murmured into the empty room, the sound brittle and small in the stillness. My hands settled on the keyboard, fingertips brushing the keys like a confession, and I typed the words that tasted like surrender: carnival disappearances masks. For the first time, I allowed myself to admit that what I was experiencing wasn't stress, or sleep deprivation, or the fraying of professional distance. It was something else.

The photograph pulsed in my periphery as if alive, drawing my gaze again and again. I picked it up, tracing the masked figure's silhouette, the unnatural tilt of its head. How many times had I heard Jason describe this exact figure—the impossible posture, the watching presence—and dismissed his words as fragmented dreams? How many patients had I reassured with written prescriptions while ignoring the rot spreading

CHAPTER 7

through my nights?

Search results flooded the screen: local carnivals, missing persons reports, urban legends about masked performers, grainy images, and news articles half-buried in digital archives. As I scrolled through page after page, my heartbeat quickened. None of it fit completely, yet none of it felt entirely separate either. In the ragged spaces in between, Jason—or what was left of him—sat. A distant recollection of a carnival at nightfall, with laughing giving way to something darker, resurfaced under the surface of the pain in my chest.

An unseen electric current buzzed in the room as I navigated the websites, heightening the tension there. Every click felt like peeling back a layer of denial, drawing closer to something that had been waiting for me to remember it.

"Come on, come on," I muttered, eyes burning from the relentless glow of the screen. Article after article blurred together, but I pushed through the exhaustion, unwilling to look away.

The masked figures, the carnival music seeping into their dreams, and the suffocating darkness that encircled their beds were all described in detail in a forum thread that piqued my interest. Reading each article made my throat tighten because the facts were too familiar. Each thread was a mirror: stories of nightmares that clung to waking life, of laughter that curdled into terror, of a slow unraveling no one else could see.

I fumbled through the stack of books on my desk, pulling one free—a worn volume on folklore and dimensional theory. My heart was racing as I scanned the index and heard the pages tremble beneath my fingertips. The entry for "The Spaces Between: Realms of Collective Fear" accelerated my heartbeat. As I perused the chapter, my breath hitched; the scholarly language couldn't mask the terror that lay beneath. It spoke of thresholds formed by shared trauma, of thin places where reality bent beneath the weight of human terror, where entities lurked—masked, waiting, pulling those they marked into shadow realms.

Sweat gathered at my temple, a cold line trailing down my face as I cross-referenced theories with the scattered browser tabs on my screen. Thread by thread, a pattern emerged—not isolated events, but a constellation of disappearances stretching back centuries. Jason's story was only the latest echo in a chorus of voices that had been ignored, dismissed, or simply erased.

Another forum entry jolted me upright: a woman in Nebraska describing masked figures trailing her down deserted streets, vanishing just as she turned; a teenager in Maine haunted by carnival music in his sleep, the melody bleeding into waking hours until he no longer knew when he was dreaming. My fingers trembled as I clicked deeper, reading a post about a boy whose room had been found undisturbed—bed perfectly made, clothes neatly folded—but whose walls were covered in drawings. There were hundreds of masks, each more twisted than the previous one.

My stomach knotted as I stared at the attached images. The sketches matched what I had seen in the mirror of my nightmares, each warped grin and hollowed eye socket an unmistakable signature.

Further down the thread, a survivor wrote, The carnival comes in dreams. At first, you can run. But the paths loop back on themselves. The watchers wait in the shadows, getting closer each time. When you finally wake, part of you stays

CHAPTER 7

behind.

I raked a shaking hand through my hair, the damp roots sticking to my fingers. These weren't just ghost stories. They were warnings, scattered like breadcrumbs through time, charting a course I had already begun to follow.

A local news article surfaced from the depths of the search, 1987, a string of vanishings near an abandoned fairground. The police had found diaries, frantic pages describing sleepless nights, paranoia, and the creeping sense of being watched by something that didn't belong in the world. My mouth went dry as I read, the edges of the room pulling inward.

I felt my teeth gnashing as the temperature dropped in the office and an electric undertone filled the air. The mesmerizing buzzing of the overhead lights matched my heartbeat.

Flick…flick…flick…

Shadows spilled over my books and coffee cup, transforming their mundane forms into something hideous. The mug's curved handle elongated into pale fingers, stretching toward my wrist. I jolted backward, scattering papers across the floor.

"Get it together," I hissed, pressing shaking hands to my temples. But when I looked up, the shadows had only deepened. They crawled up the walls, liquid and alive, pulsing with the rhythm of the failing lights.

Something moved—a flicker in the corner of my eye. My reflection blinked back at me from the black monitor, but the features weren't quite right. My mouth curled too wide, stretching past the limits of my skin. My eyes hollowed, sinking into shadow. For a breathless second, I wasn't looking at myself at all, but at one of them—porcelain skin, black wells for eyes, a smile carved in bone.

I shoved the chair away from the desk, the legs scraping loudly against the floor. The noise echoed strangely, warping at the edges into the faint tremor of carnival music, a waltz twisting out of tune. The walls rippled in my vision, swelling and falling like lungs struggling to draw breath.

With a firm grip on the desk edge, I drew my eyes away from the chaos of papers around me, wishing my thoughts would settle into their proper places. The words were hazy, vacillating between meaning and complete gibberish, while the atmosphere around me became dense and foggy. A whisper kissed my ear, so soft I nearly mistook it for the scrape of paper.

"Brooke..."

My breath caught. The whisper slithered beneath my skin, threading into old memories. I squeezed my eyes shut, praying it was nothing but exhaustion.

"Brooke... Why do you run?"

My chest tightened, a tremor rippling through me as I whipped around, eyes darting across the room. There was nothing there—just the stale hum of the lights and the faint rattle of the air vent. However, the whisper returned, curling through the silence and pressing into the cracks that I believed I had sealed long ago.

"There's no running from your past..."

I flinched, the words slicing deeper than they should have. Images surfaced unbidden—fragmented memories of a childhood carnival, of masked figures watching from the edges, of laughter splintering into silence.

"If you keep running, you might lose yourself completely..."

The voices merged, rising into a chorus that wrapped around me, drowning out thought. I clamped my hands over

CHAPTER 7

my ears, eyes squeezed tight, but the whispers seeped through, brushing against old scars and unspoken guilt.

"Come on, Brooke... Confront what you've done."

The air turned viscous, a slow drag against my skin as I moved. The shadows leaned close, murmuring truths I had buried. It struck me then, a cold jolt of clarity: this carnival of nightmares wasn't just a place—it was a reflection, a world shaped by the wounds we carried, the things we refused to face.

The reports I scoured depicted collective suffering, locations where the veil between worlds thinned, and grief and guilt nourished something that awaited recognition. I had spent years cloaking myself in reason, in clinical detachment, all the while drifting toward their open arms.

A chill traced my spine as I remembered Jason's haunted eyes, the shifting walls of his empty apartment, and the masked figures that haunted us both. They weren't just phantoms. They were predators, and they had marked me long before I'd dared admit it.

I steadied myself, fingers curling against the desk, breath shuddering through tight lungs. If I wanted to help Jason—if I wanted to survive this—I had to face the thing I had run from. I had to face myself.

With each slow step, the shadows seemed to hesitate, shrinking back like smoke in retreat. The walls no longer pulsed with menace but with challenge, waiting to see if I would break or step through.

I was done running.

Done pretending.

The carnival was calling—and I was finally ready to answer.

Chapter 8

The drive from my office to the library blurred into a haze of shifting streetlights and hollowed quiet, as though the city itself had slipped into a hush, waiting to see what I would do next. My hands tightened on the steering wheel, knuckles pale against the leather, as Jason's photo pressed like a phantom against my ribs from inside my coat pocket. At every red light, my eyes flicked to the passenger seat, half-expecting a shadow to stir beside me, half-dreading the moment it finally would. By the time I stepped from the car, the air had thickened, heavy with the scent of damp pavement and old leaves, and the towering silhouette of the library rose before me like the threshold of something I'd known all along I was meant to cross.

As I pried open the hefty oak doors, I could hear the rusty hinges making a noise as if the structure itself was reluctant to let me in. I stood before the library, a vast hall where long-lost tales lay in slumber, enveloped in an oppressive silence. Dust motes danced like lost memories in the low light pouring through grime-streaked windows as my footsteps resonated over the marble floor, rousing them. Musty parchment, disintegrating leather, and the subtle metallic tang of time slipping away created a strong aroma that permeated the

CHAPTER 8

space, along with old paper and dying hopes.

Brass wall sconces held flickering candles, their flames quivering like anxious hearts as they fought against the night but could never quite overcome it. The elongated shadows thrown by the dim, uneven light across the seemingly infinite shelves gave the impression that something was moving just beyond our field of vision. In the shadows cast by the darkness, tall bookshelves ascended like venerable guardians; their contents were shrouded in darkness as well. The atmosphere grew heavier as I descended into the depths of the void, resonating with the subtle electric charge of untold tales.

With a finger, I ran along the back of a bookcase, slicing a faint line through the decades of dust that had settled there. The silver threads of the cobwebs glistened subtly in the candlelight as they hung delicately between the bookcases, resembling beautiful lace. It was as though the reader had just gone away for a second and never came back; here and there, on broad oak tables, leather-bound books lay neglected, their yellowed pages still open, the curve of a bookmark stuck in the middle of the story. My spine tingled at the sight, and thoughts of Jason's apartment flooded my mind. There, his life seemed to have stopped in mid-motion, and the reverberation of his absence resounded more than his actual presence.

As I navigated deeper into the maze, my shadow danced across the walls, expanding and contracting in response to the shifting light. The room's vibe was far from calm, despite the polished wood beneath my fingertips feeling smooth and aged from years of hands shaping it. It was as if the stories were moving beneath my eyes as the light twisted and shivered over the open books, transforming the letters into patterns that swirled and blurred as I attempted to concentrate.

I could make out a barely audible screech, like paper rubbing against itself or the distant sound of anything moving. The shelves disappeared out of sight, and I stood there paralyzed with a knot in my throat as I stared up at the black ceiling. Something moved in the upper shadows at the very edge of my visual field, prompting my instinct to retreat. But I kept moving ahead, my feet carrying me with a mix of fear and determination.

A floorboard creaked behind me, and I spun around, heart pounding. A person materialized from the shadows created by the dancing flames. He was extremely tall, thin, and incredibly elderly. He had silver hair that fell over his shoulders like moonlight in liquid form, and his pale complexion seemed nearly glowing in the soft light. But it was his eyes that initially caught mine—deep, bottomless pits that appeared to contain all the knowledge I could ever need, as if they could expose every deceit I had told myself and the barriers I had erected to protect my reality.

"Dr. Sullivan." Like the worn and aged pages of an old book, his voice was a low murmur. There was an otherworldly energy emanating from beneath his delicate appearance, a subtle buzzing that shook the very air, as evidenced by the faint tremble in his hands as he tugged at his worn cloak. His movements were not shaky from old age but rather smooth and graceful, as if he had mastered the art of gliding across treacherous territory long ago.

His smile was neither warm nor cold, but steeped in understanding, as if he had waited for me across lifetimes. For a moment, the air seemed to still, the weight of his presence pressing gently but unmistakably against my skin. "I've been waiting," he murmured, "for someone to ask the

CHAPTER 8

right questions."

As he drew closer, the candlelight caught the silver in his hair, casting an almost ethereal halo around his head. The effect made my stomach tighten, the otherworldliness of this encounter blurring the line between dream and waking life. His voice carried the weight of inevitability. "You're seeking answers about the Realm of Illusions, aren't you?"

The words struck deep, knocking the air from my chest. I gripped the edge of a shelf, grounding myself as the room tilted beneath me. My voice was barely a whisper. "Once the carnival has you... it never truly lets go." His phrase echoed in my head, ricocheting against memories I had buried so deeply I'd convinced myself they were never mine.

He leaned in, his voice a thin thread of sound. "You've felt it, haven't you? The pull. It slips into the corners of your mind, weaving itself into your thoughts until you can't tell where it ends and you begin. The air between us thickened, heavy with the weight of unspoken truths. Around us, the candle flames bent and danced, casting fleeting images on the walls—figures twirling, masks gleaming, laughter stretched into something sharp.

"I don't..." I faltered, the clinical part of me scrabbling to assemble the pieces into a rational shape. But the image of Jason loomed large in my mind: his haunted eyes, the figure in the photograph, and the truth I had refused to face.

The historian's hand hovered near my arm, the barest suggestion of contact. "You already know," he murmured. "I can see it in you—the same look they all wore. The ones who came before."

The words burrowed beneath my skin. The ones who came before. My pulse stuttered as I realized how many others had stood where I stood, chasing logic into the dark, only to find themselves standing at the edge of the carnival's world. The room seemed to exhale around me, shadows twisting with slow intent.

Without another word, the historian drew a thick, leather-bound volume from the shelf, dust cascading in a delicate veil as he placed it on the table with a soundless finality. He opened it to pages heavy with intricate sketches—masked performers with grins stretched wide, limbs elongated, and poses bent at impossible angles. My breath hitched as I recognized them. Each figure mirrored my dreams, Jason's stories, and the chilling memories I had fought to suppress.

One drawing leapt from the page—a masked figure poised beside a striped tent, frozen in a stance identical to the one in Jason's photograph. The artist had drawn this sketch decades, perhaps even centuries, before Jason's birth.

My hands trembled as I reached out, fingertips hovering above the page. "These… they're too exact." The voice that emerged from me was thin and ragged, as if it belonged to someone else. The shapes, the postures, the emotions caught in ink—they resonated, triggering something deep and ancient in the marrow of my bones.

The historian's voice softened to a near-whisper. "You understand more than you admit. But your mind shields you from it. Protects you."

I shook my head, the reflex of denial too ingrained to discard all at once. "I can't—" But the drawings spun beneath my gaze, shifting, their expressions folding into the half-seen faces from my dreams. My throat constricted, a tremor rippling through me as memory and reality blurred together. Carnival music teased the edge of hearing, a faint, lilting tune carried on phantom wind.

The historian waited in silence, his gaze unwavering. He saw the battle flickering across my face—the crumbling foundation, the brittle shell of reason. I gripped the edge of the table until the grain bit into my palms, a desperate anchor as the world tilted on its axis.

"You're wrong," I whispered, but even to myself, the words sounded hollow. A part of me long buried stirred in protest, longing to hold on, to stay. To stop running. My chest tightened from the burden of unshed grief and unvoiced confessions.

The historian's eyes never left mine, patient and merciless all at once. His presence was a steady pull against the unraveling threads inside me. The walls I had spent years constructing to keep myself safe, composed, and untouched—they trembled now, thin as paper.

My hand drifted toward the drawing of the masked figure, fingertip brushing the page. The contact sent a jolt through me, a flash of memory half-formed—music swelling, hands reaching, laughter cracking into screams, and the cold snap of a grip slipping from mine. My breath hitched as the years collapsed inward.

The historian's fingers glided over the cracked leather binding, resting at the spine with delicate reverence. His voice was nearly a whisper. "Face it. Only then will you understand."

For a moment, the room pulsed, the flickering candlelight stretching the shadows into grotesque, fluid shapes. Jason's face flickered through my mind, his voice trembling with fear, which I had failed to calm. The dream-masked figures slid into my peripheral vision, beckoning me closer.

My grip tightened on the edge of the book, knuckles

whitening. My heartbeat thudded hard, as if responding to a call. "Tell me," I whispered, my words trembling on the edge of fear and surrender. Tell me what I need to know."

Something in the air shifted—a breath released, a current eased. The historian stepped back, his form retreating into the maze of shelves, fading like a dream at dawn. But his presence remained, coiled in the air, his words folded into the walls.

The book waited, warm under my palm, pulsing with its quiet rhythm. Around me, the library hushed, as if holding its breath. And then, from the darkness, came the whispers—not words, not entirely, but the suggestion of voices threading through the silence. The faint rustle of pages, the creak of unseen wood, and beneath it all, the delicate scrape of something waiting, echoed through the silence.

I pressed my palm to the cover, a shiver rolling through me as sensation bloomed—recognition and dread intertwined. My heartbeat surged, thundering in the hush, but the fear no longer overtook me.

The candlelight wavered, shadows peeling back for just a moment. There was a fleeting glimpse of movement. A painted grin, spinning limbs, a flash of a mask. The expression vanished once more, as if the library had absorbed it completely. But the air tasted of sugar now, cloying and sharp. Cotton candy. Summer laughter. The memory of a carnival under a twilight sky, when the night had first drawn near, lurked behind it.

"I'm ready," I murmured, the words brittle but sure.

Something shifted. The lock turned. The dark leaned closer—but this time, I didn't retreat.

My fingers closed around the spine of the book, and the

warmth surged, a quiet pulse answering my own. The whispers lifted, not as a warning, but as an invitation. I let the fear settle where it belonged, a steady pressure in my chest, no longer the chain around my ankles.

For the first time, I stopped running.

And when the dark called, I answered.

Chapter 9

The historian's words still clung to me as I left the library, a residue I couldn't wash off. I'd stepped outside expecting air—something clean, something grounding—but found only a world that felt thinner than before. The sky stretched overhead in dull gray streaks, smeared like a bruise across the horizon, and the sidewalk beneath my feet didn't feel solid anymore. The wind moved strangely, slipping beneath my coat like curious fingers. Every car that passed seemed too quiet. Every pedestrian, too distant. It felt like walking through the skin of reality, not the substance.

By the time I reached the office, my keys slipped from my hand, slick with sweat I hadn't realized was there. I couldn't remember the drive—just the dull thud of my heart, the book's weight in my bag, and the echo of the historian's final words: "Face it. Only then will you understand." They had followed me like a shadow, pressing close even after the library's ancient air had faded from my clothes. And now, standing at the door of my office, staring at the familiar brushed-metal handle, I realized I wasn't stepping back into safety.

I pushed through the office door, my lungs heaving and my heart pounding like a relentless drumbeat in my chest. The historian's voice permeated my thoughts, clinging to

CHAPTER 9

everything like cobwebs and refusing to let go. Overhead, the familiar hum of the fluorescent lights filled the room, but tonight it sounded wrong, thin, hollow, like the fading mechanical whine of something slipping toward its last breath.

The office had always been a kind of sanctuary for me, cluttered but comfortable, lined with the evidence of a life devoted to control: patient files stacked in orderly towers, research papers fanned across the desk like a fortress of facts. But now those same stacks loomed, casting jagged shadows that sliced across the room. What once gave me comfort now looked staged, hollow. The papers felt like props in a performance I could no longer remember auditioning for, let alone controlling.

Dropping into my chair, I let my trembling hands fall to the keyboard. The clack of the keys filled the silence as words spilled out, messy and frantic, racing ahead of my thoughts as if I could outpace the dread chewing its way through my chest. I had to capture it all: every half-formed memory, every fragment of the historian's warning, every whisper pulled from that dust-choked library. His voice lingered in my head, a persistent murmur, equal parts invitation and threat.

The air carried the sharp tang of old coffee and the musty smell of paper that had sat too long untouched. Mixed with it was the faint, unsettling scent from the library—something dry and old, something that clung to me like a residue I couldn't scrub away. Each word I typed felt like peeling back a layer of skin, exposing nerve after raw nerve. The historian's voice threaded through it all: the tale of the Realm of Illusions, the warnings of those who had come before, and the chilling realization that the pattern twisting through Jason's life had been waiting in mine all along.

For a moment, I froze. My gaze drifted upward, falling on the framed degrees and certifications lining the wall—once symbols of achievement, now pale trophies in a crumbling shrine. They had meant everything once, proof that I had built my life on the bedrock of reason and fact. But now they looked like window dressing, a careful illusion designed to hide the dark corners of the world I no longer had the luxury of ignoring.

"You have to face what's underneath," the historian had said. "If you don't, it'll swallow you whole."

I closed my eyes, but the words were still there, pulsing behind my eyelids like a second heartbeat. The air thickened, heavy in my lungs, as if the room itself were pressing closer. And then, almost imperceptibly, the cracks started to appear—not in the walls, but inside me.

I stared at the open research in front of me, my pulse thrumming in my ears. This is stress. Just stress. I kept repeating it as if it were a mantra, attempting to fuse the words into a solid, enduring entity. But the truth was already slipping beneath the surface, coiling tighter, an old truth I had burned deeply and now felt stirring in the darkness.

Frantic, I flipped through the studies piled on my desk—papers on sleep paralysis, neurological malfunctions, and the brain's uncanny talent for betraying itself. The explanations were cold and clinical. Lifelines. But as I skimmed the pages, the words began to blur, the paragraphs bleeding into each other, swimming in and out of focus. My fingers dug into the paper's edge as if physical pressure could keep the facts in place. My hands trembled, and my throat tightened with a dry, soundless laugh.

CHAPTER 9

"There has to be a logical explanation," I whispered, eyes locked on the pale glow of the monitor. But the sterile light only deepened the shadows pooling at the edges of the room. I drew a long, shaky breath, trying to center myself. Routine. Focus. That was the answer, wasn't it? Keep the gears turning, keep the machine running. But the machine was faltering, the parts grinding down. And the cracks—they were everywhere.

The historian's voice slipped through again, soft as a whisper against the back of my neck. "You already know why this is happening, don't you? But your mind shields you from the truth."

My jaw clenched so tight it ached. No. I wouldn't follow that thread. This was stress, pure and simple. Lack of sleep. Overwork. Nothing was waiting in the dark. No one was lurking in the shadows. No eyes were watching.

And yet, even as I fought to hold onto that belief, Jason's words came rushing back. His nightmares. His mask-haunted visions haunted him deeply. I had heard tales from individuals who had teetered on the brink of slumber and never fully emerged. The words sliced deeper than I wanted to admit, cutting into something I had buried long ago.

I shook my head sharply, trying to dislodge the thought. No. No, this wasn't real. This was exhaustion and imagination conspiring to paint monsters where none existed. I was nothing like Jason. I was still in control.

But the words were thin. They slipped through my fingers like water, leaving only cold behind.

Overhead, the lights flickered. The shadows stretched, and the sudden hush that followed made me realize just how silent the room had become.

Too silent.

A weight settled between my shoulders. There was a tingling certainty that someone was observing me.

I began to pace, each step snapping sharply against the cold tile. I paced back and forth, as if the tension coiling through the air could be broken by movement. My hair clung in damp strands to my forehead, and my nails bit into my palms where they curled into fists. Copper bloomed on my tongue where I had bitten too hard. But I couldn't stop moving. I feared that if I paused, the silence would engulf me.

I gripped the edge of the desk until my knuckles ached, the sharp bite of the wood anchoring me for a moment. Neurological misfires. Stress. Sleep paralysis. The brain was simply deceiving me. However, the more I whispered, the words grew thinner, as brittle as tissue, and ineffective against the increasing wave of unease. The room no longer felt like a safe place. It felt like a box. And somewhere in the corners, just beyond sight, something was waiting to close the lid.

The lights overhead sputtered and died for half a second.

And in that flicker of darkness, something shifted.

I whipped around so fast that the vertebrae in my neck cracked, and my breath hitched as my eyes scanned the room. For one split second, reflected in the darkened computer screen, I saw it—a face. No. Not a face. A mask.

My chest tightened, the air locking in my throat as my heart pounded a jagged rhythm. I turned in a slow, helpless circle, eyes darting from shadow to shadow. Nothing moved. Nothing came forward. However, the atmosphere felt excessively dense, the silence piercing, as if the world was stifling its breath.

I fell back into the chair, arms wrapped around myself as

CHAPTER 9

if I could press the panic back down into my chest. Just breathe. Just ground yourself. But even with my eyes shut, the images burned behind my eyelids—the masks shifting, twisting, grinning in the dark. Beneath it all, the whispers, soft and curling, infiltrated my thoughts like smoke.

The chill coursing through me was profound. I clutched my arms tighter, but the office was no longer a refuge. It was a cage. I didn't know if I had locked the door or if something else was waiting for me to close it.

My gaze fell to the old book resting on the desk, its cracked leather binding cool beneath my trembling fingers. Its presence seemed to hum in the air, a silent dare. Explore what lies beneath the surface. Uncover the secrets that fate never intended to reveal.

The walls leaned in, just a little, just enough to squeeze the breath from my lungs. This isn't in my head. It couldn't be.

Enough.

I shot to my feet, the chair scraping harshly across the floor. I couldn't stay here, hemmed in by dying fluorescent lights and the last tatters of denial. The whispers, the flickers in the shadows, the unraveling edges of reality—I had to leave before they finished weaving me into something I couldn't escape.

With a sharp motion, I snapped the book shut and shoved it deep into my bag, the motion crisp, almost angry. My hands trembled, but determination stiffened my spine. Change of clothes. I took out the car keys from the desk drawer. The motions were familiar, grounding. But this time, the destination was unknown.

The office loomed behind me, still and sterile, but every hair on my arms prickled as if unseen eyes tracked my movements.

I could feel it: that awful, crawling sensation of being watched, measured, judged. The flickering light above created sickly yellow puddles on the floor, appearing to twitch and pulse in sync with my pounding heartbeat.

Leave now, or you never will.

The metal door waited at the end of the hall, the push bar glinting dully in the dim light. My steps quickened, echoing sharply. Too sharply. There were other footsteps now, just behind mine, a heartbeat out of sync. I refused to turn. I refrained from turning my head.

I reached the door, hand poised on the handle.

And I paused.

The cold certainty enveloped me, profound and unwavering. Crossing this threshold wasn't just about leaving the building. It was about stepping into something else—something I had been circling for far too long. I could still turn back. I could go home, bury myself under the weight of routine, and pretend none of this had ever happened.

Or I could open the door.

My fingers clenched around the handle, nails biting into my palm. My chest hitched.

Behind me, the lights flickered once, twice.

Then the world behind me went dark.

I pushed the door open and stepped into the night.

The melody wasn't playing aloud, not really, but it circled in my mind, curling at the edges of my thoughts like an invisible thread pulling tighter with every mile. It clung to me, wound through the folds of memory like a stain that no amount of rationalizing could scrub away. I exhaled through clenched teeth, gripping the wheel until my knuckles ached. I could floor the gas, fly across the state, put hours between me and

CHAPTER 9

that cursed office, but deep down, I already understood the truth. The answers I sought weren't behind me, tucked safely in books or theories. They were ahead, waiting, and no matter how far I ran, every road would circle back to where it all began.

The highway unspooled before me, a twisting ribbon of asphalt shimmering under the glare of a relentless sun. At first, it was nothing—just heat rising in waves off the pavement, the mirage of motion. But then the wrongness started to creep in. The road shimmered, yet it pulsed even more, as if the earth were alive. The vehicles in front of me swayed as their edges widened and retracted. It was as if the fabric of reality were flapping apart. The landscape outside the window continued to melt as I blinked forcefully, attempting to reset the image. The trees twisted at inconceivable angles, their branches clawing at the sky like skeletal hands. Like a picture left out in the rain, the colors blended, too bright and crisp. My stomach lurched, a cold spike of panic blooming in my gut.

No. This wasn't normal.

The wrongness crawled up my spine, a whispering certainty tightening around my throat. This wasn't heat haze; it wasn't exhaustion. The world was collapsing, trapping me within its fractured structure. I hoped that by pressing down harder on the gas, I could outpace the unraveling, as my instincts surged. However, things became worse the quicker I drove. The long-gone structures on the horizon lay in a state of formless ruin, their windows wide and black, like mouths gaping open. Like water rippling under my tires, the road under me lost its weight and firmness. The air became heavier as time froze all around me. Time appeared endless, transforming the present into an unrecognizable state with every passing moment. Every breath pierced my ears with its rumbling sound.

You are not meant to be here—that was an unexpected, icy, electric idea that crept under my skin.

Following that came the whispers, which were low and curled like smoke at the periphery of hearing. Recognizable voices, the ones that had tormented me at night, crept through the cracks of this crumbling universe. I wasn't alone. I had never been alone. My throat tightened, a dry click as I forced myself to swallow, eyes locked on the warping road ahead. Every instinct screamed at me to pull over, to abandon the car, to run. But where could I go? The road behind me had already fallen away, devoured by the shifting void swallowing everything I thought was real. With every passing mile, the world broke further, slipping away in fragments.

Somewhere beyond the flickering edge of my vision, I felt it: something watching. Waiting. And I was barreling straight toward it.

My fingers dug deeper into the steering wheel, the vinyl hot and slick beneath my palms. My breath came fast, shallow, rattling through my chest as the landscape buckled. The buildings stretched, sagging like reflections smeared across water, snapping back into place with a pulse of vertigo. The trees shuddered, jerking unnaturally, as if something writhed beneath their bark. The air thickened, pressing against the car like an unseen tide. I mumbled to myself, voice shaking, "This isn't real. It's just stress… just my mind playing tricks." But the words fell flat, warped in the air, echoing back to me thin and hollow, like they didn't belong to me anymore.

A low hum began to thread through everything, rattling against my chest, buzzing in the hollow of my bones. It wasn't

CHAPTER 9

the car. It wasn't anything I could name. It was simply there, as if the world itself was coming undone at the seams. I tightened my grip, jaw clenched so hard it ached. Stress didn't do this. Stress didn't twist the road under your tires like a living thing or melt the landscape into liquid shadows.

Up ahead, a sign flickered into view—familiar, local, a marker I should have known. But as I stared, the letters twisted, writhing across the surface as if the world itself had forgotten how to form words. I blinked, heart hammering, and the sign was gone, replaced by something older, stranger, something I couldn't place but felt in the pit of my gut.

The road buckled. For one terrible instant, the car lifted, the ground falling away beneath me, and I was weightless—suspended in a void thick with color and static and something far worse. Then, just as suddenly, the world slammed back into place, rattling through the frame of the car, shuddering up my spine. I gasped, clutching the wheel, the horizon trembling before me, the sky rippling like disturbed water.

And then I heard it.

Not faint. Not distant. Not a trick of memory.

The carnival melody, the one that had haunted my dreams, was no longer behind me. It was ahead, clear and bright, drifting through the air with impossible sharpness. My chest tightened, breath catching as the asphalt warped, twisting into shapes I didn't recognize, the world tearing at its edges as I sped straight into the unraveling. There was no turning back, no brakes strong enough, no steering wheel sure enough. I was locked on this course, driving into the jaws of whatever waited at the end of this nightmare.

The light hit like a blade—searing, white-hot, cutting through my skull with blinding force. My body seized, my eyes squeezed shut, but there was no escape. And when I opened them, everything was gone.

I was no longer in the car.

I was standing in the middle of the carnival grounds.

My knees buckled, my stomach twisted in a brutal lurch, as if the world had shifted in an instant and left my body scrambling to catch up. There had been no passage of time, no sense of arrival. One blink, one breath, and I was here. The sky above stretched vast and black, a void without stars or moon, just empty nothing. And the music—oh God, the music—filled the air, crawling beneath my skin, winding through every thought, relentless and wrong.

I turned slowly, limbs stiff and trembling, searching the haze for something real, something fixed, but all I found were the figures drifting through the mist. Their masks pulsed and warped, never holding one shape for long, their edges blurred as if the very air refused to hold them still. My throat closed, a hard knot of dread settling deep in my chest. This wasn't a dream. This wasn't a hallucination. I was here. The carnival had claimed me.

I wanted to speak, to tell myself this wasn't happening, but the words dissolved before they reached my lips. The sour-sweet scent of popcorn and incense curled around me, thick and cloying, crawling into my throat until my stomach roiled. I edged forward, slow and cautious, every nerve stretched taut, terrified that the slightest movement would pull their gaze.

But maybe they were already looking. Maybe they always had been.

The carnival spread around me in impossible shapes, familiar yet twisted, a funhouse reflection of itself. Shadows

CHAPTER 9

stretched in long, unnatural arcs, swallowing paths and reshaping corners. The masked figures drifted on silent feet, grotesque faces locked in frozen leers and smirks, their presence a cruel echo of my fear. And in that moment, the realization struck, sharp and cold.

I hadn't stumbled into this. I hadn't been pulled here by accident.

I had walked right into it.

The historian's voice wrapped around me like a noose, his words curling through the haze of panic: Once the carnival marks you, it never lets you go.

Panic surged, burning in my throat, but even as my heart thundered, I knew the truth. There were no exits. No cracks in the maze. No loopholes. The world around me twisted with every desperate glance, every hopeful turn, each escape route folding in on itself, swallowed by the pulsing dark.

The masked figures drew closer, their long fingers hovering just beyond my skin, deliberate, patient. I could feel the weight of them, the press of their presence, as if they were waiting not to take me, but for me to understand. My limbs refused to move, locked beneath the suffocating weight of truth. This wasn't a hallucination or fear. This was the price of looking too long, of chasing answers I had no business demanding.

My eyes squeezed shut, the darkness behind my lids seething with afterimages—the spinning masks, the lurching shadows, the snarl of music tightening in my chest. My breath came in sharp, shallow gasps, the smell of burnt sugar searing in my nose. The whispering rose, a chorus of voices threading through every crack in my mind, winding their way around my thoughts like vines.

I had come here for answers. I had wanted the truth. But

now, staring into the faces of the carnival, I wondered if I'd ever truly wanted to know. For years, I had buried my past, locked it away like something fragile and dangerous. Digging it up now was like peeling skin from bone, raw and unbearable. And somewhere deep inside, a part of me understood.

I had been waiting for this.

The figures closed in, the air thickening, each breath tighter than the last. The music climbed, a fevered pulse, drilling into my skull until it was no longer just sound but sensation, a rhythm beating in time with my own heart. Every instinct screamed to run, to fight, to do anything—but the moment I tried to think, the world folded, warping, pulling me under.

The whispers surged. The masks loomed.

Time was gone.

It was face this or be swallowed whole.

Chapter 10

My palms pressed on an icy, unmoving surface underneath me as I gently sat up. The surface was cold to the touch and anchored me to a spot that was at once genuine and completely off-kilter. Slowly, my eyes adapted to the low light, and then, as the room began to take form, I felt a shock go through my body. Mirrors. Wall to wall, ceiling to floor. I was surrounded by endless reflections, each one twisting the world into something monstrous. My face stared back from every angle, but it was never quite right—stretched, smeared, reshaped. One version was too long, the next was too wide, and others that didn't even look human. Every reflection was a distortion, a stranger in my skin.

The overhead lights flickered, casting jagged shadows across the glass that broke and reformed like shattered memories. This wasn't my office. It wasn't my apartment. Wherever I was, it bent the rules of reality just enough to make everything feel impossible. The mirrors watched me, and I watched them, caught in a loop of fractured self-recognition. I stood slowly, legs weak and trembling, as the floor beneath me seemed to stretch with each breath I took. The shadows along the walls shifted when I moved—but worse, some shifted just before I did.

The air was thick with the cloying, sour aroma of incense and burnt sugar. At the periphery, there was a faint odor of rotting popcorn, a carnival scent, and the memory of something happy that had died a long time ago but had never ceased to decay. A low, harsh murmur, more vibration than sound, twisted across the air. Despite my inability to comprehend them, I could feel their hidden meaning. I had company. From beyond the mirrored walls, something—or—multiple somethings—observed me.

Like a person traversing a frozen lake, I stepped cautiously and unsteadily forward. The mirrors shattered my image into dozens of broken selves. A girl, young, afraid, wide-eyed. A snarling woman with teeth like knives. A hollowed-out version of myself that looked too tired to stand. I stared, breath shallow, as all of them watched me back. Each reflection was a memory I'd tried to bury, a truth I hadn't been ready to confront. They didn't blink. They just waited.

The air thickened, as if the room itself were inhaling. I turned in a slow circle, trying to orient myself, but the mirrors offered no exit, no direction, only more warped versions of me, each more disfigured than the last. Panic stirred at the base of my spine, sharp and hot. I clenched my fists, nails biting into my palms. I couldn't lose control here. Not again. I inhaled, forcing my lungs to expand against the pressure that threatened to crush them. Focus. Think. Survive.

Then came the laughter. It was distant at first, hollow and aimless, but it swelled quickly into something sharp-edged, a ring of teeth in the dark. The sound seemed to come from everywhere at once—above me, behind me, inside the walls. My breath caught in my throat as I turned again, searching, but the mirrors only reflected more versions of my fear. Each

CHAPTER 10

echo of the laugh seemed to ricochet off the glass and crawl under my skin.

I stumbled forward, hoping the movement would break the trance, but the air soured further, thick with the smell of sugar turned to ash. The scent clawed at my throat, dragging old memories to the surface—Jason's wide, haunted eyes, the torn photograph, the carnival ticket clutched in his hand. I pressed my palms to the glass, breath fogging the surface as the faces shifted again. My reflection dissolved, replaced by images I didn't want to see. A little girl weeping in silence. A grinning version of myself with hollow sockets for eyes. A creature wearing my face like a mask.

They were peeling me apart, these mirrors. Stripping me down to the bones of who I was. I backed away, heart pounding, only to find more mirrors behind me—more twisted truths, more echoes of pain. The carnival wasn't just a memory anymore. It had weight. Teeth. Intent. It wasn't pulling me in. It had already claimed me.

A flicker caught my attention—movement just beyond the glass. The performers had arrived. They emerged slowly, masks gleaming in the dim light. Their bodies moved wrong, limbs too fluid, heads tilting at angles that defied anatomy. They mouthed words I couldn't hear, but I felt them, each syllable sliding beneath my skin like cold fingers. Their masks shifted between joy and despair, rage and delight, never staying long enough to settle on one expression. I pressed my back to the mirror, hands shaking, breath coming in short bursts.

The performers glided between the glass, their presence not entirely real and yet undeniable. I tried to run, but every direction led to another reflection. The mirrors multiplied, folding space into a maze of nightmare. I stumbled, nearly falling, as the whispering rose to a chorus—soft, sibilant, persistent. It circled me, chanted my name, unspoken accusations twisting into lullabies. I shut my eyes, but it didn't help. The darkness behind my lids teemed with masks and memories.

When I opened them, they were closer. One mask hovered inches from mine, its eyes hollow, its mouth stretched wide in a grin that had nothing to do with joy. I pressed myself tighter into the corner, heart slamming against my ribs. The performers danced in slow spirals, weaving between the glass, limbs trailing like smoke. The mirrors reflected every movement, a hundred different angles of dread. The air turned syrupy, the ground uncertain beneath my feet. I couldn't breathe. Couldn't think.

And then—crack.

My fist struck the mirror without warning. A spiderweb of fractures spread outward, refracting the masked figures into kaleidoscopic nightmares. The laughter rose again, delighted, vicious. My legs gave out, and I dropped to my knees, fists clenched, teeth bared in a snarl. Tears burned my cheeks. This wasn't just a place. It was a manifestation—a living thing built from everything I had refused to face.

The performers crept closer, fingers outstretched, gentle as death. They knew who I was. What I'd done. They carried the weight of every buried memory, every broken promise, every sleepless night. I wanted to scream, but my voice caught in my throat. All I could do was stare into their masks, into myself, and see everything I had tried to bury staring back.

But beneath the terror, something else stirred. A flicker of understanding. This place wasn't trying to destroy me. It was trying to show me. To force me to look. The carnival hadn't

CHAPTER 10

created these fears—it had revealed them.

I let out a shaky breath, rising on unsteady legs. The performers didn't follow. They hovered just beyond reach, their masks flickering like candle flames in a draft. The silence pressed in, thick and total, and I understood: they were waiting for me to choose.

No more running. No more denial. I turned toward the largest mirror, the one I'd shattered, and looked again. My reflection was broken, yes—but it was mine. Every jagged piece was a part of me, and I was done pretending otherwise.

"Fine," I whispered, voice steady now. "Let's see where this goes."

The performers receded into the dark. The laughter died. The mirrors rippled once, like the surface of a disturbed lake.

And then the funhouse shifted.

Not as a prison. Not anymore.

Now it was a path.

Chapter 11

I turned another corner, my footsteps echoing through the mirrored corridor, sharp as glass and impossible to chase back to silence. Then I stopped short. In one of the warped mirrors, staring directly at me, was a version of myself, much younger. She was barefoot, wild-eyed, and unaffected by the weight I now carried. Her gaze met mine without fear, her mouth curving into a small, shy smile that felt achingly familiar. That was a smile I hadn't worn in years.

I stepped closer, fingers brushing the cool glass. The reflection didn't distort—not this time. It stayed pure, whole. The smile lingered. Open. Unscarred. The world behind the mirror shimmered like heat off pavement, and then, without warning, everything peeled away. The Funhouse vanished as effortlessly as wet paint slides off a canvas, transporting me to a completely different realm.

I was eight years old again, barefoot on warm asphalt, running through the old Paradise Fair. Strings of colored lights swung above my head on sagging wires, blue and gold and soft as starlight. Laughter rose around me, sharp and un-contained, folding into the shouts of children and the rusted groan of tired carnival rides. That old, scratchy melody—the one that always played too loud from the speakers near the

CHAPTER 11

carousel—wrapped around the memory like ribbon. And for one suspended moment, it was magic. Real magic. The kind that didn't need proving.

My small feet darted past game booths, the smell of fried dough thick in the air. I passed the ring toss stall where my father would later win me a purple unicorn. I hadn't remembered that in years. The memory struck me abruptly, a tiny, luminous fragment of the world that I had let escape my grasp. I could still feel that wonder, like a spark catching in my chest—sharp, immediate, and already fading. What had I done to it?

That feeling swelled into something heavier. Not nostalgia. Grief. I was grieving for the things I had lost and the things I had given up for safety and control. When had I stopped believing? When had wonder become something I distrusted?

The girl in the mirror still smiled, wide-eyed and untouched. She didn't know. Not yet. She hadn't learned how dark it could get. She hadn't begun constructing barriers to ward off the world. My throat tightened. Tears welled, hot and fast. She had no idea what was coming.

The mirrors around me began to ripple, as though they were breathing. The image wavered like water, and then new faces emerged. Aunt Sarah came first, her mouth drawn tight in a line of familiar disappointment. Her eyes found mine, stern but loving. I remembered the last conversation we had—her voice gentle, pleading. "Come home for Christmas. You can't keep hiding behind your work." I'd hung up on her. I told myself she didn't understand.

Another step. Another face. Marcus appeared, my college roommate's brother. The hollow look in his eyes—just like the day I found him after his suicide attempt—had never left me. I called the ambulance and stayed with him in the hospital. But afterward, when he'd reached out again, I hadn't answered. Couldn't. I had nothing left to give. The last call went to voicemail, and I never heard from him again.

Next came Dr. Chen—my mentor, my guide through the fire of medical school. Her face in the glass held more sadness than disappointment. "You're running from something, Brooke," she had said during my residency. I'd laughed it off. Burying the truth beneath awards, clinical protocols, and the false god of control.

Each reflection struck harder than the last. On the day I missed my father's funeral, my mother had tears streaking down her face as she cited a "critical case." My sister Emma, her voice brittle from years of unanswered calls, was present. Her silence was louder than any confrontation. The guilt pressed in around me, sharp and suffocating. My lungs struggled to expand under the weight of guilt.

The mirror warped again. My reflection split apart. The carnival's song twisted with it, warped and sour, grinding like a needle skipping across a broken record. A face sneered, baring teeth too sharp, too long. "Coward," it hissed. Another face joined in, blank-eyed. "Failed them all."

I staggered backward, my breath catching on the lump rising in my throat. The air thickened, damp and close, pressing down like soaked fabric. My knees buckled, and I fell to the floor. Above me, the mirrors multiplied, stretching into infinity. Every pane reflected a different version of me, each more grotesque, each more unforgiving.

The laughter returned, layered and loud, bleeding in from all sides. I slammed my hands over my ears, but it was already inside—each face, each failure, whispering variations of the

CHAPTER 11

same truth: You're broken. Your brokenness has always been present. The worst part was how much I believed that I was broken.

I curled in on myself, face pressed to the cold glass floor, the voices circling like sharks. However, just beneath the overwhelming noise, something small flickered. Small. Steady. There was a single note of resistance.

"You're not to blame," I whispered. The words felt like sandpaper on my throat, but they carried weight. The laughter faltered, stuttered like a broken transmission. I breathed in again, deeper this time. The panic didn't vanish, but it loosened its grip.

I raised my eyes to the nearest mirror. A new reflection stared back—one that merged them all. The reflection embodied my mother's sorrow. Emma's silence. Marcus's sadness. Dr. Chen's concern. All of them are woven into the person standing there. Not to accuse. They were simply there to be observed.

I stood slowly. My legs trembled, but they held. "I see you," I said, my voice steadying. "I've been running for years. From pain. From truth. But not anymore."

The glass shimmered but didn't break. Instead, it cleared. The faces softened; they faded. The faces were still present, but they had become quieter, as if they were waiting. The carnival's music, once jagged and mocking, mellowed into something wistful. The music remained strange and eerie, yet it became gentler. Almost tender.

The mirrors gradually smoothed out. The different versions of myself, which had twisted into snarls and screams, gradually eased into clarity. Not perfect. But real. I feel both scarred and exhausted. But standing. Something in my chest shifted. This shift was not an erasure of guilt but rather a repurposing of it. The grief remained, but now it felt like a weight I could carry, not a punishment I deserved.

One last face surfaced—Jenna's. She looked exactly as I remembered her from before. Laughing. Whole. No more blame. Just a presence. A goodbye, maybe. I stepped forward. The mirrors didn't fight me this time. They simply... reflected. I wasn't hiding from them anymore.

With each step, the tension eased. The air grew lighter. The whispers softened into nothing more than memory. I could feel the carnival releasing its grip, as if it had tested me and found something worth sparing.

I reached the last mirror. My reflection stared back—bruised, tear-streaked, but clear-eyed. I didn't turn away. I pressed a hand to the glass. This time, it wasn't cold. It pulsed, warm beneath my touch.

"I see you," I whispered. And I meant it.

The mirror rippled like a pond. I stepped forward. It gave way. A hush fell over the Funhouse as I passed through, the air cooling against my skin like a baptism.

Beyond the glass, the carnival waited—quieter now, changed. The lights ahead flickered, softer, creating long shadows that covered rusted rides and sagging tents. The smell of decaying sugar had vanished. What lingered now was older dust, damp earth, and time.

I looked back one last time. The Funhouse stood still, smaller now, as if it had shrunk without its power over me. Through the windows, I could still see the faces—my family, my patients, pieces of me left behind. But they didn't accuse anymore. They simply watched. And I felt their understanding.

CHAPTER 11

"Thank you," I said, my voice catching.

The weight on my shoulders remained, but it was different now. Worn like armor, not shackles. I turned toward the winding path ahead, where the carnival's shadows still curled just beyond the light.

This time, my steps didn't tremble.

This time, I wasn't walking away from the past.

I was walking toward whatever came next.

Chapter 12

As the mist rose slowly, coilingly, like fingers reaching up from below, it curled around my ankles and I stood immobile. It adhered to my flesh with a sticky tenacity, becoming thicker with each breath I took. Something had changed during the carnival, which had always been a continual din of lights and motion. The noise was no longer just loud. It was wrong. Hollow. Bent out of tune. A twisted echo of joy turned sinister.

From somewhere deeper in the haze, laughter spilled into the clearing. Not bright or warm—sharp, metallic, and layered beneath a carousel melody that stuttered in and out like a failing tape. Whispers, low and persistent, barely audible, wrapped around the sound as it twisted and folded in on itself in the air. Whenever I tried to hear or understand them, they slipped back into the fog, just out of reach.

Lights from the Ferris wheel and carousel flickered out of sync, casting erratic bursts of color across the clearing. Their shadows stretched unnaturally, jerking in staccato movements that didn't belong to anything grounded in this world. One of them slithered toward me—sharp-edged, skeletal—but before it reached my feet, it recoiled into the dark, swallowed whole.

The mist pressed higher, damp and cold, seeping into my

CHAPTER 12

shoes, but I didn't move. I stood firm. After everything I'd survived in the Funhouse, the fear here felt different. Not softer, exactly—but clearer. Like it wasn't trying to scare me anymore. It was trying to prepare me. The air pulsed with tension, as though the ground itself breathed beneath me, stretching and contracting with every flicker of those broken lights.

A calliope tune rose from the depths of the fog—quiet at first, then unmistakable. It was one I hadn't heard since childhood, but I knew it instantly. It called to something buried deep, something that had once felt like wonder. Shapes moved beyond the veil, slow and purposeful, and I watched with a heart that thudded louder than the music.

The first figure emerged with fluid grace, its robe catching fractured light and reflecting it in slick, oil-like swirls of blue and purple. My eyes caught on its mask—white bone painted with curling gold filigree, its smile wide, patient, and far too fixed. The kind of smile that pretended to comfort while hiding a blade.

Behind it came more. One mask wept frozen tears that glittered in the gloom. Another smiled endlessly, lips stretched too far, teeth too sharp. They drifted soundlessly, not walking but gliding just above the ground, their movements detached from gravity, from rules. Their eyes were voids behind the masks, dark and fathomless. Still, they watched. Not with aggression, but with intent.

The whispers thickened, threading through the clearing in waves. At first, they resembled rustling leaves, but they built into a dissonant chorus that made my skin prickle. "She remembers," one voice sang, high and lilting. "Does she?" another murmured, low and slow like rolling thunder. "Will she?" a third teased, playful but barbed.

I wanted to turn away, to plug my ears, but my limbs refused. Their words slithered into my skull, not spoken but embedded, like a song you couldn't unhear. The figure in the starlit robe drifted closer, and though its mask still wore that painted calm, the air around it shifted. Something in me leaned forward, drawn despite every instinct screaming to retreat.

"Fear not, weary traveler," it said, voice melodic and too smooth. "The truth lies within, waiting to be uncovered." Another figure stepped into the clearing, this one cloaked in darkness so dense it absorbed the surrounding light. "Listen to your memories," it intoned, a voice low and grounding. "They will guide you to clarity."

I stared at them both, my breath shallow. I tried to find a hint of humanity in the eyes behind the masks, but they remained unreadable. Still, I felt the pull. There was a stillness around them that didn't belong to this place—a silence that almost comforted, like the eye of a storm.

But just as I let my guard lower, the calm ruptured.

New figures emerged from the mist, stepping out in jagged sync. Their masks were vicious—cracked, spiked, cruel in design—and their movements held a different energy. No glide. No grace. Only hunger. Their robes absorbed all light, casting outlines like wounds against the haze.

One stepped forward, towering above the rest. Its mask was a mosaic of broken mirrors, catching my reflection in shards, slicing it into a dozen fractured images—every one of them afraid. "You can't outrun your guilt," it rasped, voice like shattered glass scraping tile. "And you can't hide from the truths that bind you."

The air thickened with static. It crawled over my skin like

CHAPTER 12

invisible electricity, the hairs on my arms rising in warning. The carnival's music dropped to a hum, a low vibration I could feel in my ribs. Each masked figure pulsed faintly in time with my heartbeat, as though drawing power from my fear.

They circled, slow and deliberate, until I stood boxed in, the mist now a cage. My legs threatened to buckle, but I held firm as the figures began to speak—each voice joining a symphony of riddles and warning.

"You must find what is lost to truly know yourself," one whispered, its tone metallic and biting.

"What you cling to as safe holds the key to your escape," another added, voice slow as molasses.

"The truth lies in what you've hidden."

"Your sanctuary is your prison."

"Remember what you chose to forget."

The words pierced me—sharp, deliberate. They didn't feel like riddles anymore. They felt like instructions. Or confessions. My body swayed with their rhythm, the voices wrapping around me like thread pulling taut. Each one echoed a piece of something I'd buried. My office, my routines, my endless analysis—they weren't safety nets. They were blindfolds.

They moved closer, cloaks brushing against my arms, soft but ice-cold. The scent of rotting sugar and old wood filled my lungs, and my breath came ragged. The guilt rose in tandem with the mist. Flashes of faces—Jenna, my mother, Marcus, Sarah—struck like lightning behind my eyes. Their disappointment, their hurt, everything I'd locked away, poured in.

I gritted my teeth, pressing shaking hands against my temples. "No more running," I whispered, barely audible.

But the words were true. This time, I meant them.

The figures froze, as if testing my resolve. Their heads tilted in eerie unison. The silence that followed should have felt empty, but instead it pulsed—charged and waiting. I paced the edge of the clearing, watching them, feeling out the rhythm of their appearances.

Each mask seemed to align with a memory, a thought, a wound. The midnight figure had appeared when I thought of Jenna. The mirror-faced one when I'd doubted myself. The weeping mask when I'd touched on childhood. They weren't random. They were responses—reflections of the pain I carried.

"You're not monsters," I said aloud. "You're memories. Manifestations." The mist thickened in reply, but no one moved to stop me. They watched as I spoke. Waiting.

I recalled their earlier words: "What you think is safe holds the key to your escape." My safe place—my office, my routines, my denial—had become my prison. It all connected.

Each mask flickered now, showing hints of familiar places—Jenna's smile, my office door, my old house. I wasn't surrounded by strangers. I was surrounded by myself.

"Show me," I said, voice louder now. "Whatever it is. I'm ready."

The one with the shattered mirror tilted its head, reflecting me back in fragments. "Are you certain?" it asked. "Some truths cut deep."

"I've been cut before," I replied. "I can take this one."

The figures began to move again, swirling in a slow, tight pattern around me. The lights pulsed in time with their steps, and the music swelled—not chaotic now, but purposeful. Their masks glowed faintly, each flickering with images I

CHAPTER 12

didn't yet understand. A dance, no longer one of torment, but one of revelation.

"Follow the path your mind has hidden," they chanted, their voices folding into one harmonious thread.

I took a breath, steady and deep, and stepped forward. The figures parted, robes fluttering like banners in a storm. They formed an aisle of shadow and memory, one I had no choice but to walk.

But for the first time, I didn't dread what waited at the end.

I moved into the mist, past the masks and into the unknown—not as a woman fractured, but as someone finally whole enough to see the truth.

Chapter 13

The mist was waiting for me.

As I stepped beyond the ring of masked figures, the last tendrils of their swirling dance melting back into shadow, a stillness settled over the clearing—dense and knowing. My breath curled in the cold air, each exhale vanishing into the low, heavy fog that clung to the ground. The silence that followed was not peace, but anticipation, as if the carnival itself had pulled back, making space for whatever came next. And I knew, deep in the marrow of my bones, that this was not the end of something.

The fog thickened as I moved forward, curling around my ankles with slow deliberation, like it knew I was there and wasn't ready to let go. I paused, heart rattling in my chest, watching the mist twist and roll across the path, pulling me closer to the distant glow of the carnival lights. The brightness bled through the haze in strange, unnatural streaks—bold reds and yellows smeared like wet paint, their edges too sharp against the dim gray. They pulsed and shifted, watercolors on a canvas that couldn't decide what it was supposed to be.

I squinted through the gloom. Were those performers? Patrons? Shapes moved at the edges of my vision, half-formed and flickering, refusing to hold still. Faces folded

CHAPTER 13

at the wrong angles. Limbs bent where there shouldn't be joints. The harder I stared, the more the shapes unraveled into impossibilities.

A child's laughter rang out to my left, high and bright—but hollow. I spun toward it, only to find nothing but the mist and the echo it left behind. The sound hung in the air like a ghost of joy, the final note of a lullaby no one remembered how to finish. Above me, the carnival's electric glow tried to push back the fog, casting halos of color that only deepened the dark. Shadows shifted through it—some tall, some small, all just out of reach. No matter how hard I looked, they vanished the moment I tried to name them.

I hugged my arms around myself and took another step. The air felt colder here, thicker, as if the mist wasn't just weather but memory. The rides and booths rose like broken monuments through the haze. I caught sight of a Ferris wheel—tall and skeletal—but when I turned again, it had shifted, now behind me and stretching even farther into the sky, its spokes cutting through the dark like bone.

"I know this place," I whispered, the words trembling as they left me. I didn't know how or why, but those feelings felt true. This wasn't a dream. This was not a hallucination. This was memory made real—cracked and warped, yes—but rooted in something I'd once lived. Something I'd tried to forget.

The fog pulled tighter around me, and I kept walking. My footsteps were slow, unsure. The air pressed down on me with every step. Then the music came again, threading through the mist—soft, almost melodic, just out of tune. At first, it was beautiful. Familiar. Then it shifted, jarring and discordant, as if someone had taken something lovely and twisted it until it broke.

The voices followed.

They slipped through the fog like silk torn down the middle—one moment smooth, the next abrasive. They moved in waves, rising and falling in eerie harmony until a single word cut through.

"Jenna."

I stopped breathing. The name slammed into me with the force of a wave, and I staggered back, wind knocked from my lungs. The fog vibrated with it, the lights pulsing in time with the sound.

"Jenna... Jenna... Jenna..."

Over and over, the name looped—taunting, mourning, calling. I slapped my hands over my ears, but it was no use. The chant lived inside me now, deep in the hollow place I'd refused to acknowledge. My knees buckled, dropping me to the cold, damp ground. The fog spun tighter, swirling like a storm, and the name pushed harder, dragging up everything I'd locked away.

Jenna was laughing beneath the carnival lights, her head tilted back, that streak of color across her cheek making her look half-human, half-phantom. Her fingers curled around my wrist, tugging me toward the Ferris wheel. "Come on, Brooke! Don't be such a scaredy-cat!" I could still hear her voice—bright, teasing, whole.

More memories rushed in, wild and unforgiving. Under the string lights, Jenna spun in circles, her sundress catching the wind and her hair tangled like silk in the breeze. Cotton candy stuck to both her fingers and mine, and I laughed in response to her laughter. Her joy embodied gravity, and I was too young to comprehend the possibility of such joy dissipating.

But it did.

CHAPTER 13

The memories shifted. The color drained. The music warped again, sour and broken. Jenna's laughter echoed one last time—then curdled into silence. The lights dimmed. Shadows bled through the edges of my memory, swallowing her in pieces.

I crouched low, trying to hold onto something real, but the voices only grew louder. Her name repeatedly echoed in my mind. My body shook. My heart beat wild and uneven, and for a moment, I couldn't breathe.

But then, something in the noise changed.

Under the chant and beneath the grief, a whisper rose. Not from them. From within me. A question.

What are they trying to show you?

I stilled, hands falling from my head. The fog was still thick, the voices still a storm—but I listened. Not to the sound, but to what it pointed to.

"Jenna..." I cried out, my voice barely audible.

The mist trembled. The shadows stopped shifting.

"Jenna, I need to remember!" I said again, louder. My voice cracked, but I didn't care. I stood slowly, trembling, heart thudding, and shouted her name into the fog.

"JENNA!"

The name hit the air like thunder. It cracked through the noise, split the chant in two.

And the carnival changed.

The fog parted slightly. The masked figures returned—but this time, their edges were clear, their movements slower. One wore yellow. Jenna's sundress. My breath hitched.

I moved toward her, or what I hoped was her. The mist pulled at my feet, the music spun louder, faster. The masked figures turned, their faces flickering—smiling, sobbing, sneering—but they didn't block me. They watched. Waiting.

My fingers reached for the figure in yellow, heart clawing at my ribs. I had to see. I had to know.

The music rose to a crescendo, a cacophony of screams dressed as song.

Then—her voice.

"You have to let go, B."

Everything stopped. My body, my breath, my thoughts. Only that voice. That name.

No one called me B but her.

"Jenna?" My voice cracked open with the word.

"I'm here," she said. "But you have to remember."

The sound of her steadied me. It wrapped around the panic, held it still. Not gone—but quieter. Contained.

Memories surfaced again—but softer now. Gentler. The Ferris wheel. The string lights. The laughter. Her hand in mine.

The grief stayed, but it changed. It didn't drown me this time.

It showed me.

I stood taller. The masked figures stilled. The music fell to a hush. Only the fog and her voice remained.

"I hear you," I whispered. "I'm ready."

The carnival responded—not with menace, but with permission. The lights dimmed, the spinning ceased. The figures didn't vanish. They simply waited, quiet now. Listening.

And in the stillness, I finally understood.

It had never been chasing me.

It had been leading me here.

To this moment.

CHAPTER 13

I faced the figures, the shadows, the weight. Not to run. Not to escape.

To remember.

To accept.

"Show me everything," I said.

And the carnival exhaled.

Chapter 14

The fog wrapped around my ankles, cold and damp, resisting each step I took. I couldn't discern if I was moving forward or merely circling the same patch of ground; everything appeared identical—fog and shadow stretching endlessly in every direction.

Reaching out, my fingers met only wet air clinging to my skin, cold and clammy like hospital sheets—a thought that churned my stomach.

Above, the lights pulsed—red, blue, green, yellow—steady and slow. They weren't cheerful or playful; instead, they felt alive, breathing in rhythm with me. The cadence made my head swim, prompting me to squeeze my eyes shut to halt the spinning.

When I reopened them, the shadows had shifted. They stretched long and thin, pulsing with the lights, almost human before melting back into the fog. Every booth, every corner of the carnival blurred at the edges—a game stall became a figure, a figure became nothing at all.

The air thickened, heavy like the deep end of a pool. Each breath tasted charged, electric, as if the entire place held its breath. Whatever I was meant to find was here—somewhere within this warped space.

CHAPTER 14

Shapes moved through the fog, slow and deliberate. My breath caught as the first figure stepped into view. A mask—ornate, shifting with the pulse of the lights. The smile stretched too wide, gold paint catching the glow, making it shimmer as if breathing.

More followed, slipping out of the mist one by one. Each mask stranger than the last—some locked in grief, others twisted into sharp, unsettling grins. Their costumes whispered as they circled me—silk and velvet sliding against the heavy, wet air. They moved like dancers: slow, precise, measured. Behind every mask, I felt it—the focus, the hunger. Their eyes tracked me through narrow slits, watching.

Then the whispering began. Soft at first, buried beneath the carnival's broken tune. Others joined, weaving into a melody that tugged at me, making my head swim. No words, just sound, pulling at something deep inside, begging me to step forward.

Part of me wanted to. The other part—the one that trusted logic, diagnosis, and charts—screamed to hold my ground. This wasn't mere theater; it was a lure.

Clenching my fists, torn between instinct and training, I stood frozen as they circled tighter, their quiet song curling closer. An image surfaced—me, leaning over charts, rattling off symptoms to Dr. Edwards as he watched carefully, concern tucked behind every nod.

Then Jenna. Her face, her laugh—exactly as I remembered. Coffee cup in hand, teasing me in the break room. Her laughter spilled out through the light, too real, too sharp. It wrapped around me, pulling like gravity. I could almost step through, almost go back.

The figure's hand remained steady, waiting. The doorway

pulsed—soft, steady, like a heartbeat. It showed me what I wanted, what I missed, what I'd been chasing since all this began. And still, it waited.

The images warped, slow and sickening, like photos left to blister under the sun. The break room stretched and bled into black; the walls rippled, swallowing color. Jenna's laugh soured—bitter and sharp, echoing back with something rotten underneath. My office folded in on itself, a cage of sterile walls and buzzing lights. Fluorescents stuttered overhead, casting hard, unforgiving beams on stacks of patient files rising like headstones—towering, endless. Each one heavy, each whispering the same thing: failure.

Dr. Edwards' gentle concern darkened, eyes narrowing, warmth gone—just quiet disappointment staring straight through me. His face blurred at the edges until all I could see was judgment. The masked figures swayed closer, moving with the distortions, feeding them. Every memory turned colder, darker.

Jenna's smile warped, accusing. The coffee cup in her hand cast a deep, red-black shadow across the floor. Her laughter fractured, breaking into a whisper that licked at my ears: "You should have known. Should have seen. Should have helped."

I tried to turn away, but the figures wouldn't let me. They peeled everything back, every cherished moment stripped bare, exposing something darker underneath. A knot twisted in my chest, tight and breathless. Was this the truth? Had I painted over it all to survive? I felt myself slipping, untethered. They couldn't be real—not like this. Could they?

The masked figures spoke in unison now, weaving memories I didn't recognize. "Remember when you missed the diagnosis?" one hissed, mask bending into a cruel sneer. "You

CHAPTER 14

could've saved them—if you'd paid attention."

I shook my head hard, trying to clear the fog pressing against my skull. "No... no, that's not real." But the scene unspooled anyway—my supervisor's face, tight and disappointed; the sting of harsh words echoing down a sterile hallway. It felt too real. The guilt clung like fresh bruises, sharp and familiar, though some part of me knew it wasn't mine.

Another figure stepped closer, wearing Jenna's face, her voice. "You left me," it whispered. "When I needed you most." But the tone was wrong—warped and hollow. "I reached out to you that night, but you were too wrapped up in your work to answer my call."

The accusation hit like a physical blow. Had there been a call? I could almost hear the phone ringing, see myself ignoring it as I pored over patient files. The memory crystallized with such clarity that, for a moment, I believed it. But something in my gut recoiled. "Stop it," I whispered.

They didn't. The figures kept circling, feeding me their twisted parade of false memories—each one sharper, more vivid than the last. Conversations I'd never had, mistakes I never made, betrayals that weren't mine—stitched together into a story that felt too real. That was the worst part. They didn't just lie; they wove the lies through truth—tight, seamless.

Jenna's laugh, her smile as she handed me coffee after a long shift—real. I knew that. But then—her face tight with anger, her voice accusing. I never let her down like that. Did I? My head throbbed, trying to untangle it. Truth slipped through my fingers, replaced by something darker, heavier. The more I fought it, the more it bled away.

I pressed my palms to my temples, desperate to pull something simple from the static. The receptionist at my office—Sarah? No—Sandra? Her face was clear, but her name darted just out of reach. The barista who always smiled when handing me coffee—had we ever exchanged names? "Jason," I whispered, grabbing at the memory like it might slip away.

Jason, sitting across from me, hands fidgeting, talking about the masks, about being watched. But the words fell apart, static swallowing them before I could hold onto anything real. Panic bloomed in my chest, tight and fast. More memories peeled away—my mother's eyes, my best friend's laugh, the smell of my favorite café—all blurred at the edges like watercolor rinsed from the page. I shook my head, hard, like I could slam the pieces back into place. But it only scattered them further.

The memory of my med school graduation—the way my gown clung to my knees in the wind, the exact shade of lipstick I had worn for the photos—faded into something hazy, stripped of detail. The sense of pride I'd once carried in my chest? Gone, reduced to the echo of a feeling. The triumph of my first patient consultation dimmed too, replaced with blank walls and the sterile click of my own shoes down the hall.

The fog drew tighter.

It curled into my ribs and licked at my ears, muffling the world. And in the vacuum left behind, the masked figures advanced, slipping from the periphery into my path like dreams solidifying into nightmare. The one closest to me leaned in, so close I could see my own face warped in its surface.

"Let it go," it said again. "You don't have to hurt anymore."

Its voice was soft. Sweet. A lullaby sung in reverse.

CHAPTER 14

And for a terrifying moment, I wanted to.

I wanted to give in, let them take the weight I'd carried all these years—the guilt, the pressure, the silence between me and the people I'd failed. Let the masks rewrite it all. Smooth the jagged edges.

A world where I could still walk into my office and believe I was making a difference.

The temptation laced through the air like perfume, subtle but cloying. I swayed toward it.

And then—I remembered.

The Funhouse. The fractured mirrors. The moment I'd faced my reflection and saw not a monster, not a mask, but someone still fighting. Someone still standing. I had earned that. That clarity hadn't come easy, and I wouldn't trade it now for a lie wrapped in comfort.

"No," I said aloud. Not loud. But firm.

The masked figure tilted its head. The cracks in its painted lips deepened.

"I said no."

The others stilled. The lullaby stopped.

They didn't retreat. Not yet. But they blinked—one by one—like resetting clocks, mechanical and slow. Their masks shimmered in the pulsing light, the porcelain sheen flickering with images. The images of Jenna, Jason, my mother, Dr. Edwards, and Sarah flickered through the static.

"You can't scare me into forgetting," I said, straighter now. "You can't tempt me into surrender. I know what's real."

The figure nearest to me gave the faintest shake of its head, almost... amused.

"You think truth protects you," it said. "But truth is where pain lives. You'll see."

"No," I said again. "I already have. I've seen what you are."

The shadows quivered. The illusion of calm cracked.

"You feed on the cracks," I continued, louder now. "On grief, on doubt. But you only have power when I run from it."

I stepped forward. Not away. Toward them.

"I'm not running anymore."

The masks flickered again—some twisted, others slackened in something like surprise. Their perfect, hollow faces couldn't hide it. Something was changing.

"I remember who I am," I said, my voice clear despite the pulse pounding in my ears. "And I remember who I lost. I remember Jenna."

And as I said her name, something in the fog stilled. The color deepened. The lights overhead stopped flickering, pausing in a moment of held breath.

I could feel her there—somewhere in the current beneath it all. Not a ghost. Not a hallucination. But the shape of what she had meant to me. The mark she left.

I closed my eyes. Just for a moment. And I let myself remember not just the loss, but the joy. Her laugh. The way she'd braid her hair in the mirror before rounds. The way she'd call me "B" and shove protein bars into my coat pocket on double shifts.

The pain was still there—but it no longer drowned me.

When I opened my eyes again, the masks were retreating. Not fleeing. Just... fading. Like smoke losing its shape.

And then, only one remained.

It didn't move. Didn't speak. Its mask was plain white. No smile. No tears. No cracks. Just a mirror.

And in it—I saw myself. Not fractured. Not warped. Just... me.

CHAPTER 14

For the first time, I didn't look away.

The figure raised its hand and pointed into the fog behind it. I followed the gesture, heart steady, breath slow.

There, just beyond the mist, was a path. Not clear. But visible.

Chapter 15

I was increasingly disoriented as I made my way through the maze-like pathways of the carnival. The worn and twisted surfaces of the wooden boards beneath my feet were a testament to the years of abuse they had endured. A suffocating fog hung in the air, clinging to my flesh and eventually permeating my clothing and sinking into my very bones. Following an invisible current, I continued on until I accidentally entered a hall adorned with reflections.

These mirrors were not your typical ones. From floor to ceiling, enormous slabs of glass undulated like agitated water. As I walked further, my reflection increasingly distorted and twisted into hideous caricatures that vaguely resembled me. The carnival lights produced an eerie radiance, their hues transferring to the mirrors and further warping them. Condensation formed on the glass with each breath as the air cooled.

At the corridor's end stood a mirror larger than the rest, its surface pulsing with a dull, rhythmic light. A strange, pulsating light seemed to match my heartbeat as it radiated out from it. I stepped carefully closer, the mirror's pulse becoming louder with each stride. The only sound that remained after the deafening roar of the carnival had dissipated was my

CHAPTER 15

breathing.

As I reached out to touch the mirror, its surface yielded under my fingers, warm and pliant like flesh. The surface of the mirror shook wildly, and a surge of electricity traveled up my arm. The mirror jolted me back to long-forgotten memories and events that I had wished would simply fade away. In my mind, I was at a coffee shop with Sarah and Mike, laughing to hide my underlying worry. Then I see a younger me at a carnival, where the atmosphere is one of carefree joy and the lights are dazzling.

Scenes changed quickly, growing increasingly disturbing as they went. Jenna and I were back in my office, where we had been before, organizing the bookshelves. Seated opposite from me, Jason narrated his nightmares, his eyes wide with horror. Colors melted and faces stretched into unidentifiable shapes as the images bled and blended together. Anxiety was like a drumming in my ears, and my heart was racing.

Suddenly, the mirror presented a hospital room, sterile and cold. The smell of antiseptic was almost tangible, and the fluorescent lights cast harsh shadows across the linoleum floor. In the center of the room lay a hospital bed, its sheets pristine and tightly tucked. I stepped closer, dread pooling in my stomach. The figure in the bed was me—pale, motionless, and entangled in a web of tubes and wires.

A nurse entered the room, adjusted an IV bag, and scribbled notes on a clipboard before disappearing. The machines beeped steadily, a cruel reminder of life hanging by a thread. I pressed my hand against the mirror, the cold surface grounding me as I stared at my comatose form. Tears welled up, blurring my vision. "Why did I survive?" I whispered, the words barely audible.

The mirror's surface shimmered, and the hospital room dissolved into a chaotic swirl of colors. The carnival reemerged, its lights glaring and distorted. The mirror cracked, fractures spiderwebbing across its surface. Each shard reflected a different memory—Jenna's laughter, the crash, my own guilt-ridden face. I backed away, the weight of the memories pressing down on me.

"I remember," I choked out, the admission freeing and terrifying. The mirror's fragments pulsed with light before fading into darkness. The carnival's illusions persisted, but now I saw them for what they were—distorted echoes of a past I could no longer escape. I turned away, the path ahead uncertain but my resolve stronger than before.

The path behind me seemed to close in, swallowed by the fog and fractured lights of the carnival. I didn't need to look back to know that the mirror—the hospital bed, the stillness of my body, the failure, the guilt—was still there, pulsing behind me like a second heartbeat. But I kept walking. My boots thudded against the wooden boards, each step a silent rebellion against the pull of the past.

The sounds of the carnival began to bleed back into the world. But they weren't the same. The laughter that once echoed like broken music was lower now, strained, as if the place itself was tired of pretending. The calliope groaned through a tune that didn't know how to end. Lights flickered and blinked out, casting long fingers of shadow that danced over booths and twisted rides. And through it all, the mist still clung to the ground like regret.

I passed a row of abandoned stalls—one with a ring toss game where every bottle had been knocked over, another with stuffed animals slumped in piles like discarded dreams.

CHAPTER 15

My hand brushed a faded prize on one table, and it disintegrated under my touch. Everything here was falling apart. Everything was crumbling.

But I wasn't.

Not anymore.

The confrontation in the mirror had carved something open in me, yes, but it had also cauterized something else. I had looked straight into the ugliest part of my story and hadn't shattered. Maybe I was still bleeding inside, still brittle in places I didn't yet understand—but I hadn't broken. I had remembered, and I was still moving.

The maze of the carnival gave way to a clearing, wide and oddly quiet. A carousel stood at its center, its horses caught mid-prance, paint peeling, manes faded from red to rust. The music leaking from its cracked speakers was slow and discordant, but strangely beautiful in a broken sort of way. Like a lullaby someone had forgotten how to sing properly but couldn't stop humming anyway.

I stepped toward it, drawn without knowing why. As I approached, the air changed again—less like a haunted breath on my neck, more like a held breath waiting to be released. I reached out and touched one of the horses. Its chipped glass eyes stared back at me, hollow and blank, but not unkind. The platform beneath my feet vibrated slightly, not enough to startle, just enough to remind me that this place was still alive.

I closed my eyes and let the sounds wash over me: the wind whispering secrets through the sagging tents, the music wheezing from the carousel, the faint buzz of dying lights. It was a symphony of decay, and yet it didn't repel me. It resonated. This was what the carnival had always been—an echo chamber for the pieces we tried not to look at. A place where the parts of ourselves we buried found shape and voice.

And maybe… maybe that meant it was also a place of reckoning.

I opened my eyes and climbed onto one of the horses. The moment I did, the carousel lurched into motion, slow at first, then steady. The lights above me brightened—not garish this time, but warm. The music steadied, just slightly. It didn't become whole, but it stopped breaking apart. And for the first time since I stepped into this twisted dream, I let myself breathe.

The carnival wasn't gone. The mirrors still stood behind me, their memories ready to slice open fresh wounds if I let them. The guilt hadn't evaporated, and the past couldn't be unwritten. But I had faced it. I had claimed it.

I leaned forward, the carousel spinning me through the mist, and whispered to the dark, "I'm still here."

It wasn't defiance. It wasn't triumph. It was something quieter. Something truer.

It was survival.

And as the carousel turned, dragging the fog into wider circles and pushing the shadows to the edges, I felt something shift—not outside, but within.

Chapter 16

The carnival stretched before me, its once-vibrant hues now muted under a sky smeared with bruised clouds. Each step I took sank into the gravel path, the crunch beneath my boots echoing like brittle bones snapping under pressure. The air hung heavy, syrup-thick, clinging to my skin and weighing down my limbs. The mirror's revelations clung to me, not as fleeting memories but as a living entity, entwined with the very fabric of this twisted realm.

Above, the lights flickered erratically, casting the carnival in sickly reds and pallid greens. Shadows danced and recoiled with each pulse of light, their movements predatory, as if waiting for the opportune moment to strike. The absence of sound was deafening—no carnival barkers, no distorted calliope melodies, no warped laughter of children. The silence pressed in, suffocating and absolute, amplifying the eerie stillness that surrounded me.

The storm clouds overhead loomed ominously, casting the landscape in a perpetual twilight. The air tasted metallic, reminiscent of blood on a split lip, and carried the scent of impending rain. I continued forward, navigating the serpentine paths that twisted deeper into the carnival's heart. The shadows elongated, reaching across the midway like tendrils, retreating and advancing with each flicker of light. I wrapped my arms around myself, seeking warmth not from the cold, but from the unsettling familiarity that permeated the air—a presence that knew me intimately.

My footsteps resonated sharply, the only sound in the oppressive hush. The surroundings—the tattered banners, the sagging tents, the abandoned prize booths—appeared as faded remnants of a forgotten dream. Everything exuded decay, a veneer of festivity barely concealing the rot beneath.

At a fork in the path, I hesitated, eyes darting between two equally uninviting routes. Both vanished into the same murky fog, offering no indication of safety. The silence intensified, wrapping around my throat like an invisible noose. In the distance, a metal ride groaned, its creak reminiscent of a dying breath.

The carnival seemed to hold its breath, anticipating my next move.

My mind, a fractured reel, replayed snapshots I had long suppressed. The night of the accident surged forth, raw and unfiltered. My hands gripped the steering wheel, knuckles white with tension. Jenna's laughter, bright and carefree, echoed in my ears. Then—headlights. Blinding, fast, unavoidable.

I stumbled, colliding with a railing, pain radiating up my arm—a penance I welcomed.

The carnival warped around me, colors intensifying to feverish hues. Reds like fresh wounds, yellows like festering infections. Lights flashed like sirens, spinning in a chaotic dance. I bent over, gasping for breath, the air thick with the acrid taste of fear and remorse.

Then, the memories overwhelmed me.

CHAPTER 16

Tires screeched. A moment of weightlessness. Jenna's scream, abruptly silenced. The crunch of metal, the shatter of glass, the world tilting violently. I crawled from the wreckage, while she remained motionless—silent.

Guilt surged, choking me. I clutched my head, pressing against my temples, desperate to contain the onslaught of memories.

Sirens wailed—whether real or imagined, I couldn't discern. Flashing lights pierced the fog, blurring the lines between carnival and catastrophe. And Jenna—pale, broken, still.

"I'm sorry," I whispered, the words feeble and inadequate. "I'm so sorry, Jenna."

The fog remained indifferent, closing in with suffocating finality.

I froze, paralyzed by a sound that transcended memory—a visceral, haunting screech of tires on wet asphalt. My hands clenched instinctively, gripping an invisible steering wheel. The carnival's lights distorted, morphing into blinding headlights. The scent of rain on pavement, sharp and metallic, filled my nostrils.

"Watch out!" Jenna's voice pierced the haze, sharp and terrified.

The scene replayed in my mind—a cruel montage of laughter turned to horror. Her hand reaching out, the glint of water on the windshield, brake lights too close, too fast. The car veered, tires losing traction, and then—

Impact.

The grotesque symphony of metal contorting, glass exploding, and the world unraveling.

I collapsed to my knees, the ground beneath me indistinct—gravel or glass, it didn't matter.

Ahead, the funhouse loomed, its distorted mirrors reflecting fragmented versions of myself. But all I saw was the crash—the mangled vehicle, the hissing steam, and Jenna.

The memories persisted, relentless. Sirens blared, rain obscured my vision, and my face was wet—tears or rain, indistinguishable.

I remembered every detail, every agonizing second.

And I knew, with unwavering certainty, that I could never escape it.

I squeezed my eyes shut, attempting to block out the cacophony—the lights, the fog, the haunting laughter. But the silence only amplified the internal chaos.

Then, she appeared.

Jenna.

So vivid, so real, it stole my breath.

She sat beside me in the passenger seat, illuminated by the dashboard's soft glow. Her smile—radiant and genuine—lit up her face, her eyes crinkling with mirth.

She laughed, a sound that once brought me solace. "You're such a dork, B," she teased, nudging my arm playfully. I could still feel the gentle jab, still smell her perfume—a blend of vanilla and something sweetly decaying.

For a fleeting moment, warmth enveloped me. Familiarity.

Then, the shift.

Her smile faded, replaced by a look of terror. Her eyes widened, fixated on something ahead. The dashboard's glow cast her face in an eerie green hue as headlights approached—blinding and swift. Her mouth opened, not for laughter, but a scream.

"Brooke!"

Her voice shattered the illusion, anchoring me in the

CHAPTER 16

present. I felt her fingers brush my arm, reaching out—

And then, nothing.

Her scream echoed, drowning out the carnival's ambient noise. The bar, the jokes, the shared laughter—all twisted into a cruel jest. Her joy transformed into horror, her laughter into a scream.

I crumpled, pressing my hands against my temples, desperate to silence the memories.

But they intensified—her smile, her laugh, her scream.

And I realized, with painful clarity, that I had been the architect of this nightmare.

The carnival's colors faded, bleeding into the background as the memory consumed me. It didn't creep in; it crashed down, unrelenting.

I was back in that parking lot.

Gravel underfoot, keys jingling in my hand, the cold air biting after a night of indulgence.

Jenna stood before me, her smile wide yet tinged with apprehension. Her hair tousled, her eyes searching.

"Let me drive," she offered, hand extended. "Come on, B. I'm not even buzzed."

She lied—not maliciously, but out of concern. I knew her tells—the glint in her eyes, the tilt of her head. I almost acquiesced.

But I didn't.

"No," I chuckled, feigning confidence. "I've got us. I'm good. I swear."

She hesitated, her hand hovering before she sighed, relenting. "Alright. But you owe me pancakes in the morning."

That was Jenna—gracious even in surrender.

I smiled, unaware of the impending tragedy.

I took the wheel. I started the engine. I laughed at her jokes as we drove into the night.

And when the headlights blinded us, when the rain slicked the road, when everything spiraled—I was the one in control.

She trusted me.

And I failed her.

The carnival responded, its lights pulsing erratically, casting distorted reflections in the puddles. I saw myself—drenched, disheveled, broken.

Then, the whispers returned.

Not gentle, but accusatory, wrapping around me like smoke.

"Coward," they hissed. "You let her die because you were too scared to love her."

I clamped my hands over my ears, but the voices persisted, internal and unyielding.

Figures emerged from the shadows—the masked ones. Their costumes, once whimsical, now menacing. Their movements deliberate, predatory.

Another leaned in, its breath a sickly sweet rot. Its mask bore Jenna's face, twisted into a grotesque parody.

They encircled me, their robes brushing against me—cold, invasive. Each mask reflected a version of me.

The coward.

The failure.

The driver.

And amidst them—Jenna.

I curled into myself, trembling, as the carnival's lights strobed overhead, transforming the world into a nightmarish carousel of guilt and regret. Their faces blurred—Jenna's, mine, strangers from my nightmares. All bore the same expression:

CHAPTER 16

Disappointment.

I had been running long before that fateful night.

I recalled her across a coffee shop table, hands wrapped around a mug, eyes probing. Her fingers brushed mine when we laughed—always laughing, as if humor could shield us from reality.

But it couldn't.

I believed guilt would consume me, and for a time, it did. But now, it evolved—into regret.

That was the burden I carried, the unspoken truth.

For the first time, her laughter resonated within me, not as a torment, but as a comfort. That warm, genuine laugh—I had lived for it, unknowingly. Now, it uplifted me.

The carnival's menace diminished. Still surreal, still unsettling, but subdued. The ride was winding down.

The shadows receded, reluctant but yielding. They remained, lurking, but their oppressive weight lifted.

And I breathed—truly breathed—for the first time in what felt like years. The air that filled my lungs wasn't pure or clean or new. It was heavy with salt and soot and memory, but it was mine. It was real. And I hadn't realized until that moment just how long I'd been holding my breath.

I rose slowly, my legs trembling beneath me like they hadn't gotten the message yet, like they still remembered the crash and the weight and the fear. But they held. They held because I needed them to. My hands, scratched and trembling, hung at my sides like they didn't know what to do next. But that was okay. I didn't need to know the next step yet. It was enough just to be standing.

Around me, the carnival sighed. That was the only way I could describe it—a long exhale, like some hidden machinery was powering down after running too long, too hot. The lights, once manic and strobing, steadied into something softer. Not comforting, exactly, but no longer hostile. They reminded me of nightlights left on in quiet hallways—not because you believed in monsters, but because you weren't ready to believe they were gone.

The masked figures didn't vanish, but they stopped moving. They stood like statues now, scattered across the midway in faded colors and sagging silks. Their masks no longer leered. Their presence wasn't threatening anymore. It was mournful. As if they had been hollowing out the worst parts of me not to hurt me—but to show me the shape of what I'd been carrying.

I looked at them and didn't feel afraid. I felt… seen. Not by them, exactly. By myself. By the part of me that had been buried so deep I thought I'd lost her.

"I'm still here," I said out loud, and the sound of my voice startled me. It sounded stronger than I expected. Not defiant. Not triumphant. Just steady. Certain.

I looked around the midway—the torn tents, the rusted rides, the fog still curling low to the ground like something with claws. None of it scared me anymore. It was ugly and broken, but it was familiar. This place had torn me open, yes. But it had also shown me something I'd never let myself see before.

It had shown me the truth.

And now that I had it, I wasn't letting it go.

A breeze picked up, soft but unmistakable, and the fog began to lift—not all at once, but in tendrils, like smoke leaving a battlefield. The way ahead was still shadowed, still uncertain, but I could see it. A path. A way forward. It didn't promise anything, not peace, not closure. Just motion. Just choice.

CHAPTER 16

And maybe that was enough.

Behind me, the funhouse stood quiet. The cracked mirror I'd once pressed my face to now glinted dull and still, no longer pulling at me. I didn't need it to. I knew what was behind the glass now. I knew what I'd survived. I knew what I'd lost.

And I knew what I was walking toward.

I turned from it, slow and sure, each step peeling a layer of weight from my shoulders. The carnival would always be here, I understood that now. In some way, it was a part of me. A haunted place, a remembering place. But I didn't have to live in it anymore.

I could walk through it.

And I could leave it behind.

As I crossed the threshold of the midway, the lights dimmed one final time. Not extinguished. Not snuffed out. Just quieted, as though the carnival itself understood what had changed.

And for the first time since Jenna died—since I died with her in every way that mattered—I stepped into the dark not as a ghost, but as someone alive.

Not healed. But whole.

The gravel path beneath my feet leveled out, the crunch of stone giving way to packed dirt. With every step, the noise of the carnival faded further behind me—no more warped calliope music, no mocking whispers, no flickering lights breathing down my neck. Just wind. Just the sound of my own breath, rhythmic and steady, threading through the hush like something sacred.

The night was still thick around me, the fog trailing like reluctant smoke, but it no longer pressed in with the same suffocating grip. It gave space now. A corridor. A clearing.

The kind of stillness that doesn't come from absence, but from aftermath. Like the quiet that follows a storm once it's finally run out of anger.

I passed what might once have been a fortune teller's tent—now sagging with time and moisture, its sign faded to illegibility. A deck of warped tarot cards lay scattered beneath the canvas, the edges curling like petals. I didn't stop to gather them. I didn't need to know what the future held anymore. I wasn't asking for answers. I was learning how to live with the questions.

The path twisted again, narrowing as it ran beneath an arch of iron ribs—the remains of a ride maybe, or just another dream turned skeleton. Beneath it, the breeze turned cooler. Cleaner. It smelled less like rust and sugar and more like the edge of something real. Like soil. Like rain. Like waking up.

Chapter 17

The carnival lights pulsed rhythmically with the pounding in my chest, resembling a dying heartbeat. Each burst of neon sent the shadows dancing across the cracked pavement—jagged, twitchy things that moved like they were on strings held by someone with a sick sense of humor.

I stood frozen, feet planted like they'd grown roots, staring into the thick pockets of darkness that stretched between the rides. It wasn't just dark—it was the kind of dark that seemed to breathe. To watch.

Somewhere behind me, the carousel music drifted through the air, slow and slurred. The tune was familiar, almost comforting... almost. But the notes bent in strange ways, like a record warping in the sun. It sounded like a lullaby that'd been left out in the rain too long—soggy and wrong.

I hugged myself tight, trying to shake the cold crawling up my spine. It wasn't the kind of cold you feel on your skin. No, this one wrapped around your bones. It weighed heavily on your chest. Every breath I took felt like I was pulling the whole damn carnival inside me, and it would rather not come easy.

The string lights above flickered and buzzed, carving faces into the dark—faces that seemed to grin and leer every time

I blinked. I heard laughter, but not the kind that made you feel warm or safe. This laughter was hollow. Unhinged. Like something laughing at its own bad joke just a little too loud, a little too long.

Off to my left, the cotton candy stand glowed pink, casting a weird light that made everything look bruised. The shadows near it twisted into long fingers, reaching for nothing and pulling back like they were shy. Perhaps they were simply patient.

I don't know how else to explain it, but the place felt alive. It was alive, but not in a whimsical, storybook way. More like a dog that's been mistreated too long—quiet, crouched in the corner, just waiting to snap.

Something was coming. I could feel it crawling through the ground, coiling in the air. The music picked up pace, matching my heartbeat, and the lights flickered like they were panicking. And that's when I knew.

The carnival wasn't broken.

It was waking up.

Something moved in the mist.

Not fast. Not loud. The sound was just loud enough to cause my eyes to twitch. That's all it took. It was just a flicker of shape in the gray.

And there it was.

My breath caught like a blow to the ribs.

A car—or what was left of one—sat crumpled in the clearing, half-swallowed by the fog. Not just any car. My car. The car was bent and folded in on itself, as if a giant fist had picked it up and squeezed until it screamed. The metal gleamed wet under the flickering carnival lights, as if the crash had just happened. As if it were still bleeding.

CHAPTER 17

I took a step. Then another. Each one felt like I was wading through molasses. It felt cold, suffocating, and burdensome. The closer I got, the more wrong it all looked. The driver's door hung open like a broken jaw, the airbag limp and yellowed, splashed with a rust-colored stain I didn't want to look at too closely.

Jenna's blood.

The world tilted slightly, causing the mist to rush in and swallow the wreck as if it had never existed. As the fog thinned, the garish carnival lights faded, replaced by the sterile glow of fluorescent bulbs. The scent of antiseptic filled my nostrils, and the distant beeping of monitors echoed in my ears. I was no longer in the carnival; I was back in the hospital.

The smell hit me first.

Bleach and plastic. It emitted a sharp, sanitized tang that is only found in hospitals. It stuck in the back of my throat. I felt nauseous.

Beep. Beep. Beep.

Monitors. I knew those sounds. Too well. The room's mechanical heartbeat lacked the strength to maintain rhythm on its own. The walls exuded a stark whiteness that left you feeling as if they had erased your existence. And yeah—I knew this place.

ICU.

Something fluttered at my feet.

I looked down.

Photographs.

They were everywhere. I crouched and picked one up, hands shaking. Jenna smiled back at me—sun in her hair, arm slung around my shoulders like she belonged there. Like she always had.

Ferris wheel in the background. The carnival lights behind us, instead of being warped and cruel like they are now, were warm and inviting. Inviting.

The timestamp in the corner? The date was three days prior to the crash.

I swallowed hard.

Another photo. Then another. At the beach, Jenna and I are both sunburned and beaming with joy. It's graduation day—caps off, drinks in hand. We were enjoying ice cream on a summer sidewalk, both of us dripping wet and laughing uncontrollably.

Each image cut deeper than the last.

Those smiles? Those moments?

They were ghosts. All of them. Still wearing the faces of the people we used to be, back before everything shattered.

And now? Now they just watched me.

Mocked me.

Reminded me exactly what I'd lost—and exactly who I'd been before I let it all slip through my fingers.

The photos slipped from my hands like dead leaves, scattering across the ground in a soft, papery hiss.

That's when they came.

Dark shapes peeled themselves from the shadows, one after another, like they'd been waiting there the whole time—lurking just out of sight. Watching. Waiting.

My breath hitched.

The masked figures glided forward, their long, flowing costumes moving like ink in water. I recognized them. Of course I did. They'd haunted the edges of this nightmare since the beginning. But something had changed.

Their masks weren't just eerie now.

CHAPTER 17

They were furious.

Snarling smiles stretched into grotesque sneers. Hollow eyes burned with rage. They looked like porcelain demons caught halfway between laughter and violence.

"Stay with us, Brooke," they said, voices stitched together in a hideous harmony that made my stomach churn. "You belong here, where the pain can't find you."

I backed away—tried to, anyway—but they moved in with the elegance of sharks circling a wounded swimmer. The lights overhead flickered like a dying pulse, catching their masks in quick flashes. Every grin sharpened. Every sneer deepened. It felt like the carnival itself was tightening around me.

"You can't run from your past!" one hissed, lunging forward with a jerk that made me flinch. The mask warped as it moved—features bending into something jagged, something wrong. Its voice sounded like steel dragged across stone, and it drilled straight into my spine.

I turned to run, but cold fingers clamped down on my shoulder.

Not fingers, exactly. More like claws. They were long and pale, each one jointed in too many places, curling around me like a spider's legs. I froze. My blood turned to ice water.

It pulled.

Not hard—just enough to let me know I wasn't going anywhere.

The air thickened around me, pressing down like wet wool. I couldn't get a full breath. My chest ached. My ribs screamed.

The voices rose.

Not shouting—chanting. A thousand whispers woven together into something loud enough to shake the ground.

Accusing. Demanding. Punishing. Every syllable scraped along the raw edges of my conscience.

At my feet, the photographs glowed faintly, like they'd caught fire from within. Jenna's face stared up at me—still smiling, still whole. That smile used to feel like sunlight.

Now it felt like a goodbye.

The whispers got louder. Not like voices in a crowded room, not like murmurs behind your back. No—these were surgical. Precise. Each one struck like a hammer to the skull, a wave slamming into a cliff that's been eroding for years. You think it'll hold... right up until it doesn't.

I tried to remember who I was. Brooke Sullivan. That name had always carried weight. Sleep therapist. Rational thinker. Survivor. But now? The syllables rang hollow, like I was saying someone else's name out loud and hoping it would stick.

I squeezed my eyes shut.

Tried to picture my office. It was there—sort of. Beige walls. A potted plant that was half-dead, but I kept forgetting to water. Diplomas framed and straight. But then... they weren't diplomas anymore. They were posters. Garish things. Carnival clowns that never blinked. The walls twisted. Mirrors replaced windows. Shadows danced where sunlight should've been.

My patients... God. Their faces blurred. Their stories bled together like spilled ink. A mother with night terrors. A vet who hadn't slept more than two hours in a decade. A teenage girl who woke up screaming every night at 2:17. But now they were laughing. Laughing. And their mouths were sewn shut.

"Who am I?" I asked, or maybe whimpered. My voice didn't even sound like my own anymore.

CHAPTER 17

The masked figures pressed in, close enough to steal my breath. The air turned thick and syrupy. My lungs burned with every shallow inhale.

"I'm…" I tried again. But the words caught, like they'd hit barbed wire on the way out.

Was I a therapist? Had I ever been? Or was that just another trick of this place—a role written for me by the carnival and performed until the curtain dropped?

Jenna's face flickered. My anchor. My north star.

But even that started to melt.

Her mouth curled into a smile too wide for any human face. Her eyes went glassy. Empty. Like windows into a house that hadn't been lived in for years.

The memories—God help me, even the accident—started to unspool. One thread at a time. Late nights talking about the future, gone. Long walks with coffee and aching feet, gone. That last laugh before the headlights, gone.

I grabbed my head. Fingernails dug in. Anything to stay here. Anything to feel real.

The ground rippled under my knees. Not dirt. Not pavement. Just… texture. A suggestion of substance. Lights flared in my peripheral vision, stuttering in and out like dying stars. Patterns swirled across the dark, curling toward me like fingers made of color and sound.

"Stay with us," the figures whispered.

No—not whispered. Chanted. Hypnotic and unrelenting, like a lullaby written in hell.

"Let go of who you were. Become part of the carnival's eternal dance."

I was slipping. I could feel it. My sense of self, of time, of anything real—fracturing. Crumbling. Being scooped out of me like ice cream in summer. Too fast. Too easy.

The carnival spun on.

And I?

I couldn't tell anymore if I was still Brooke Sullivan...

...or just another mask waiting to be worn.

My heart was trying to punch a hole through my chest when the truth finally landed. Not softly, either. This wasn't some gentle epiphany handed to me by a kindly therapist over chamomile tea. No, this thing slammed into me like a freight train. Because of the carnival? The warped rides, the crooked music, the masks with too many teeth and not enough soul.

It was me.

All of it.

Every flickering light, every distorted whisper, every mirror that showed me a face I didn't want to claim—born straight outta my own head. My own fears. My own failures. My own grief, dressed up in funhouse drag.

The realization knocked the breath clean outta me. I staggered, legs giving a little, knees catching just short of the ground. Because all this time, I thought I was being haunted. Hunted. Tortured by some outside force I couldn't explain.

But no.

I'd done it. Me. Brooke Sullivan, licensed sleep therapist and full-time coward, had built this twisted place brick by guilt-soaked brick.

The masked figures? They weren't monsters. They were my fears, my doubts, my refusal to admit what I'd done—or more accurately, what I hadn't done.

The shadows flinched. The lights above flared like dying stars. The air itself seemed to recoil, like it wasn't used to honesty. Like the truth had never echoed through these

CHAPTER 17

grounds before.

"I'm not afraid!" The words felt foreign, a desperate attempt to mask the fear still clawing at my insides. But as they hung in the air, something shifted—a flicker of courage igniting amidst the shadows.

The echo bounced through the carnival like a wrecking ball, shattering the silence that had been closing in like a noose. The rides groaned. The mirrors cracked. The masked figures backed away like they'd been slapped—because maybe, in a way, they had.

And then the world—my world—started to fall apart.

Not collapse exactly. More like... bleed.

Carousel horses melted into hospital beds. The cotton candy sky wept morphine and iodine. The laughter of unseen children curled in on itself until it was nothing but the beep-beep-beep of a heart monitor in a room too bright, too cold.

Every lie I'd told myself collided with the things I couldn't forget.

I didn't run this time.

I stood there, fists clenched, lungs burning like I'd swallowed fire. Reality twisted around me, but I stayed put. Because this wasn't just about escaping some haunted circus act—it was about owning it. Owning all of it.

The guilt. The silence. The moment I pulled my hand away from Jenna's. The second I turned the key in the ignition.

This wasn't a carnival.

It was a confession.

And I was done hiding from it.

The carnival was tearing itself apart, and it wasn't going quietly.

Lights burst overhead with a series of sharp cracks, spitting sparks that hissed as they scattered across the fractured pavement. The Ferris wheel—once a slow-turning monument to summer nights and sticky fingers—howled like something alive. Its cars twisted and swung in wild arcs, the groan of metal and the snap of shearing bolts slicing through the thick air. Every creak and shudder felt like a death rattle. The air smelled of burning sugar and something darker. Something old. Something that had been waiting too long to break free.

The ground trembled, fissures snaking across the pavement, each one a testament to the unraveling world around me. I felt every vibration in my bones, each fissure spreading out like a map of every bad choice I'd ever made. The funhouse mirrors lining the midway shattered in rapid succession, each one detonating with a sharp crack that echoed through the chaos. Jagged shards rained down, catching the flickering glow of the dying carnival lights. For a split second, I saw myself reflected in the broken glass—twisted, fragmented, but still standing.

The masked figures? Gone. Vanished into the darkness where nightmares belong, their whispers swallowed by the deafening roar of a world finally tearing itself apart.

Good. Let it fall.

My breath came hard and fast, but I stood my ground.

Memories flashed like strobe lights through the chaos—Jenna's laugh, so bright and carefree; the shriek of tires on pavement; the sterile glow of hospital lights that had burned into my retinas while I drifted somewhere between life and death. Each memory hit like a punch to the gut, but I didn't flinch.

Because they were mine.

Every one of them.

The carnival had no claim on them now. No claim on me.

CHAPTER 17

I sucked in a breath—deep and steady, tasting ozone and cotton candy and something electric that made the hairs on the back of my neck stand up. My fists clenched at my sides, nails biting into my palms just enough to keep me grounded. The chaos surged around me, but I found the stillness within.

"Show me," I whispered, barely louder than the pounding of my heart.

The carnival didn't like that.

The wind howled, tearing at my clothes. The lights strobed wildly, casting warped shadows that danced like phantoms. But I didn't move. I stared straight into the heart of the madness, where the center of the carnival pulsed like a living thing.

"Show me everything."

The words carried more weight than they should have, as if the ground itself had been waiting for me to speak them.

And then... the world listened.

The chaos didn't stop—it intensified. But this time, I was ready.

The truth was there, buried beneath the wreckage and the lies I'd told myself. It had always been there, waiting for me to stop running long enough to see it.

My pulse thundered in my ears as the carnival responded—not with words, but with something deeper.

Chapter 18

The masked performers jerked upright in unison, and every nerve in my body screamed for flight. Their movements no longer mimicked anything human—too seamless, too slick—like puppets that had cut their own strings but kept moving anyway. My breath locked in my throat as their faces began to twist, flesh—if it was flesh—stretching and folding in ways that mocked anatomy. The masks, once unnervingly beautiful, sagged and ran like candle wax, giving way to malformed visages that should never have existed outside a nightmare.

"Poor little Brooke," one of them purred, and bile rose in my throat. The voice—it was Jenna's laugh, bent and spoiled, curling through the dark like smoke laced with ammonia. "Still running, even now."

A second figure spun past me, close enough that its fingertips grazed my arm. The touch was damp and tacky, like the skin of something long dead but not fully rotted. "You can't hide," it breathed, words coiling through my ear canal and lodging somewhere cold and permanent behind my eyes.

I staggered back, but it didn't matter. They were everywhere—sliding through the Funhouse like they'd been born inside its bones. They wove between warping mirrors and narrow passageways with a disturbing, sinuous grace.

CHAPTER 18

Their bodies bent at unnatural angles, jointless and boneless, like ink poured into cracks that had no business opening.

And then came the laughter. Not above me or behind me, but inside the walls, inside the glass, inside my head. It bounced from mirror to mirror until the whole place was alive with it—cackling, jeering, gasping with cruel delight. One voice became ten, then a hundred, until it sounded like my own reflection had turned against me. The noise tunneled under my skin, nested behind my ribs, cold and persistent as rot.

The voices layered atop one another like mismatched harmonies—clashing, colliding, refusing to blend. Some were airy, high-pitched giggles, the kind you'd hear from children shrieking through a summer lawn sprinkler. Innocent, at first. Until you heard the undertone—like something gurgling beneath the laughter, thick and wet. Others were deep, rasping things, crawling up from places where light didn't go. Together they didn't just sound wrong. They sounded designed to unravel something inside me—notes chosen not for melody, but to dismantle sanity one nerve-ending at a time.

"Stop," I said, but my voice was a thread in a hurricane—fragile, swallowed before it had a chance to land.

One figure snapped its head toward me, eyes wide and wild beneath a melting mask. "Did you hear that?" it hissed, voice cracking like ice. "She wants us to stop."

Another cackled, its grin splitting across its jaw like a wound. "Should we, sisters? Brothers?"

"NEVER stop!" they shrieked in unison, their chorus jagged and off-key, more scream than song. "Chase her! Chase her until the memories come bleeding out!"

They moved through the walls like they weren't even there, slipping between seams in the air, gliding around corners no wider than a breath. Every instinct screamed to run, but I could feel them gaining—cold breath tickling the back of my neck, fingers brushing across my shoulders like cobwebs strung from bone. Their touch was light, but each graze turned my blood to ice, and their laughter—God, that laughter—dug into my spine like wire.

Around us, the carnival music spiraled into chaos. What had once been a broken lullaby now screeched into a jagged, fevered refrain, each note pitching upward, needle-sharp and brain-deep. And the performers? They weren't just chasing me.

They were hunting me. Playing. And they were enjoying every second of it.

Like cats circling a wounded bird, savoring the fear, feeding off it. I was the mouse, and they were taking their time. Enjoying it.

I spun around, lungs hitching on ragged breaths, vision tunneling as my gaze darted left, right, back again. Looking. Hoping. Begging for a way out. But the corridor kept stretching, long and wrong, angles buckling like heat mirages. The walls didn't just enclose—they pulsed. In and out. Like lungs drawing breath. Like the entire Funhouse was alive and exhaling over my skin.

"Move," I told myself, barely a whisper.

And I did.

I ran, shoes slamming against the warped boards, the sound too loud—too sharp—ricocheting off every mirrored surface. It wasn't just echoing. It was mocking me. The Funhouse didn't reflect sound. It fed on it. Laughed it back in distorted, jagged loops.

"You can't escape us!" The voices curled through the corridors like smoke, slipping under my skin, whispering from corners that didn't exist.

I pushed harder. My lungs clawed for air. My calves screamed with every turn. But the maze never shifted in my favor. I passed the same cracked mirror—again. Same fracture in the corner, same fingerprint smudge just beneath it. A mocking breadcrumb.

"No." The word scratched from my throat.

Another turn. Another mirror.

"No, no, no—" The syllables tore loose as the truth struck like a gut-punch.

I wasn't escaping.

I was looping.

The Funhouse wasn't trapping me anymore.

It was digesting me.

The air thickened, congealing around me with the weight of something wet and unseen. Each breath dragged like it had to claw its way through molasses. The walls narrowed with every step, folding inward—not physically, but perceptually. Like the Funhouse wasn't just closing in. It was inhaling me.

I turned a corner. There it was again.

The spinning platform.

I'd passed it—what, three times? Five? I couldn't tell anymore. The colors had bled together into streaks of rusted red and spoiled yellow, like carnival paint running through sewer water. The platform turned slowly now, heavy and indifferent, as if bored with the chase. As if it had been waiting for me to give up.

The music twisted. Notes folded in on themselves, warped

into something sharp and unnatural. Not melody. Not memory. Just noise with teeth. The kind that crawled into your ears and stayed there, shivering against the nerves like static and razor wire.

"Round and round she goes…"

The voices slithered through the corridors like perfume spilled on rotting lace—sweet and rancid all at once. Light. Mocking.

"Where she stops…"

The air tightened around my ribs.

"Nobody knows."

Laughter followed. Not around me—within me. It vibrated through my skull like I'd swallowed a speaker playing back every awful thing I'd tried not to remember. It settled behind my eyes, echoed in my jaw. I couldn't tell where it stopped and I began.

Maybe I wasn't beginning anymore.

Maybe I was dissolving.

I clapped my hands over my ears, hard enough to hurt, but the sound didn't stop. It pressed inward, worming past bone, threading itself into the folds of my brain like cold fingers made of static and memory. I stumbled forward, teeth clenched, eyes wide, bracing for more—anything but what came next.

Then it cut through. A voice. Sharp. Familiar.

"B! Help me!"

Jenna.

Not some echo from the fog. Not the whisper of grief pretending to be something else. It was her voice—raw with panic, cracking at the edges. But underneath that was something smaller. The tremor. The one she never let anyone hear unless things were bad. Really bad.

My chest tightened, breath catching in my throat like a hook had been lodged there and yanked. That voice didn't belong to the thing that had worn her face. This wasn't a carnival trick.

It was Jenna. Or it was close enough to break me.

"Jenna?" The name barely escaped me, hoarse and fragile, vanishing into the electric throb of my heartbeat.

The masked figures circled still, a grotesque ballet in slow motion, but their movements lost urgency. They flickered at the edges of my vision, reduced to afterthoughts, as if the world had narrowed into a tunnel with one endpoint—her voice.

"B, please!" The cry echoed again, rising through the thick air like a flare. It wasn't just desperate—it was breaking.

My body moved before my mind gave permission. A step. Then another. Drawn not by reason, but by that aching instinct that knew her pain better than my own name.

Every rational part of me screamed to stop. This was the carnival's doing—a place built to deceive, to tear at the seams of reason and memory until nothing true remained. I knew that. But it didn't matter.

Jenna's voice pulled me forward, not gently, but like a hook buried deep beneath my ribs. It tore through logic like it wasn't even there. I knew that tremble in her voice, that thread of panic stretched thin. It was the same fear I'd heard the night everything shattered.

"I'm coming!" I shouted, the words ragged, voice frayed with something between desperation and defiance.

Around me, the masked figures stirred, slow and serpentine, their whispers swelling like a storm surge. They laughed, shrill and shrieking, the sound threading under my skin like cold wire—but I didn't flinch. Her voice was louder now. It cut through the noise like light in fog.

"B, hurry!"

Her voice split the air—urgent, cracked with fear—and it hit me like a rush of adrenaline straight to the chest. Her panic was tangible, bitter as old blood on the back of my tongue. I pushed forward, legs heavy as if the floor itself had turned to sludge, dragging against every stride.

The walls of the Funhouse seemed to contract, the corridor narrowing with each step. The air thickened—dense, syrupy—as if the whole place had lungs, and I was breathing in its fear.

Still, I moved.

Because illusion or not, I wasn't going to abandon her again.

The fog curled tighter, spiraling with a strange awareness, and from its center, a figure began to form—slender, familiar, impossibly real.

My heart kicked hard against my ribs.

Jenna.

I knew that silhouette. The tilt of her head. The easy sway of her stride. The way her arms swung like she was walking downhill, smiling at something just behind her. All of it etched into memory so deeply that I didn't need light to recognize her. But beneath that surge of recognition came a stab of unease.

Something wasn't right.

My gut twisted with a certainty that didn't need proof. This wasn't her—not really.

As she stepped into the light, the carnival glow flickered across her face—and my breath stopped dead in my throat.

Jesus.

CHAPTER 18

Her smile split wide, too wide, carving through her face like a fracture in porcelain. The corners of her mouth dragged unnaturally toward her ears, revealing a row of teeth that seemed to multiply with every blink—razored and crammed together like broken glass. Her eyes... Christ. Her eyes weren't eyes anymore. They were pits. Black and bottomless, drawing everything in like gravity gone wrong.

I couldn't look away.

"Help me, B..."

Her voice, that voice—it was perfect. Almost. The same shaky desperation I remembered from the crash, threaded with panic. But beneath the plea was something else. Something that oozed, thick and slow, curling under her words like smoke in a locked room. It whispered with hunger.

I stumbled back.

Jenna—or the thing pretending to be her—rippled like heat rising off asphalt. One moment, she was laughing, alive, the exact memory I'd carried for years. The next, her form twisted, skin rippling as if something inside it writhed for escape. Her hair undulated in the strobing light—not like silk, but like a nest of serpents, alive and watching.

"Please, B... don't leave me again."

The words cut straight through me, carving into a place I thought I'd buried for good. My breath hitched. A fresh wave of guilt crashed in, sharp and immediate, dragging me under. I wanted to believe. God, I wanted to run to her—throw my arms around her and promise I'd never let go again. That this time would be different. That I'd do it right.

But I didn't move.

Because some part of me, the part that still knew how to tell truth from fantasy, was already screaming.

This wasn't Jenna.

Whatever stood in front of me wore her face like a borrowed costume, twisting her voice into a scalpel and aiming straight for the softest part of me.

My heart hammered, fast and erratic. I felt frozen and flayed open, like every nerve had been stripped raw. The lights around her pulsed, casting her features in short, stuttering frames, like a film reel skipping on broken glass.

And that's when it landed—not soft or slow, but with a jolt.

This wasn't Jenna.

This was the carnival again. My grief dressed in skin and memory, coiling around my guilt like a predator. And I'd nearly let it in.

"No…"

The word came out rough, scraped raw from somewhere deep in my chest. It wasn't a scream or a shout—it didn't need to be. It was a boundary. A refusal. I stepped back, legs trembling but firm enough to hold. "You're not her."

The creature's smile widened, slow and grotesque. Flesh stretched past its limits, corners of the mouth peeling toward the jawline as if the skin were nothing more than damp canvas pulled too tight. Its face cracked under the strain, and beneath it—those eyes. Not Jenna's eyes. Not warm and teasing, full of light and memory. No. These were voids. Oil-slick and bottomless. They didn't see me. They devoured.

"B…" it purred, mimicking Jenna's voice so well it almost broke me again. Almost. "Don't you love me anymore?"

The cadence was right. The softness. Even that familiar dip she always had when she teased me. But it was hollow—lacking the spark that made Jenna real. The voice was an echo, a clever imitation draped in something cold and insidious. It slithered through my bones, burrowing into every crack the real Jenna had once healed.

My vision blurred, but I didn't blink. Didn't dare. Because for one breathless, dangerous moment, I wanted to believe it. I wanted to run to her, wrap my arms around her and pretend the crash had never happened. Pretend the last few years were just a bad dream I could wake up from.

But that's all this was—a dream.

"You're not real."

The words tasted like metal. Like guilt. My voice wavered, but it didn't break. I wiped my face, dragging the sleeve of my coat across skin that felt fevered and ice-cold all at once. Then I looked it in the eye—the monster wearing her—and stepped back again.

"You're just another trick," I said, my voice low, steady now. "Another lie dressed in her skin."

The thing cocked its head, the motion sharp and unnatural, like a puppet whose strings had been pulled by hands that didn't understand the limits of a human body. There was a crack—wet and brittle—like cartilage giving out. The sound echoed through the Funhouse, bouncing off the mirrored walls like a dare.

"But don't you want me to be real, B?"

The question came softly now, not with malice but with calculated tenderness. That voice, so close to Jenna's it made my ribs ache. Pleading, almost—but not quite. There was a slickness to it. A practiced mimicry that struck deeper than any accusation.

"Don't you want a chance to fix it?"

And there it was. The bait.

The carnival wasn't just tormenting me. It wasn't just some

malicious machine grinding up my memories for its own amusement. It had studied me. It knew me. This wasn't about fear anymore. It was about longing. About regret so sharp it carved out space inside your chest and asked you to live there anyway.

Of course I wanted a second chance. Of course I wanted to undo that night. To hear her laugh again—really laugh, not this parody of joy made sinister by whatever was puppeting her image.

But that's how it worked. That's how this place kept you. It didn't need to chain you down. It only had to show you the thing you wanted most, and let you reach for it until your hands bled.

I tore my gaze away from the thing that wore Jenna's smile like a stolen mask. The movement broke something loose in my chest—my pulse surged, crashing against my ribs like surf in a storm. The Funhouse warped around me, the floors tilting, the mirrors blinking with warped reflections of panic. But all I could hear was the music.

That carnival melody had turned to shriek—not from volume, but from pitch. It had climbed so high it felt like it was drilling into my skull. Violins on the verge of snapping. Calliope pipes bending into discord. Every note scraped across my nerves, stripping away thought until only one word remained.

Run.

I didn't choose it. My body launched forward like it had been waiting for permission. The floor beneath my boots gave slightly, as if the whole structure was breathing underfoot. Echoes chased me—footfalls not my own. They multiplied, overlapping in syncopated rhythm, too many to count.

CHAPTER 18

And that laughter. It clawed after me. Not just mocking—relentless. Glee stripped of joy.

"Running again, Brooke?"

The words oozed through the walls, spoken not from one mouth but from dozens—layered, wet, familiar. My name wasn't an accusation. It was a taunt. A leash. And I could feel it tightening.

I careened around the corner, lungs straining, vision tunneling—only to freeze mid-step.

They were waiting.

Three masked figures loomed in the corridor ahead, arms spread like grotesque hosts offering an embrace that promised only ruin. Their hands twitched, fingers unfurling like insect legs—segmented, glistening, inhuman. The movement was too smooth, too intentional. My stomach twisted as their shadows stretched toward me, thin and boneless.

"Stay with us forever," they whispered, and the words didn't echo. They landed. Heavy. Final.

Their masks convulsed, not shifting but seizing—teeth blooming from porcelain, eyes expanding into voids. Expressions flipped between manic joy and dead-eyed menace with the flicker of strobe lights, as though they were sampling from the greatest hits of my worst dreams.

I spun on instinct, heart hammering, and took the nearest exit. Another corridor. Same story. More of them emerged from the seams of the walls, peeling out of shadow like smoke turning solid. Each turn brought more faceless tormentors, more reaching hands.

The Funhouse was no longer a maze. It was a trap. And it had closed.

The mirrors multiplied along the corridor walls, gleaming

like predators' eyes in the half-light, each one holding not a reflection, but a thousand versions of me unraveling. My face appeared again and again—drawn, haunted, increasingly fractured, like I was watching my own sanity splinter in real time.

The exits had vanished. Where once there had been doorways or turns, now there were only blank, bone-smooth walls. The maze had rewritten itself while I wasn't looking.

Then came the voice.

"B, please don't leave me again..."

Jenna. But not.

Her voice carried that aching, unmistakable edge of heartbreak, but now it bent beneath something venomous—like grief that had turned in on itself and grown teeth.

My lungs forgot how to work. I knew she was behind me. I didn't need to turn to feel it—her presence was a chill stitched into the very air, pressing against the back of my neck like the cold barrel of a gun.

The masked figures poured through the gaps in the walls like ink spilled in water, slipping into the space around me with a grotesque fluidity that defied human movement. They didn't walk—they seeped, their bodies elongating, stretching, as though the Funhouse itself had sculpted them from shadow and grief.

Their laughter ricocheted through the corridor—a high, fragmented shriek—layered and warped like a chorus of children imitating madness. The mirrors turned it into a surround-sound hallucination, bouncing it between a thousand distorted versions of myself, all of us trapped in the same collapsing spiral.

No matter where I turned, they were there. Blocking my

path, reaching for me with too-thin fingers, their masks twitching between expressions I didn't want to decipher.

The Funhouse had shed its disguise. It was no longer a carnival attraction. It was a predator. And I was its prey.

Doors slammed shut in quick succession—bang, bang, bang—each one a final punctuation mark. The floor rippled underfoot as the corridors began to bend, folding in on themselves like paper warped by heat.

I wasn't running anymore.

I was being herded.

And I had no idea what waited for me at the end of the line.

My legs burned, but something shifted deep inside, a flicker of warmth cutting through the icy grip of fear. The warped carnival music still shrieked through the air, and the laughter echoed louder with every step, but it didn't hit the same anymore. Not after I remembered.

Jenna's real smile.

Not that grotesque parody they'd twisted her into. Not that thing wearing her face like a mask. I saw her as she really was—bright and fearless, with that stubborn streak that had always been a mile wide. She never backed down. Not once.

"You wouldn't want me to give up," I whispered, breath ragged, voice barely more than a ghost in the noise. But saying it made something lock into place. As if her hand had closed around mine again, grounding me. "You'd tell me to fight."

Around me, the masked figures surged, their movements twitchier now, desperate. They grasped at empty air where I'd just been—arms outstretched, too eager. But I wasn't running blind anymore. The panic had cooled, forged into something harder. Not just courage. Defiance.

"You can't have me!" I roared, the words ripping from my

chest like they'd been waiting years to be spoken. They echoed through the corridor, crashing off mirrors like a battle cry. I dropped low, twisted under a clutching hand, and shoved forward into the chaos.

Let them wear her face. Let them steal her laugh. They could twist every memory into something grotesque—but they couldn't own her.

Jenna wasn't here. Not in this nightmare. Not in these tricks. She lived in the laughter that still echoed in my bones, in the stubborn spark that refused to die no matter how dark it got.

The funhouse convulsed, the walls buckling inward like a beast in pain. The mirrored surfaces warped and flared, showing glimpses of all the versions of me that had stumbled here—afraid, broken, lost. But my feet didn't falter. The air still rippled, the ground still tried to slide out from under me, but my footing held.

I wasn't running anymore. I was advancing.

Behind me, the thing still wearing Jenna's voice shrieked my name, but it hit different now. Too shrill. Too ragged. Not a cry of power, but of desperation—like a puppet realizing its strings were snapping.

I didn't turn around. Didn't give it the dignity of a glance.

"You're not her," I said, and my voice rang out clearer this time. Stronger. "The real Jenna wouldn't want me stuck here, locked in a lie."

Her memory flickered behind my eyes—smirking over pancakes, calling my bluff at midnight, yanking me back from the edge with a joke only she could get away with.

Keep going, B.

I felt it like a hand at my back. Not a whisper this time, but

CHAPTER 18

a push.

My chest filled—not with fear, but with fire. Not with dread, but with something steadier. The kind of love that refuses to quit. The kind that walks into the dark and dares it to blink first.

"I won't be your prisoner," I said, jaw clenched. "And I won't bury her memory in your lies."

The air thickened around me, but I pushed into it like wind in a storm, muscles tight, heart surging. This place didn't want me strong. Didn't want me angry. But I was both.

Jenna wouldn't have folded.

And now—neither would I.

The corridor still writhed ahead of me, its shape never holding for more than a second, but I wasn't lost. Not anymore. The maze could shift and snarl all it wanted—I knew now there was a way out.

And I was going to find it.

Not just for Jenna.

For the version of me that forgot she deserved saving too.

I kept moving, even as my legs begged for mercy. The walls twisted. The mirrors multiplied, each one reflecting my fear, my doubt—my own face looking back at me, wide-eyed and trembling. But that wasn't all they showed.

They showed the truth.

The guilt. The silence. The night I let Jenna down—and the mornings after, when I lied to myself about why. I buried it all so deep it rotted. And here it was, clawing to the surface.

My steps slowed, my breath ragged. The figures circled again, their laughter spiraling up like smoke. They shrieked, taunted, tried to make the air vibrate with panic.

But I stood still.

Because I finally understood.

"Enough."

The word wasn't loud. It didn't have to be. It dropped like a stone into deep water, and everything else rippled around it.

The laughter cracked, faltered mid-note. The figures jerked and twitched, no longer graceful. No longer in control.

"I said enough."

This time, it echoed like thunder.

My fists clenched at my sides. I could feel their presence pressing in, feel the weight of every lie I'd told myself for years. But it didn't matter. They were shadows. Smoke.

Chapter 19

I stood in the center of the room, breath quick and shallow, each inhale thick with the stale weight of the air. It pressed against my skin like damp velvet—suffocating, heavy. Overhead, bulbs flickered and buzzed, casting long, jagged shadows that jittered across the floor. The mirrors loomed like vultures, their tarnished glass reflecting a thousand warped versions of myself. I wasn't just surrounded—I was being swallowed.

These weren't idle memories. They were grotesque caricatures—funhouse mutations that twisted me into something barely human. There was one that showed me when I was younger, with my eyes wide open and my heart filled with anxiety, just like the child who would hide under the blankets if the night became too quiet. Another showed me older, worn down and hollow, her face etched with grief and years of unspoken regret. Others showed… things I didn't want to name.

My pulse hammered in my ears, matching the uneven flicker of the lights. I tried not to look too closely, but the images pulled at me, dragging my gaze from one nightmare to the next. They weren't just reflections. They were echoes—fragments of everything I'd buried, everything I'd been too afraid to face.

And the frames...

The intricate patterns that should've been ornate and beautiful twisted in my peripheral vision, writhing like living things. It was as if they were breathing alongside me, taking in my anxiety and releasing something more sinister.

My throat was as dry as sandpaper as I forced myself to swallow. As I lifted my hand, my fingertips lightly brushed over the surface of one of the mirrors. I was completely unaware of this as it occurred. As if water had been disturbed by a breeze, the glass rippled in a way that was gentle and fluid. But it wasn't cool. It was warm. Alive.

A shiver crawled down my spine as I yanked my hand back. These weren't just mirrors.

They were watching.

And they knew me. Knew every crack, every hidden fear, every damn thing I'd been trying to outrun.

I wasn't standing in a funhouse.

I was standing in a trap. And the walls were closing in.

I couldn't shut my eyes. My thoughts scattered like startled birds, each one dragging me deeper into memories I wasn't ready to face. To my left, there was a young Brooke. Her hair was pulled back into pigtails, and she had a broad grin on her face. Her eyes were filled with a mixture of wonder and mischief. I could almost hear her laughing, that carefree chuckle that used to reverberate through the afternoons of summer, even if she was not directly speaking to me. My chest ached at the sight, a long so sharp it felt like a knife twisting under my ribs.

In the mirror straight ahead, I saw who I used to be just a few years ago. Standing in my new office, the diploma hanging neatly behind me, its polished frame catching the light. That version of me stood tall, her shoulders back, her smile filled with purpose and confidence. she was prepared to assist other people and had the desire to make a difference. Unburdened by the burden that I carried now, her eyes shone with a gleaming brightness.

However, the reflection that was to my right was the one that came so close to removing the air from my lungs. Her eyes were hollow and faraway, and tears were streaking down her face. Her shoulders sagged under a weight that was all too familiar—grief. Guilt. The crushing emptiness that had settled into my bones after Jenna's death. I could feel it radiating through the glass, thick and suffocating, trying to pull me back into that dark place.

And then... there was the mirror behind me.

I turned slowly, dread curling in my stomach, and came face-to-face with a version of myself I didn't like to acknowledge. Her jaw was clenched so tight I thought her teeth might crack. Her fists were balled at other sides, knuckles white with tension. Fury burned in her eyes—raw, unfiltered rage. Rage at herself. At fate. At the cruel joke that had left me standing while Jenna...

As I moved, the reflections shifted with me, reacting as if they could feel my presence. When I drew closer to the grieving version, the angry one's scowl deepened, her body practically vibrating with fury. The little girl's smile wavered, her innocence dimming as she sensed the storm swirling around her. Even the confident version of me, the one standing tall in her office, began to falter, her shoulders dipping under the weight of the others.

It was like watching ripples spread across a pond—each reflection touching and changing the others, a constant push and pull of emotion. They weren't just fragments of me. They were all me. The joy, the hope, the grief, and the anger. Swirling together. Feeding off one another.

And standing in the middle of it all, I could feel the chaos mirrored inside me, a storm I'd been trying to outrun for far too long.

It was as if a tsunami of blame and regret was washing over me all at once, and the voices came at me all at once. It was as if the weight of their words was pressing down on me, and I staggered back, my breath seizing as it did so. It was so powerful that the mirrors began to vibrate, and the glass began to hum like a tuning fork that had been hammered too hard. Their mouths moved in perfect sync, a cruel chorus that echoed louder with each passing second.

"Why didn't you stop us?"

The first voice was my younger self. Her wide, tear-filled eyes stared back at me, her pigtails swinging slightly as if caught in a breeze that didn't exist. Her voice cracked with something worse than sadness—betrayal. The kind of betrayal that cut deep and left scars no amount of time could erase.

"You let us go. you didn't stop it."

My throat tightened, but before I could even form a thought, the version of me from the office spoke up. When she spoke, her voice, which had been filled with hope and drive in the past, suddenly dripped with letdown. Her reflection appeared to be the same, with her stance remaining the same and her diploma hanging on the wall behind her. However, her grin had vanished, and it was replaced with something bitter.

"You gave up on us," she charged, her eyes appearing lifeless and hollow. "You let the darkness win."

The next voice hit me like a punch to the gut. The grieving

CHAPTER 19

version of me. Her face was streaked with fresh tears, her shoulders shaking under the weight of sorrow.

Her pain was unbearable, and I felt it like a physical ache in my chest. But then came the worst of them all—the angry version.

"This is all your fault!"

The scream that she let out ripped through the room, resonating off the mirrors until it seemed as though the walls themselves were yelling at me. Her jaw was clenched so tightly that I feared her teeth might break, and her eyes looked like they were on fire with rage.

"You're weak," she spewed out, her reflection shaking with anger about the situation. "You allowed her to pass away. And what about now? You are now too much of a coward to attempt to change any of it any more."

An explosion of accusations that swelled up into a deafening boom was produced by the voices that overlapped each other. At this point, every reflection spoke at the same time, and their voices blended together to form a nightmare chorus of self-loathing and remorse. I was no longer able to differentiate between the speakers' voices. It seemed as if a constant drumbeat was beating at my head even though they had blended into a single force.

"Your fault. You failed her. Coward. Weak."

I clamped my hands over my ears, but it didn't help. The voices weren't just noise—they were inside me, reverberating through bone, screaming beneath my skin. The pressure built fast, sharp, like my skull might split from the weight of it.

"Stop," I whispered, my voice barely audible against the storm of accusations.

But the voices didn't stop. They wouldn't stop. This

continued until I confronted them.

I slammed into the nearest mirror, shoulder-first, putting every ounce of desperation into the hit. Pain shot through me, a jolt that rattled my teeth and made my bones ache, but the glass didn't shatter. It didn't even crack. The surface rippled like a pond disturbed by a thrown stone, distorting my reflection before settling back into place.

Without taking a breath, I mumbled, "No." Panic began to wriggle its way up my throat, and my chest began to heave.

I pounded the mirror again and again, fists aching, skin splitting. The surface flexed beneath my hands—unnaturally pliant, like flesh over bone—but it wouldn't break. It should've shattered. Glass shouldn't move like that.

Behind the glass, my reflection didn't just stare back—it watched. I could see it in her eyes. There was a glint of knowing in her eyes. She appeared to be anticipating my understanding.

Then the laughter began.

The girl with the pigtails initially let out a soft giggle. But there was nothing innocent in the sound. It was hollow. Cold. The others joined in, one by one, until the room swelled with the sound of my voice in every octave. Twisting. Mocking. The air thickened with a sour, wet smell reminiscent of rot. As it reverberated off the mirrors, the volume eventually reached a point where it felt as though it was within my skull.

"Just stop!" I screamed, fists hammering the glass fierce enough to bruise. The mirror continued to ripple, teasing me with its unbelievable flexibility, even though my knuckles were throbbing and the flesh was tearing.

The reflections swayed with the motion, their distorted faces twisting with delight. Their laughter grew more manic, a chorus of derision that made the air thick and difficult to breathe.

"LET ME OUT!" I hurled myself towards the mirror, exerting all my weight on it. For a fleeting instant, I was under the impression that I felt it give, even a little bit, but then it took a strong push back. In that moment, the glass bounced like elastic, pushing me away as if I were nothing, causing me to falter and come dangerously close to falling to my knees.

The reflections laughed even louder, their wicked delight spreading across their faces as they stood there. It was no longer only that they were laughing at me. They were taking pleasure in this. I am allowing my irritation, anxiety, and desperation to fuel my behavior.

I was able to sense it. I found that the more I struggled, the more powerful they got. Despite my best efforts, this nightmare continued to suck me down further and deeper.

I couldn't stop.

But I wouldn't give in either.

If I did, they'd win. And I wouldn't let them.

I stumbled back, barely staying on my feet as the mirrors around me blazed to life. The light was blinding, but I didn't need to see to know what was coming. I felt it—an electric pulse in the air that made my skin prickle and my stomach drop.

Then the crash returned—merciless.

Each mirror replayed it from a new angle, as if daring me to look away. The nightmare I'd escaped for all these years was now reflected in glass and filled with guilt. Headlights burst through the darkness, glaring and merciless, just like that night. The screech of tires tore through the silence, sending a spike of dread straight through me.

And then I saw her.

Jenna.

The gentle brightness of the dashboard illuminated her face, and as the dawn of realization approached, her grin began to fade. As her look changed from one of amusement to one of wide-eyed dread, I watched in excruciating slow motion as everything changed. Her lips formed the shape of my name.

"B!"

The sound of the impact followed a heartbeat later, a sickening, bone-deep thud that echoed through my body like a punch to the chest. Glass exploded outward, shimmering in the headlights like stars before they sliced through the night. I could hear the metal groan and crumple, folding in on itself with a finality that made my knees go weak.

"Stop," I whispered, my voice barely more than a breath. But the mirrors didn't listen. They never listened.

The crash looped. Over and over.

"Jenna…" Her name cracked in my throat, lost beneath the sound of tires shrieking, glass shattering, metal folding in on itself. The sounds I'd never been able to forget. The sounds I'd never stopped hearing.

The mirrors pulsed with every shattering replay. Light flashed in time with the sound of twisting metal and breaking glass, sycning perfectly with the moment where everything had gone so wrong.

"I'm sorry," I whispered, the words tasting like ash. My throat was tight, my eyes burning with tears that refused to fall.

But the mirrors didn't care.

Jenna's face filled every reflection, her terror locked in a

CHAPTER 19

loop that refused to end. Her wide, pleading eyes met mine again and again, pulling me back into that moment—into the guilt, the helplessness, the unbearable weight of everything I'd lost.

The mirrors weren't just showing me the past.

They were making me live it.

I couldn't hold myself up anymore. My legs gave out, and I collapsed to the floor, the cold seeping up through my jeans and settling into my bones.

I curled into myself, knees drawn tight against my chest, as if making myself smaller could somehow make the memories stop. But they didn't stop. They kept coming, hammering at me with the force of a freight train, each one worse than the last.

"I can't," I whispered, my voice barely more than a breath. It was all I could manage. My throat was raw, tight with emotion, and the words tasted like defeat. "I can't take this anymore."

The mirrors didn't care. They didn't stop.

I shook with sobs too deep for sound. Each one hollowed me out, scraping at my ribs from the inside. I pressed my forehead against my knees, trying to block it all out, but the memories clawed their way in anyway.

"Stop," I begged, my voice muffled against my knees. But the mirrors didn't stop. They just kept replaying it, feeding me the same nightmare on an endless loop, as if they were trying to break me.

And maybe they had broken me. Maybe that was the point.

Because I couldn't fight it anymore.

The cold seeped deeper, numbing me from the inside out, and the room spun around me, tilting and twisting until I didn't know which way was up. My heart pounded in my ears, but it was distant now, barely a whisper against the roar of everything I'd been trying to outrun.

I was drowning in it.

And for the first time... I didn't have the strength to swim.

My body was trembling under the weight of all that was going on, and I remained there with my knees pressed against the chilly floor. Even though my fingers were entangled in my hair and my nails were digging into my scalp, I felt as though I could somehow anchor myself, grab on to something—anything—to halt the torrent of emotions that threatened to consume me completely. This nightmare that I couldn't seem to get out of was the only thing that felt real to me, and it was the coolness of the floor underneath me that helped me feel grounded.

"I'm sorry," I mumbled, but the words were barely audible over the sound of a breath. My throat was tight with emotion, and the words that I was trying to say came out ragged and broken. "I'm so sorry, Jenna."

But saying it didn't make it better. Didn't make it go away. The apology felt hollow, too little and way too late. Years of running, of convincing myself I'd done all I could, of building walls around the truth so thick that even I couldn't see through them—those walls were gone now. Crumbled into dust. So what was left?

It's just me. Broken. Exposed.

I looked up through blurred vision, and for the first time, I didn't flinch. My reflections looked back, their faces still etched with accusation, but... something was missing. The heat in their eyes had subsided slightly. The anger wasn't gone, but it wasn't all-consuming anymore. Maybe it was my surrender—my willingness to finally see them—but they weren't enemies now.

Their faces—mine—watched in silence. Not enemies. Not monsters. Something worse. They were me. Every bruised memory. Every broken version I'd tried to forget.

The ache in my chest remained, sharp and hollow—but something flickered beneath it. Not peace. Not relief. But recognition. A fragile thread of acceptance, thin as breath, buried deep in the rubble of everything I'd been avoiding.

I couldn't break the mirrors. Couldn't silence the voices. Because they weren't distortions. They were me. The truths I'd exiled. The grief I'd starved until it grew fangs. The fear I dressed in logic and called control.

My breath stuttered once, caught in my throat—but I let it go. Shoulders sagging. Chest aching. And with that breath, something shifted. The weight didn't vanish, but it no longer threatened to crush me.

I raised my eyes, meeting each reflection in turn. Grief. Rage. Innocence. Hope. All watching. All waiting. Not monsters. Not curses. Just the truth of who I'd been. Who I still was.

"I can't change it," I said, voice rough but steady. "But I can stop pretending I already died with her."

Through the haze of tears, something shifted in the mirror farthest from me.

It wasn't the usual parade of blame and bitterness. No accusation, no hollow echoes of Jenna's scream. This was different.

The little girl stared back at me, the one with the wide, innocent eyes and the pigtails tied just a little too tight. Her head tilted ever so slightly, the way Jenna used to do when she was about to tell me to stop beating myself up. That look—

half patience, half exasperation—hit me harder than any of the accusations had.

"Maybe she never wanted me to carry this," I whispered, softer this time. "Maybe she wanted me to find a way back."

The words felt strange coming out, like saying them aloud made them real. But they were true. I could feel it, deep down, like a match sparking to life in the dark. A small, flickering flame, but steady. Refusing to go out.

Jenna wouldn't want this. Not the endless cycle of guilt and regret, not me punishing myself for something I couldn't change. I thought of her laugh, the one that could turn even the worst day into something bearable. Even that night—before the crash, before everything fell apart—she'd been trying to cheer me up, cracking jokes and pulling me out of my own head.

Would she want me stuck here? Trapped in this twisted funhouse of guilt and sorrow.

The angry version of me, the one who'd been screaming blame from her side of the glass, faltered. Her scowl softened, just for a moment, and for the first time, I saw something besides rage in her eyes. Uncertainty.

The grieving reflection, the one who'd been sobbing and crumbling under the weight of loss, quieted too. Her shoulders still shook, but the echo of her pain wasn't as sharp, wasn't as all-consuming.

Something changed. The air thinned, like the room had been holding its breath and finally let it go. The silence between heartbeats stretched longer. Gentler.

I breathed in, and it didn't slice on the way down. It stayed. It steadied.

My hands pressed against the cold floor, the chill cutting

through the numbness that had settled in my bones. The echoes of the crash, the accusations, all the voices screaming my failures still churned around me, but they felt... different now. Not gone, but distant. Like thunder grumbling on the horizon after a storm had torn through, still echoing in the air but losing its power with each passing moment. The storm had done its worst, and while the damage was undeniable, the chaos was beginning to settle. I looked at the reflections again, really looked this time.

They stared back, eyes filled with pain and shadows, but the fury was fading. The grief still lingered, raw and heavy, but it wasn't all-consuming anymore. The guild hadn't vanished—it probably never would—but it wasn't strangling me like it had been moments ago.

They were still me. All of them. The scared kid who didn't know how to stop the inevitable. The determined woman who'd built walls so high she couldn't see past them. The broken, grieving version who'd been drowning under the weight of it all.

But I wasn't afraid of them now.

I didn't need to outrun them. I needed to listen. To remember. To grieve without burying myself beside her. And maybe—just maybe—learn how to carry the weight without letting it break me.

The mirrors hadn't been my prison.

They were the map.

Chapter 20

The carnival music spiraled into chaos, each note colliding with the next in a discordant surge that scraped at my nerves. I clamped my hands over my ears, but it was no use—the sound wasn't just around me. It was in me, vibrating in my chest, threading through my bones like static.

And that's when I saw her.

She stepped out of the fog like a half-forgotten memory, familiar in shape but off around the edges. Jenna—but blurred, distorted, like an old photograph left out in the rain. She was there, but not all the way. Her glow was soft, almost too perfect.

I couldn't move. Couldn't breathe.

Jenna drifted through the maze of mirrors with an eerie grace, her movements too fluid, too smooth, like she was part of this place. Like the Funhouse had claimed her. Her reflection bounced around me, dozens of Jennas gliding along the glass, each one a distorted echo of the friend I'd loved and lost. And I couldn't tear my eyes away.

When she turned to face me, my chest clenched so tight it felt like a fist was squeezing the air out of my lungs. Her expression was a perfect storm of sorrow and sweetness—Jenna, just as I remembered her. But there was something

CHAPTER 20

underneath. Something wrong. Like a smile that didn't quite reach her eyes, or a laugh that came half a second too late.

"Jenna?" I barely recognized my own voice. It was cracked and hollow. I took a step forward, my hand reaching out on instinct, but she was just beyond my grasp. Always just beyond.

Her eyes met mine, and for a heartbeat—just one—I thought I saw her. The real her. A flicker of warmth, of recognition. But then it was gone, replaced by a sadness so deep it made my knees weak.

She opened her mouth, and nothing came out. No words. Just silence. Thick. Suffocating. And then the music rose again, louder and more obnoxious, as if the Funhouse was mocking me. The lights pulsed in rhythm with the twisted melody, splashing red, blue, and green across her face, making her look even less like Jenna and more like something... other.

I stood frozen, breath shallow, unable to move as her form faded. My legs ached to run, to reach, to do something—but the air itself had turned to glue, rooting me to the floor. I was trapped, caught between the living and the dead, as Jenna's figure began to dissolve back into the fog.

Her eyes never left mine.

And I felt it. That ache deep in my bones. The knowledge that I was losing her all over again.

But this time... it was worse.

Because this time, I wasn't sure I'd ever get her back.

Jenna's voice rang out through the Funhouse, faint but insistent, breaking through the twisted carnival music and the suffocating weight of my guilt.

"You need to remember, B. You have to face it."

My heart constricted as the words stirred something deep

within me that I had kept hidden for far too long. Fear gripped at my chest, wrapping icy fingers over my ribs and squeezing until I felt unable to breathe. But it wasn't all terror. No. Something dark stirred beneath it. Guilt. The sort that digs deep, embeds itself in your bones, and whispers in your ear when you are alone at night. And longing—the longing.

This wasn't how it was supposed to be.

Jenna wasn't supposed to be a flickering shadow, her warmth drained away, her laughter replaced by this hollow ache. She wasn't supposed to be a ghost, trapped in this twisted nightmare, looking at me with eyes that begged me to do… what? Fix it? Change the past? I couldn't even save her that night. What the hell did she expect me to do now?

But her eyes held mine, and the air shifted.

The Funhouse pressed in closer, the walls breathing like a living thing. The mirrors seemed to hum with a subtle, vibrating tension, as if they were expecting something. The lights dimmed, their sickening glow softened, and the twisted music slowed—it was no longer a frenetic, mocking mess. It was now sadder. Almost… mournful. Like a funeral dirge played on a broken music box.

I tried to speak. I tried to tell her I was sorry, that I didn't know how to fix any of this. But the words stuck in my throat, choking me. What could I possibly say to her? To her—my best friend, the one I'd let down when it mattered most. The weight of it pressed down on me, heavy as the wreckage that had crushed us both that night.

Jenna's expression softened, just for a moment. And I saw her again. Not this ghostly version, but the real Jenna—the girl who had laughed with me until our sides hurt, who had always believed in me, even when I didn't believe in myself.

CHAPTER 20

That smile, the one that could melt away my fears, flickered across her face. But it was gone almost as quickly as it came, replaced by something that shattered me.

Sorrow.

"I don't know how," I whispered, barely louder than a breath. My voice cracked, heavy with the weight of years of regret. "I don't know how to face it. It's... it's all my fault."

Jenna shook her head, slow and deliberate, her image flickering like a candle caught in a breeze. "It's not your fault, B." Her voice was softer now, almost tender, but there was an edge to it—an urgency that sent a chill down my spine. "You have to let go. You have to remember the truth."

The truth.

Her words hit me like a punch to the gut, knocking the air right out of me. I did remember. I'd just spent so long trying not to that it had twisted itself into something else—something easier to carry. But now... now the memories stirred, and the Funhouse began to shift around me. The walls warped, the mirrors vibrating as the air grew thicker. I could feel it happening, feel myself being pulled back.

Back to that night.

The lights of the Funhouse dimmed, but they didn't go out. No. They shifted, brightening into something harsher. Headlights.

I blinked, and suddenly, I wasn't in the Funhouse anymore. I was back on that road, the night air thick with the smell of burning rubber and gasoline. I heard the screech of tires, the sickening crunch of metal folding in on itself, and the shatter of glass raining down like deadly confetti.

And Jenna's scream.

Oh God, her scream.

I squeezed my eyes shut, trying to block it out, trying to will myself back to the Funhouse, back to the safety of not remembering. But it was too late. The past had its claws in me now, and it wasn't letting go.

"Face it," Jenna's voice echoed in my mind, softer now, almost pleading.

I had no choice. The memories were dragging me under, pulling me back to the moment that had changed everything. And this time... there was no running.

I had to remember.

Whether I wanted to or not.

The question clawed its way up my throat, raw and burning, begging to be set free after years of being buried so damn deep. My hands shook as I faced Jenna's ghost, her face caught between the warm glow of memory and the cold, distorted light of the Funhouse. The mirrors around us pulsed with that same unnatural energy, like they were holding their breath. Like everything was holding its breath. Waiting.

Just say it.

"What really happened that night?"

The words scraped out of me, barely louder than a whisper, but they felt like broken glass in my mouth. Shards slicing their way free, each one cutting deeper on its way out. My chest tightened, my heart pounding so hard I swore it was trying to break loose.

Jenna's form wavered, her edges flickering like a candle too close to a draft. But it was her eyes that gutted me. That sadness... the same sadness I'd tried to outrun, the same one that had haunted me in every nightmare and quiet moment. It was still there, staring back at me with the weight of everything I'd been too much of a coward to face.

CHAPTER 20

I put my arms around myself, attempting to hold everything in and prevent the jagged shards from splitting apart. But it was futile. The weight of whispered facts pressed down on me, heavy and depressing. I could feel it squeezing air from my lungs, making each breath more difficult than the last.

"I've been so afraid," I confessed, the words rushing out before I could stop them. My voice crackled, almost holding together. "Afraid of remembering. I'm afraid to know." The confession hit me like a punch in the belly, and I stumbled beneath its weight. "But I can't... I can't keep running."

Saying it out loud felt like finally letting go of a breath I didn't even realize I'd been holding. Terrifying. Liberating. Like standing on the edge of a cliff, toes hanging over, knowing the fall was inevitable but no longer caring.

The Funhouse responded.

The carnival music, that warped, sickly tune that had been a constant backdrop, faded into a distant hum. The silence that followed was worse—thick and heavy, pressing down on me like the air before a storm. My breathing echoed off the warped mirrors, ragged and uneven, and those mirrors... they weren't helping. Each reflection stared back at me with a different version of my fear—wide, terrified eyes, lips trembling, tears threatening to spill. It was like standing in a room full of ghosts, every one of them carrying a different piece of weight I'd been dragging for years.

But I forced myself to look away from them. I forced myself to look at her.

Jenna.

"Please," I whispered, my voice barely holding on, barely louder than the pounding of my heart. The word stuck in my throat, thick and heavy, almost choking me as it came out. "I need to know... the truth."

The silence stretched, and for a moment, I thought she wouldn't answer. Thought maybe this was another trick, another cruel illusion conjured by the Funhouse to break me down. But then...

Jenna's eyes met mine, and something shifted.

A tremor ran through the air, subtle but impossible to miss. The mirrors quivered, and the fog that had been swirling around thickened, curling tighter as if it, too, was bracing for what was coming.

Her lips parted.

And I knew—I knew—that whatever came next would change everything.

The carnival groaned, like an old house settling in a storm, as if it had heard me and decided—finally—that I was ready. Or maybe it was just tired of playing with me. Either way, the ground beneath my feet began to tremble, a low, steady vibration that matched the frantic thud of my heart. The air shifted. Thicker now. Heavier. Like I was breathing through gauze.

And then... the sounds.

Not the warped, distorted carnival noises I'd grown used to—the ones that scraped at the edges of my sanity. No, these were different. Real. Too real.

Laughter. High-pitched and pure. Children running between rides, their shoes scuffing against the pavement. The murmur of voices, excited and carefree, blended with the distant, lilting melody of carousel music. Not the sick, broken version that had followed me through this nightmare... this was the real thing. Bright and lively. Nostalgic in a way that made my chest ache.

CHAPTER 20

I turned, and the mirrors rippled like rain hitting a pond.

At first, I thought it was just another trick. But then... the images came.

Jenna's sweater. That familiar, vivid red that stood out no matter where we went, like a beacon. It bled into the harsh yellow glow of streetlights, the colors swirling together like oil on water. Dizzying. Disorienting. But I couldn't look away.

Flashes.

Our laughter echoed in the car. The headlights coming too fast. Tires screeching. I gripped the wheel tightly, my knuckles turning white. My voice—screaming her name—lost in the chaos.

Each memory hit like a gut punch. Crystal clear one moment, dissolving into the next before I could process it. Like the universe was fast-forwarding through the worst night of my life, making me relive it all over again without giving me the chance to breathe.

"This way," the carnival seemed to whisper. The voice was everywhere and nowhere, slipping into my ears like a lover's secret. I didn't trust it, not for a second. But I didn't have a choice.

The path shifted beneath my feet. The wooden planks groaned and twisted, rearranging themselves with a sick, organic fluidity. They stretched forward, pulling me deeper into the Funhouse—or maybe into the darkest corners of my mind. I couldn't tell anymore. The line between them had blurred long ago.

Moving was not my desire. Every nerve in my body screamed for me to stop, turn around, and run. But something stronger than fear drew at me. Something more profound.

The desire to know. To eventually witness what I had spent so many years trying to overlook.

So I took a step forward.

And the air grew heavier. More dense. Pressing down like a weight, I was unable to move on my chest. The pressure rose with every step, forcing air out of my lungs. However, I continued to move. Because I was forced to.

The sounds grew louder, layering over each other like an orchestra tuning before a show. Laughter. Screams. The sound of tires squealing on wet pavement filled the air. Snatches of conversation. Jenna's voice was calling my name.

A symphony of forgotten moments.

And I was walking straight into the heart of it.

The world tilted, twisted, and folded in on itself. The carnival lights dimmed, their garish glow bleeding into the fog, and suddenly… I was there. Back in Jenna's car. The scent hit me first—vanilla air freshener mixed with the faint musk of leather seats that had soaked up too many summer afternoons. It was so real, so immediate, that my chest clenched, and for a moment, I couldn't breathe.

Music drifted through the speakers. That damn song. The one about dancing in the moonlight. She loved it. Played it constantly, singing along even though she couldn't carry a tune to save her life. I could hear her now—off-key, laughing, her voice full of so much joy it didn't matter. The kind of joy that made everything feel okay, even when the world wasn't.

God, I didn't want to be here. Not again.

The streetlights flashed across her face as we drove, painting her features in shifting patterns—gold and shadow, light and dark. She looked so alive. Carefree. But I knew what was coming. I could feel it, like a storm building on the horizon.

CHAPTER 20

And I was powerless to stop it.

The music cut out. Just... gone. It felt as though someone had abruptly ended the most joyful time in my life.

Then came the screech of tires.

My body went rigid. I knew what was next. But knowing didn't make it any easier. Jenna's laughter dissolved into a sharp intake of breath, her smile vanishing as fear flooded her eyes. She looked at me—just for a second—but it was enough. She was wide-eyed, terrified, and aware.

No. No, not again.

The impact hit like a freight train. I felt it in my bones—the crunch of metal twisting, glass exploding in a shower of deadly stars. My head snapped forward, then back, the seatbelt biting into my shoulder like a claw. And through the chaos, I heard her scream my name.

B.

Not angry. Not blaming. Just... scared. For me. Even in her final moments, she was thinking of me.

The memories didn't just play out. They consumed me. Every sensation was amplified, magnified by the carnival's sick influence. The taste of blood flooded my mouth, sharp and metallic. The smell—burning rubber and scorched metal—clawed at my throat. My vision blurred, doubled, then fractured, as if the Funhouse mirrors had followed me into this nightmare.

I tried to close my eyes to block it out, but the carnival wouldn't let me. No, it held me there, like a sadistic puppeteer forcing me to watch the show play out again. Every crash. Every scream. Every second that led to Jenna's last breath.

Tears streamed down my face, hot and relentless, as the weight of it all crushed down on me. I could feel it pressing against my chest, making it hard for me to breathe and think. It wasn't just guilt anymore. It was grief, raw and bleeding, pouring out of wounds I'd tried to pretend had healed.

But through it all, Jenna was still there. Or... what was left of her.

She stood just beyond the chaos, her ethereal form flickering like a candle caught in a breeze. Her smile was soft. Sad. And somehow... understanding. She knew how much this was tearing me apart, but she also knew it was the only way forward.

The Funhouse pulsed around us, the warped reality feeding off the truth finally being dragged into the light. And for the first time... I wasn't sure if the carnival was torturing me or helping me. Because of facing this? Remembering this?

It felt like dying.

Jenna's form shimmered, her edges blurred by the shifting light, but her presence was steady—more solid than it had been before. Like she was rooting for me. Like she knew this moment was the one I'd been running from for too long.

And I felt it too. Something is shifting deep inside. The crushing weight that had lived in my chest since that night—guilt so thick and heavy it felt like I'd been dragging around a corpse—started to crack. Not gone. Not even close. But... different. Changing.

"I've been running," I said, the words landing like stones dropped into still water. "Not just from that night. From me. From the truth I would rather not name."

My voice didn't shake this time. It was steady, carrying the weight of the truth I'd been too afraid to speak. And the carnival? It felt it too. I could feel it in the air, like the whole place was holding its breath. The lights overhead pulsed, not

CHAPTER 20

erratic and chaotic like before, but slower. Measured. Like they were listening.

The mirrors around me shifted. Their endless parade of distorted versions of myself didn't feel like accusations anymore. They were... reflections. Windows. And as painful as it was to look at them, I knew I had to. I had to stop seeing them as punishments and start treating them like what they were—pieces of a puzzle I'd been too scared to finish.

"I need to see it all," I told her. My eyes locked on hers, and for a moment, I swear I could feel the warmth that used to radiate from her. "Every detail. Every decision. Every second of that night." I took a shaky breath, but I didn't waver. "Not because I want to punish myself anymore." My jaw clenched as I forced out the next words. "Because I need to understand."

The air around me thickened, charged with something electric. The Funhouse didn't fight me on this. It... shifted. Responded. Like it was waiting for this moment all along. The warped, sickly music that had haunted me since I stepped into this nightmare started to change. The notes cleared, sharpening into something almost recognizable. Still twisted, but focused. Like a radio dial tuning in, zeroing in on something real.

Jenna's smile was soft, touched with that familiar sadness, but there was something else too. Pride, maybe. Or hope. Or both. And if that didn't give me strength.

This wasn't about drowning in guilt anymore. It wasn't about letting the past keep me chained to the wreckage of that night.

It was about finding my way through.

The mirrors shifted. Not warping, but focusing. Flashes of that night—headlights, laughter, the split-second panic—

flickered into place like glass settling into a broken frame.

I took another breath. This time, it's deeper. The type that filled my lungs and kept me grounded. The air seemed heated, pulsing with expectancy.

"Let's finish this," I said softly, more to myself than her.

And for the first time, I was prepared.

I took a step.

Just one. But it felt like crossing a damn chasm.

The warped ground beneath me began to steady, its pulse syncing with my own. It felt as though the Funhouse was no longer opposing me but responding to my resolve.

The whispers persisted, transforming from a cacophony of torment into a gentle murmur, guiding me forward with unexpected tenderness. The sound wrapped around me, not taunting, not mocking—just leading. like breadcrumbs left behind to guide me out of the dark.

The mirrors, too. They didn't distort and twist me into some nightmare anymore. They still pulsed, their glass surfaces shifting like water, but it wasn't wrong this time. They were showing me something. Offering glimpses, fragments of what was to come. The truth I'd been running from wasn't lurking in the shadows anymore. It was waiting. And I was finally ready to meet it head-on.

As Jenna's silhouette faded into the mist, her features softened until only a warm glow remained. Instead of panic, a calm acceptance settled over me—she was no longer a haunting memory but a comforting presence within me. Her presence lingered, threaded through the air like a familiar scent that sticks around long after someone's left the room. Her smile, the last thing I saw before she faded completely, stayed with me. Gentle. Encouraging.

CHAPTER 20

"You've got this, B."

The path ahead twisted and turned, winding deeper into the carnival's heart. I couldn't see where it led, but I could feel what was waiting. Memories. Choices. All the things I'd buried so deep I'd convinced myself were gone. But it wasn't. It had been present all along, patiently waiting for me to be prepared.

And I was.

I placed a hand over my heart, where guilt had once anchored me. Now, it felt less like a burden and more like a reminder—a part of me, but no longer defining me. Shifting. It wasn't an anchor anymore, holding me down. It was fuel. Pushing me forward.

The whispers coalesced into a melody of meaning—not in words, but in emotions that resonated within me, urging me toward truths I'd long evaded.

I took another step, and the mist ahead of me... parted.

Chapter 21

The darkness enveloped me—not suffocating, but heavy, like a damp, familiar blanket.

And then I heard it.

Not the warped carnival music. Not the distorted whispers or mocking laughter.

The sound of tires on asphalt filled the air. A steady, rhythmic hum that vibrated in my bones, familiar in a way that made my heart pound harder and faster.

My breath caught as the scent hit me next—vanilla. Jenna's perfume. The scent was soft and sweet, with a subtle hint of something warm underneath. The subtle leather aroma of her car seats blended with the scent of her ChapStick. The one she always kept in the center console, swearing it was "just in case," but somehow, she went through a tube a week.

The darkness peeled back, not all at once but in layers, like fog lifting in the early morning. The world reassembled itself, piece by piece, each detail sharp enough to cut. The glow of streetlights painted streaks of gold and shadow across the windshield. I could feel the cool breeze from the AC brushing against my face, hear the low hum of the engine vibrating through the car like a heartbeat.

My fingers brushed against the texture of the seat—smooth,

CHAPTER 21

worn just enough where it had been gripped too hard during one of her infamous "Jenna takes a corner like she's in a Fast and Furious movie" moments. And there was my phone, resting in my lap, the weight of it grounding me even as the memory dragged me deeper.

Time slowed.

I didn't just see it—I was there.

Jenna was humming softly, her voice barely louder than the radio, a habit she had when she was completely at ease. Her eyes, focused but distant, watching the road but somewhere else entirely.

God, it felt so real.

Not like the nightmares that had haunted me for years—those fragmented, jagged things that left me sweating and gasping in the dark. This was whole. Complete. Every sound, every sensation… it was all there. The weight of the night pressing down, the quiet comfort of Jenna's presence filling the space between us.

But underneath it all, something buzzed. A tension.

A countdown.

I could feel it building.

Each breath echoed louder in the confined space, every second stretching out, ticking by with a precision that made my skin crawl. I knew what was coming. I knew. But this time… I wasn't just an observer. I was in it, living it again in agonizing detail.

The Funhouse was still with me. I could feel its hold, lurking just beyond the edges of the memory, like a puppeteer watching, waiting. But it wasn't manipulating me now. It was letting this happen, guiding me back to where everything had gone wrong.

And I was powerless to stop it.

The dashboard lights cast a soft blue glow. Jenna sang along to the radio, off-key but brimming with joy—a carefree energy I always envied.

The heater hummed softly, filling the car with a warmth that felt almost too good, like the universe was trying to lull me into a false sense of safety. Outside, autumn pressed against the glass, cool and crisp, but in here? It was just us. Cozy. Safe.

And then there was that smell—sticky sweet, like cherries and syrup. The Cherry Coke.

We'd hit that pothole earlier, laughing like idiots as our drinks went airborne, soaking the console and splashing on the leather seats. "Guess the car's thirsty too," Jenna had joked, her grin wide enough to light up the night. The memory hit me like a sucker punch, sharp and vivid, the kind of thing that sticks with you long after the moment's gone.

I shifted in my seat, and the leather gave a familiar creak, the residue from that spill still tacky under my fingertips. Her shoes brushed against crumpled candy wrappers on the floor—remnants from our convenience store run after the party. We'd grabbed everything in sight, giggling like kids who'd just discovered sugar for the first time. Sour Patch Kids. Peanut M&Ms. Those weird little gummy worms Jenna loved but never finished.

The radio played that song. Our song. The one Jenna always claimed was our anthem. I couldn't remember the name now, but I'd know it anywhere—those opening chords, the steady beat, and Jenna's immediate reaction. She cranked the volume, her bangles jingling as she tapped the rhythm against the dashboard, her grin practically daring me to join in.

CHAPTER 21

"Come on, B!" she'd said, her eyes sparkling in the passing streetlights. "Don't make me do a solo!"

Everything had felt so normal. So... easy.

That peculiar intimacy of late-night car rides wrapped around us like a warm blanket, where time slowed and the world outside didn't matter. Conversations flowed effortlessly from one topic to the next, the kind of moments that etched themselves into your mind without you ever realizing it.

But now...

Those nuances suddenly felt heavier. Like anchors drawing me down, each one bringing me closer to what was next.

The half-empty water bottle rolling around in the backseat. The way Jenna's hair caught the light, strands glowing gold in the soft flicker of the streetlights. The slight skip in the CD player—just a hiccup, something we always meant to fix but never got around to.

Even the sound of our laughter echoed differently now.

I wanted to hold onto that moment forever, to freeze us right there in that perfect bubble of before. But time doesn't care about what you want. It just keeps moving, dragging you toward the inevitable.

And the inevitable was coming. Fast.

The buzz of the motor, the comfortable background noise that had lulled me into a false sense of security, vanished in an instant. A flash of light. Bright. Too bright. My heart slammed into my ribs, my brain struggling to catch up as the two beams carved through the night ahead, growing impossibly larger.

"Jenna!" I heard my own voice, distant and distorted, like I was underwater. The word tore itself from my throat, raw and instinctual, but it felt useless. Too late. Too late.

The headlights took us completely, turning the windshield into a blinding wall of white. Everything changed in that moment, as if reality itself tipped on its axis. My fingers pushed into the steering wheel, grasping it as if it were a lifeline, and my knuckles turned white. But there was no saving us. Not now.

My gasp sliced through the chaos as I yanked the wheel, my movements sharp and desperate. The world tilted violently to the right, my stomach dropping like I'd been flung off the edge of a cliff. Tires screamed against the asphalt, that high-pitched wail that burrows into your brain and stays there. Forever.

The laughter we'd shared just moments ago? Gone. Snatched away and replaced by terror that tasted like metal on my tongue.

Time didn't slow. Not really. But everything… sharpened. Crystal clear. Every detail seared into my memory like a brand.

The CD skipped. That stupid CD. The music cut out mid-chorus, leaving behind a void that made the chaos feel even louder.

The half-empty water bottle, in the backseat, shot forward, weightless for a heartbeat, like it was suspended in the air by some cruel cosmic joke.

And the lights. Jesus, the lights.

They stretched, warped, until they consumed everything. Blinding beams of white that burned into my eyes, searing their shape into the backs of my eyelids. I could feel them even when I blinked, like afterimages etched into my retinas.

My pulse pounded in my ears, louder than the screeching tires, louder than the panicked rhythm of my own breathing. Every sound seemed magnified, every sensation amplified, like the universe was making sure I wouldn't forget a single second of this nightmare.

The acrid stench of burning rubber permeated the car, combining with Jenna's perfume's overly sweet vanilla—a horrible combination that turned my stomach. The air felt thicker and heavier, as if the atmosphere had turned against us, pressing down and squeezing the air from my lungs.

Our small world, which had been safe, warm, and pleasant, was disintegrating. I could feel it unravelling around me, thread by thread. I couldn't stop it.

I was just there. Helpless. Watching everything go to hell.

The moment went on and on, as if the universe wanted me to experience every ounce of horror and powerlessness. And then…

Impact.

The crash hit like a thunderclap. Metal shrieked as the front of the car crumpled, the sound piercing through my skull.

My chest slammed against the seatbelt, the force knocking the air from my lungs with a soundless gasp. For a split second, the world went completely silent, as if the universe had sucked all the sound away just to make what came next hit harder.

Then everything exploded.

Glass burst around us in a thousand glittering fragments, catching the headlights as they flew. For a moment, it was almost… beautiful. Like tiny stars, falling in slow motion. but beauty had no place here. Not in this chaos. Not in the thick of this horror.

My head snapped forward, chin smashing down hard before whipping back around. Pain surged through my neck, hot and piercing, leaving a trail of fire down my spine. My eyesight dimmed, everything reduced to dashes of light and shadow as the automobile whirled madly, a terrible merry-go-round with life or death stakes.

I tasted copper, bitter, and metallic, and it flooded my mouth where I had bit my tongue. It combined with the acrid odor of burning rubber, heated metal, and something else—a chemical that burnt the back of my throat. The odor was everywhere, stifling me and making it impossible to take a complete breath.

The airbag deployed with the force of a shotgun blast, slamming into me at bone-crushing speed. White powder entered the automobile, forming a dense cloud that combined with the smoke and shattered glass dust, transforming the interior into a swirling fog. I coughed, but it was drowned out by the roar of destruction.

My body jerked and twisted against the restraints, and the seatbelt dug deep into my shoulder, leaving a scorching line of pain that felt like it was slicing through flesh and bone. My fingers scrabbled, looking for something firm to grab onto. However, everything was happening too quickly, and the world was spinning out of control. Gravity twisted in on itself, tugging me in directions that made no sense, each lurch sending a new wave of sickness through my stomach.

The dashboard collapsed inward, folding like aluminum foil and groaning as it came closer. My eyes burned as the air became thick with smoke and chemical residue, and the stinging mist coated my throat and lungs, making each breath seem like inhaling fire.

Jenna's piercing, horrified shriek cut over the boom of crumbling metal and shattered glass. But her speech was almost instantly swallowed up by the unrelenting scream of the universe tearing itself apart.

The scraping of metal against asphalt was relentless, a

CHAPTER 21

grating grinding noise that seemed to go on forever. It wasn't simply a sound in the air; it crawled under my skin, vibrating through my bones, making me feel as if I were being torn apart alongside the car.

My heart raced in my ears, and the rhythm was wild and unpredictable, producing a desperate, fearful beat. Adrenaline rushed through my veins, hot and electric, yet I could do nothing. There's no way to stop the madness.

The automobile kept spinning and turning, pulling us deeper into the darkness.

And I couldn't stop it. I couldn't save her.

We were helpless to save each other.

The world had gone still. Too still. The kind of silence that doesn't feel natural, that feels like something is holding its breath. My ears rang, a high-pitched whine that buzzed in the back of my skull, but beneath that... nothing. No sounds. No movement. Just... emptiness.

I turned, every nerve screaming at me not to look. But I had to.

"Jenna?" My voice was barely a whisper, a broken thing that barely crossed the space between us. But there was no answer—just that suffocating silence pressing down on me.

My head throbbed as I forced myself to look. And what I saw made my blood run ice-cold.

The passenger side was... gone. Or what was left of it barely resembled what it had been just minutes before. The entire side of the car had caved in, crushed like an aluminum can that had been stomped underfoot. Twisted metal, jagged shards of glass, and torn leather turned the space where Jenna had been, into a nightmare.

And the blood.

Dark red smeared across the pale leather of the seat, seeping into the cracks, spreading like ink spilled on paper. It was everywhere.

For a moment, my brain refused to process it. It had to be something else, right? Oil. Or... or maybe the Cherry Coke we'd spilled earlier. Yeah. That had to be it. But deep down, I knew. I knew. And that knowledge curdled in my stomach, making bile crawl up the back of my throat.

Jenna's seat was pushed inward at an impossible angle, crumpled and twisted until there was barely any space left where a person could be. The dashboard had collapsed, folding inward like a paper accordion, pressing into where her legs should've been. My mind painted images I didn't want to see—images of her pinned there, trapped, helpless.

I couldn't see her. Not really.

But I could see everything else.

Her phone lay face-down near the floor, the screen shattered but still flickering weakly, casting a faint blue glow over the wreckage. It blinked on and off, as if trying to cling to life—just like I was.

My hands shook as I reached for it, but I couldn't bring myself to pick it up. The weight of it—of everything—was too much. My chest tightened, my breaths coming too fast, too shallow.

"Jenna..."

Her name was a ghost in the silence, barely louder than the whisper of wind through the shattered glass. But no matter how many times I said it, there was no answer.

Just that awful, crushing silence.

And the horrible truth is settling in my bones.

She wasn't coming back.

CHAPTER 21

Not this time.

Through the haze—smoke, glass, blood, God-knows-what—I squinted, trying to find her. My head felt like it had been split open with a sledgehammer, and every nerve in my body screamed when I moved. But I didn't care. I had to see her. Had to know.

"Jenna?" My voice came out dry and cracked, like old paper. I barely recognized it. Hell, I barely recognized myself. The only sounds were the tick-tick-tick of the ruined engine trying to die and the distant wail of sirens, still too far away to matter.

And then—her voice. Thin. Fragile. But there. "Hey, B…"

It wasn't much, barely louder than a sigh, but it was her. And it cut through the wreckage and the smoke and the panic like a thread of gold in a coal mine. "You're gonna be okay," she whispered. "Just… just keep your eyes open for me, okay?"

B. She still called me that. Like we were still us. Like we were still in her room on a Friday night, talking about boys and sneaking sips of wine coolers and pretending we weren't scared of growing up. Like we weren't trapped inside a dying car on a nameless road with blood on the dash and glass in our hair.

But this wasn't comfort. Not really. There was something different in her voice now—soft, sure, but… distant. Tired. Like she was already somewhere else and just leaning back for one last goodbye. I heard it, even if I didn't want to. And it made my blood freeze in my veins.

I turned my head, biting back a groan. The pain was everywhere, like my whole body had been put through a meat grinder. But I had to see her.

And there she was.

Through the dust and the smoke and that weird golden

light that sometimes comes right before dawn—or maybe just before death—I saw her eyes. Still hers, still Jenna's. But different. The mischief was gone, snuffed out like a candle, and in its place was something else. Sadness. Serenity. Some kind of terrible knowing.

She was smiling. Or trying to. I could see the pain in it. The effort it took just to lift the corners of her mouth. Like even that was costing her.

Our eyes locked. And everything else—the noise, the stink, the sirens, the searing pain—it all went away. It was just us again.

And I knew. I knew.

She wasn't asking me to stay awake. Not really. She was saying goodbye. Her last gift.

Keep your eyes open for me.

And I would. For her, I would. Even if I didn't know how to live without her. Even if the thought of breathing without her next to me felt like a joke.

I blinked, and she was still there. Watching me. Holding on. But just barely.

The weight of her words hit me harder than the crash ever could. Not loud. Not dramatic. Just real. Like the moment when a storm breaks and everything's suddenly too quiet.

I wanted to move, to reach for her hand and hold it like that would be enough to keep her here. Keep her real. But I couldn't. My body wouldn't cooperate. It was like being pinned under the entire world.

"No, no, you're fine," I said, or tried to. It came out half a sob, half a lie. "They're coming, Jenna. The ambulance is coming. I can hear them."

And I could—those far-off sirens, howling like wolves at

CHAPTER 21

the edge of the woods. But they didn't sound like salvation. They sounded like a punchline. Like the universe laughing.

She was struggling to breathe. I could see it now. Every shallow pull of air was war. And that cracked hone on the floor—hers—was still flickering, painting her face in cold, stuttering blue light. It made her look... not peaceful, exactly. But still. Too still.

That wasn't her. That wasn't my Jenna. The girl who dragged me out of my comfort zone, who danced in parking lots and made up songs about gas station snacks. The girl who dared the world to try and bring her down.

"B," she whispered, barely audible. "You're stronger than you know. Hold on to that."

I wanted to scream. I wanted to shake her and shout, No. You don't get to talk like that. You don't get to say goodbye.

"Stop it," I choked. "Just stop. We're both getting out of here. You hear me? Both of us. Together."

But I knew. I already knew.

I saw it in her eyes. Not fear, not pain—but distance. Like she was already halfway gone, looking past me at something I couldn't see. Something was calling her name.

Her eyes—those stupid, beautiful eyes that had once dared me to steal a traffic cone for no reason at all—were dimming. Fading like old photographs left out in the sun. And I couldn't stop it. Couldn't hold her here with willpower and words. Couldn't bargain with whatever force had decided that she got the short straw and I didn't.

And there it was. The worst truth of all. I would be the one left behind. To explain. To remember. To carry this night around like a broken rib—hidden, sharp, always hurting.

I was going to live.

She wasn't.

And I hated it.

The truth hit me like a freight train—no warning, no mercy.

Watching the light drain from Jenna's eyes… it was like watching the sun blink out. One second, she was there. The next—just gone. And me? I was still breathing. That was the worst part. I was still breathing.

All this time, I'd clung to this stupid, fragile idea that I could've changed things. Maybe the crash wouldn't have happened. Maybe she'd still be here. Laughing. Living.

But here, reliving it in brutal high-def clarity, I saw it for what it was: a car spinning on asphalt, two kids caught in a moment too fast to fix, and the universe not caring about what was fair.

There was nothing I could've done.

That hit harder than any wreck. The breath went right out of me, like someone punched me in the lungs. The air felt thick, syrupy. My chest, a lead box. I was drowning on dry land.

The memories returned—not as fleeting echoes, but as permanent residents. The screech of tires, the shattering glass, her voice calling my name—a haunting goodbye.

And me—alive.

Still alive.

My fingers trembled as I reached out, knowing damn well there was nothing to reach for. Just smoke and ghosts. Her face flickered like an old film reel, frame by frame, beautiful and breaking.

"I'm sorry," I whispered, the words catching in my throat. "I'm so sorry."

It didn't feel like enough. Nothing ever did. You could

scream it into the void a thousand times, and it wouldn't bring her back. Wouldn't fix it.

The guilt? It was in my blood now. In the marrow. I'd worn it so long it had become part of my skin. A second skeleton. And now it creaked and groaned under the weight of that one impossible truth—she died and I didn't.

And that was the sentence I'd been living ever since.

The carnival world pulsed around me—lights flickering like dying stars, mirrors reflecting a girl I barely recognized. And still, somehow, the loneliest thing was knowing I'd keep waking up. I'd keep walking, keep breathing. And she wouldn't.

I was the one who got to remember.

And maybe that was the real punishment.

The memory slips through my fingers like wet sand—there one moment, then gone, just the ghost of an impression left behind. It dissolves like watercolor in the rain, the edges bleeding out, the colors smearing together until I'm left standing in the wreckage of not-quite-real and too true.

The smell of burnt rubber fades first. Thank God for that. Then the glass, the twisted metal, the white-hot flash of headlights. But her voice—Jenna's voice—sticks.

"Just keep your eyes open for me."

Still echoing, even now. Especially now. It hangs there in the stale carnival air like smoke that refuses to rise. A whisper made of razor blades.

My legs shake. Not like a leaf in the wind—no, more like a building that knows it's about to collapse. The funhouse lights twitch overhead, flickering with that busted-neon buzz, throwing jittery shadows across my hands. They're trembling. I don't even try to hide it. Why bother?

I can still feel the steering wheel pressing into my palms. The belt was digging into my chest like a warning I didn't take. But those things—they're fading. Drifting out of focus like the last scene in a dream. The kind you wake from gasping.

"Jenna," I breathe. Just her name, nothing else. But it lands like a brick in my throat. It tastes different now. Heavier. Honest. Like it belongs to someone who's finally stopped lying to herself.

All this time, I've been sprinting blindfolded through the dark, trying not to remember, trying harder not to feel. Guilt's a hell of a drug, and I've been mainlining it for years.

But I can't outrun her voice.

My lungs burn, screaming for air. The carnival pulses around me, warped and twitching like it's alive. I drop to my knees. Not dramatically. Just… because I can't stay standing anymore. My body's done pretending it's fine.

I reach out, thinking maybe I'll feel her. Some trace of her warmth, her presence. But there's nothing. Just air. Heavy, electric, empty.

And then it hits—really hits.

I couldn't have saved her. That's the knife in the chest. That's the part I never let myself say out loud. Not until now. Not until this moment when everything is stripped bare.

Some things are out of our hands. Some tragedies don't come with explanations or a villain to blame. She's gone. And I'm still here.

But that doesn't make me guilty. Just… alive.

The truth rushes in, fast and brutal. No filters. No safe distance. It shatters every lie I've told myself for years and leaves me raw and gasping.

And standing in the middle of this twisted funhouse—with

CHAPTER 21

its warped mirrors and pulsing lights—I finally see it all. Clear as broken glass in a beam of light.

  She's gone.

Chapter 22

The silence after the truth is deafening. It wraps around me, thick and suffocating, pressing in from all sides. For a breath—a heartbeat—I let it settle. Let myself exist in the wreckage of what I finally admitted. But grief isn't still. It doesn't sit quietly with you. It claws. It thrashes. And before I even realize it, I'm moving—feet pounding against the warped boards of the funhouse, running like I can outrun the truth that just gutted me. I feel as though I can surpass the ghosts that have suddenly appeared everywhere.

Every breath feels like fire, raw and scraping down my throat. My lungs scream for mercy, but I can't stop. Won't stop. The shadows here move like they've got a pulse, stretching across the walls in long, bony fingers. They reach for me. I swear, they reach.

"B, don't leave me..."

Jenna's voice, soft and thin, threads through the dark like a fishing line hooked straight through my spine.

"You need to stay..."

Cold. That's what her voice feels like. Ice sliding down my ribs. I want to scream, but I just run faster. My legs threaten to fold beneath me, and still I keep going. "Because if I stop, the memories will catch me, and I'll drown in them."

CHAPTER 22

The mirrors blur past, revealing a distorted version of me—mouth agape, eyes hollow, a silent scream frozen in glass. Her eyes are empty holes. Her face bends in ways skin shouldn't bend. She's laughing. Or screaming. I can't tell.

I round a corner—too sharp, almost lose my footing—and there it is. Another hallway. The hallway appears endless, empty, and familiar in an unsettling way. I spin, looking for another path, another choice. But they all look the same. No, not the same. Worse. It feels as though the walls are gradually enclosing us, all the while beaming with happiness.

"No, no, no," I gasp. It's barely a whisper. It's as if I'm praying for the house to hear me and grant me mercy. Stupid.

The whispers grow louder now. The voice no longer belongs to Jenna. Or maybe still Jenna. Or maybe all of them. Versions of her. Of me. Voices bounce off the cracked funhouse glass like rubber balls.

The shadows move again. Closer now. I can feel the chill of them, brushing the hairs on my arm, my neck. My heart thrashes against my ribs, a captive desperate for escape. It might succeed.

Then—slam. I hit a wall. No, a mirror. My palms slap against it, and it's cold. Not like glass should be, but something deeper. A kind of cold that remembers things.

My reflection stares back at me. She's scared. Twisted. Eyes wide, mouth open in a silent scream that might be mine. Might not.

And from behind me, that voice again. Closer now. Almost gentle.

"Stay with us, B... stay..."

And for one long, terrible second—I want to.

The whispers are at my heels now. Closer. Louder. Not

whispers anymore—screams with broken teeth, voices flayed raw. They bounce off the funhouse walls, doubling, tripling, becoming a twisted chorus that wraps around my head like barbed wire.

"You can't escape!"

"It's your fault she's gone," the voice hissed, each word a dagger to my conscience.

I run, lungs burning. A fleeting thought surfaces—Jenna's laugh, the warmth of her presence—but I push it aside. I can't afford to stop. I remember.

Her laugh, bright and wild, tumbling through the car like music on a summer night. Then the sudden silence. The color was draining from her face. "B—" she'd said. Just that. Nothing more. And then the world went black.

I squeeze my eyes shut. "No. Please." But the walls don't care, and neither do the voices.

They howl louder.

"You killed her!"

"You killed her!"

The guilt settles on me like a lead coat, dragging at my legs, turning my knees to jelly. The air thickens—like breathing soup through a straw—and I can feel the floor shifting underfoot, tilting like the world wants to throw me off.

I stumble again, hit the wall, smear a handprint across the glass. My reflection grins back at me—only it isn't me. Her eyes are black holes. Her mouth keeps moving with the chant.

"You killed her!"

Over and over. Over and over.

"I didn't mean to!" I scream, but it sounds like someone else's voice. Too high. Too broken.

The funhouse sways. The mirrors warp. The whispers curl

CHAPTER 22

around my ears like steam from a boiling kettle. Jenna's voice threads through the noise—just a whisper now, soft as ash.

"Keep your eyes open, B..."

But I don't know if it's her anymore. Or just guilt wearing her voice like a mask.

And still, the memories spin around me like knives in a blender—each one sharper, crueler, more precise. No escape. No pause. Just the truth, hot and heavy, pressing down from all sides.

God help me.

I'm not sure I can outrun it anymore.

Through the warped glass and choking dark, it appears—a glint of gold, like a coin tossed into the bottom of a whining well. A door. Real, or close enough. My breath hitches. It's the kind of sight that shouldn't exist here, in this funhouse hell of whispers and twisted reflections. But there it is, shining like salvation, like mercy wrapped in oak and firelight.

I lurch forward. "Almost there," I rasp, though I'm not sure if I'm saying it to myself or Jenna or the ghosts in the walls.

Behind me, the voices rise to a fever pitch, no longer content to whisper. Now they scream. Every step I take toward that door seems to provoke them, like rats scattering from the light. "You don't deserve it!" one howls. "She died and you ran!" screams another.

But I don't stop. Can't stop. My legs are jelly and fire, every tendon stretched thin, but that light—it's pulling me. It's everything the rest of this place isn't. Warm. Steady. Honest.

I stagger, my hand slamming into a mirror for balance. My reflection doesn't look like me anymore—eyes too wide, mouth open in some silent scream—but I don't linger. The mirror ripples at my touch, the surface shivering like it knows

I'm about to break free.

The closer I get, the more the door seems to breathe. I swear it breathes. It's golden trim pulses with a heartbeat of its own, patterns crawling and coiling across the wood like they're alive. Not welcoming exactly—but not malicious either. Just… watching. Waiting.

My feet drag, but I don't stop. The air hums around me now, thick with energy, heavy with meaning. This is it. This is the moment the maze ends, not with a scream, but with a choice.

A few more steps.

And then—god help me—I'll open it.

The doorknob jerks under my grip, slick with sweat and as cold as the breath of something dead. I twist harder, knuckles white, shoulder pressed into the frame. Nothing. Not even a creak. It's like the door was never meant to open in the first place—just another illusion, another trick.

"No, no, no—they can't catch me!" The words tumble from my mouth like a child's prayer, frantic and useless. They bounce off the funhouse walls, twisted in the mirrors until they no longer sound like me. The echoes answer back, not with sympathy, but with laughter.

Low at first. Then louder. Until it becomes a wall of sound that presses in from every side, like the house itself is laughing at me.

And I know those voices.

Not just strangers, not just figments. They were the voices of people I've loved, people I've lost. Jenna's giggle warped into something sharp. My mother's disappointed sigh, strung out into a chuckle. Even my laughter—bitter and cracked—joins the symphony.

CHAPTER 22

I slam my forehead against the door, the sharp bite of pain grounding me for a second, but not long enough. The carnival music starts up again, more twisted and haunting than before. Slower. Meaner. It slithers between the laughter like a snake in tall grass, coiling tighter and tighter around my throat. I can't breathe.

Movement flickers at the edge of my vision. They're coming.

Masked figures step out of the darkness like dancers hitting their mark on a stage no one wants tickets to. Their costumes shimmer with old glitter and new malice, all sequins and shadow. Their movements are too smooth, like joints unhinged from human limits. Masks leer and twitch, grinning one second, grimacing the next.

They're not rushing. They don't need to. I'm already cornered. Already broken.

The music and the laughter merge now, a single discordant wail that makes my teeth ache and my knees wobble. It's in my bones, that sound—like they've found the frequency of my fear and tuned themselves to it.

And the door?

Still won't open. Of course it won't. It's not here to save me. It's here to keep me in.

The laughter doesn't trail off. It snaps—gone in an instant, like someone slamming shut a door behind you in a house you didn't realize you'd entered.

And just like that, the silence sets in.

Not peaceful silence. Not the kind you get on Sunday mornings with coffee and birdsong. This one's thick, predatory. It hums under the skin like a coming migraine. The kind of quiet that listens back.

I go still. Not because I want to, but because something primal in me decides it's the only option. A chill snakes down the hallway, wraps itself around my ankles like smoke. My breath fogs the air, hanging there, suspended—as if even the cold isn't sure it wants to touch this moment.

The masked figures—dozens, maybe more—stop in unison. Their heads droop, their bodies twitch once, and then... they begin to melt. That's the only word for it. Like candle wax sloughing off a shape, pooling into something black and pulsing on the floor. Their forms blur together, a writhing, shapeless tide of velvet and bone-white porcelain.

And out of that mass... she comes.

No footsteps. No sound. Just sudden presence, like turning a corner and finding the moon waiting for you on the ground.

I stop breathing.

It's me. But not.

She's draped in what used to be my white coat—only now it's turned into something from a fever dream, stitched together with shadows and carnival silk, the seams embroidered in gold thread that twinkles like star dust dying out. The coat floats around her like it's underwater, caught in some current I can't see.

The mask she wears is carved, delicate, with a smile too wide, too permanent. The kind of smile you wear to funerals because people are watching. The kind of smile that doesn't quite reach the eyes.

And the eyes... they're mine. That's the worst part. Because it's not just resemblance—it's recognition. She's not some doppelganger conjured up by the carnival's twisted illusions.

She embodies the parts of me I've tried to forget—grief personified, guilt incarnate, self-loathing given form. And

CHAPTER 22

more. Something... else. Something that looks at me like I'm the one wearing the mask. Like she's the real one, and I've been pretending this whole time.

The rest of the shadows bow. Not dramatically. Just a slow lowering of heads, like they're offering tribute. Or surrender.

The Ringleader tilts her head, and I feel it in my bones—that same awful feeling I had when I first saw Jenna's empty seat. Like I'm about to understand something I'll never be able to un-know. Like this... is what I came here to find.

I try to move. To run, scram, breathe—anything. But I'm frozen. Caught in the web of my reflection. Because facing her isn't just looking at a darker version of myself.

It's realizing that she's been there all along. Waiting. Watching. Growing stronger every time I lied to myself about what happened.

And now, she's ready.

I don't move.

I want to reach out. Her hand is right there, steady and still, as if all I have to do is close the distance between us and I can finally rest. No more memories clawing at the edges of my sleep. No more waking up with a scream half-formed in my throat and no one beside me to hear it. No more dragging Jenna's ghost behind me like a second spine.

Just peace.

But there's something in her eyes—my eyes—that stops me. It's not comfort. Not really. It's hunger. That cold, unblinking kind that doesn't need to chase because it knows you'll come crawling eventually.

"I don't belong here," I whisper, though my voice trembles with doubt. The words feel weak, like I'm trying them on for size but haven't committed to wearing them yet.

The Ringleader tilts her head. The smile never changes.

"You came here on your own," she says, tone like velvet soaked in poison. "You built this place, brick by brick. Every guilty thought. Every unspoken regret. Every lie you told yourself to make it through the day."

And she's not wrong. That's the worst part. Every twisted hallway, every reflection that screamed instead of speaking—it's all mine. My shame. My silence. My grief, shaped into walls and mirrors and doors that don't open.

"I didn't know what else to do," I say. It comes out like a confession.

"You survived," she replies. "And that terrified you more than dying ever did."

I flinch. Because that hits too close. That's the wound I never wanted to look at directly—the fact that when I crawled out of the wreckage and heard they'd pulled Jenna out cold and lifeless, some part of me wanted to trade places. Some part of me still does.

The Ringleader steps closer. I don't back away.

"Let it go," she says, her hand still waiting. "Let her go."

But that's the thing. Jenna's already gone.

The person I'm holding onto—the guilt, the pain, the constant ache of not being enough—that's not her. That's me. That's what this thing feeds on. It wraps itself around the worst version of my grief and offers it back to me dressed up as absolution.

I stare at the hand, those perfect fingers, and suddenly it doesn't look like salvation anymore.

It looks like surrender.

"I'm tired," I whisper.

The Ringleader nods, like she understands.

CHAPTER 22

But then I shake my head. "No. Not tired enough to become you."

Her eyes flash—just for a second—and the mask twitches at the corners, as if the smile's cracking.

"You'll be back," she says, the words low and venomous.

"Maybe," I answer. "But not today."

And then I turn my back on her. My knees almost give out from the effort, but I take one step. Then another.

The air shifts. The shadows hiss.

But I keep walking.

The past is etched into me, unchangeable. But I can choose to step forward, carrying its lessons without being bound by its chains.

I stumble back, nearly losing my footing, the door at my spine like a lifeline. My pulse hammers so loud it drowns out everything else—the whispers, the music, the shadows crawling like insects along the walls. I see her hand still outstretched, patient as death. And for a second, I almost take it.

Then Jenna's real smile flashes behind my eyes. Not the grotesque carnival mimicry, not the half-decayed ghost begging me to stay. No, her. That sun-soaked laugh, that eye-roll when I said something stupid, that warmth that made you feel like maybe the world wasn't such a terrible place after all. That memory tears through the fog like a lightning bolt, searing and clean.

"No!" The scream rips out of me, hoarse and guttural. It echoes like a gunshot in the Funhouse air, bouncing off warped glass and twisted metal.

The masked figures recoil slightly—a subtle movement, but enough to signal a shift. That synchronized puppet show stutters, the illusion bending at the seams. For the first time, they flinch.

The Ringleader tilts her head, and the smile—my smile—flickers. Just once. Her coat flutters like a flag in some invisible wind, shadows crawling across it like spilled ink. "You can't escape what you are," she says, and it's still my voice—but thinner now. Wavering.

I slam my palm against the door behind me. The wood is solid. Real. And I cling to it like a drowning woman clings to the last rung of a broken ladder.

"This isn't what I am," I shout, my voice cracking like dry wood. "This is what I was afraid of becoming."

Her posture shifts. Just slightly. That mask with the eternal smile doesn't move, but something behind it... softens. Or maybe fractures.

"You're not me," I hiss. "You're what I let happen. The guilt. The silence. The running. You fed on it, didn't you?"

The air shivers.

"I'm not hiding anymore."

And suddenly, I'm moving. I don't know where the strength comes from. It isn't courage—not really. It's rage. Not just at her. At me. For every night I sat in the dark and let this thing take root. For every time I lied and said I was okay when I wasn't. Every time I remembered the crash, but told myself it didn't matter.

I step forward. One foot, then the other. It's like wading through cement, the air thick with resistance, but I do it anyway. The other masked figures fall away, melting into shadow, like they were never there at all.

It's just me now.

Me, and the worst version of myself.

CHAPTER 22

"I choose to remember—not to punish myself, but to honor her. I choose to live, carrying her memory as strength, not burden. I choose to leave, stepping into a future she would have wanted for me."

The Ringleader's mask twitches again. Just the slightest tremble at the corners of her lips. And then, beneath the porcelain facade, I see it.

Fear.

Not mine.

Hers.

Because I'm not afraid of her anymore.

Because she knows—finally—I'm the one walking away.

They come at me like a wave, a tsunami of limbs and teeth and screaming mouths. The masked figures, once content to lurk and leer from the edges, surge forward in a blur of shadow and madness. They're not separate anymore—just one writhing thing, all twisted legs and hungry hands, like guilt given form. And that sound—Jesus. The laughter's gone, replaced by something worse. Screaming. Not theirs. Mine. Dozens of versions of it, howling from every corner of the Funhouse, echoing through my ribcage.

Their masks boil and bubble like wax in a fire, melting into flashes of memories I never wanted to see again. There's Jenna, smiling—no, grimacing—no, dying. The hospital lights blink red and green like twisted Christmas ornaments. The beep-beep-beep of a flatline. Metal crunching. Glass shattering. My fault. My voice, screaming her name like a broken record stuck in hell's jukebox.

And then the Ringleader lifts her arms.

The world tilts.

The carnival... changes.

The lights don't twinkle anymore—they flicker like dying bulbs in a backroom freezer. Sickly yellow, then nothing. The walls squeeze inward. I swear I can hear them breathing. The mirrors start to ripple and blur, showing me versions of myself I don't recognize—eyes wide, mouth frozen in that silent "why?" over and over. Each reflection a cell. A lock. A sentence.

"You cannot escape what you've done," they chant. Together. One voice made of a thousand nightmares. "Stay. Become what you are. Let it in."

Their hands reach for me. Not flesh and bone. Smoke. Cold. Like frostbite creeping up your skin with fingers made of ash and regret. One brushes my cheek and I flinch, because with it comes another one—another flash—her voice, Jenna's soft and shaking: "You're gonna be okay, B..." And I can't breathe, can't think—

But then—

Then something digs in from deep inside me. A spark. A flicker. Not rage, not grief. Something harder. Something that doesn't break easily.

No.

I grit my teeth. Ball my fists. I feel my nails break skin, dig into the soft meat of my palms, and I welcome the pain. It hurts. Good. It means I'm here. It means I'm still fighting.

Because this—this place, these masks, these shadows—they aren't death.

They're me.

The worst parts of me, sure. The fear. The guilt. The coward who ran. But they're still just reflections. Mirrors. They don't own me.

I look up, breath ragged, heart a jackhammer behind my

CHAPTER 22

ribs.

And I whisper—maybe to them, maybe to Jenna, maybe to myself—

"Not this time."

Chapter 23

My knees give out, and I hit the floor hard, knees cracking against the cold like snapped twigs. There is pain—of course, there is pain—but it feels distant, as if it is happening to someone else. Not me. Not really. Pain no longer holds any significance for me.

I suck in air like I've been drowning. Maybe I have been. Every breath is fire. My lungs burn, my throat's raw, and it still feels like I can't get enough oxygen. Like the darkness is taking it for itself.

It swirls around me, thick and heavy, like smoke from a house fire. I can't see more than a few feet ahead, but it doesn't matter—what would I even look for? A way out? A reason to keep moving? Something in me already knows: there's nothing out there but more of this.

Sweat and tears cling to my skin like a second layer of grime. My hair's a wet mess stuck to my cheeks, knotted and sticky. I try to wipe it away, but my hands won't stop shaking—little tremors that move up my arms and into my chest like I'm falling apart from the inside out.

My heartbeat pounds like a relentless war drum—boom, boom, boom—echoing in my ears without respite. It drowns out everything else, even the carnival's twisted lullaby. The

CHAPTER 23

taste in my mouth is a combination of salt, dirt, and an unidentified bitterness.

A tidal wave of suppressed emotions—guilt, fear, grief—crashes over me, each one a weight I've carried silently, now demanding acknowledgement. Even as my arms tremble, trying to keep me upright, it feels like a battle I'm too tired to face.

My head drops. Chin to chest. I watch a tear hit the ground like it means something. Like the floor might care. More follow, sliding off my face and splattering on the warped boards beneath me. I'm unraveling one drop at a time.

The cold seeps through my clothes, sinking into my skin, settling deep within my bones, a chilling reminder of my isolation. It's everywhere now. And I can't move. I don't want to. What would be the point?

My fingers spread against the floor, searching for something—anything—real. Solid. But even that feels like it's slipping away. Like I'm dissolving into the dark.

And the worst part?

For a second, I think I'm okay with it.

Through the blur of tears, I see her shadow slither across the floor—long and hungry, swallowing the light like it's starving. The Ringleader. My shadow. My face.

It's me staring back through the mask, only… wrong. The eyes are too sharp. The mouth is too cruel. Like someone took my reflection and twisted it just far enough to make it monstrous.

"You're the reason she's dead," she says, and her voice—it isn't a voice. It's syrup and venom, sweet and sick all at once. It slides into my ears, sticky and slow, wrapping around my spine like a snake. "You don't deserve to wake up."

The words hit harder than fists. Every syllable lands in my chest like a hammer blow, cracking something that was barely holding together to begin with. My arms give out. My legs fold. And just like that, I'm down—face pressed to the cold floor, breath coming in shallow, wheezing gulps.

Because, deep down, I fear she's right—that my survival came at too great a cost.

Her laughter comes next, high and sharp, and it echoes off the mirrors in every direction like shrapnel. It bounces and ricochets, and suddenly the walls aren't walls anymore—they're funhouse glass, endless reflections of her. Of me. Of both. A thousand versions of my face, smirking like they know the punchline to a joke that ends with a body in a grave.

"No," I try to say, but the word's paper-thin, a whisper lost in the sound of my own unraveling. It doesn't even make a dent.

The ringleader crouches. Slow. Deliberate. Her mask inches from mine. And those eyes... my eyes... they're filled with something black and bottomless. I can't look away. I want to, but I can't.

"You killed her," she whispers, her breath icy against my cheek, each word a dagger of truth piercing my defenses. "Your best friend. Your Jenna. Dead because of you."

I squeeze my eyes shut like it'll help, but it doesn't. The words have already made it in, worming their way through the cracks. They bounce around inside my skull, louder with every pass, until they're screaming. And I believe them. That's the worst part—I believe them.

Because I was there. Because I lived. Because she didn't.

And now I'm on the floor, curled in on myself like a dying thing, shaking too hard to stand, too hollow to speak. Guilt manifests beside me, no longer an emotion but a shadowy companion. It's her. Me. Us. And it's winning.

It's always been winning.

My fingers claw at the gritty floor, dragging through dust and broken glass, desperate for something solid, something real. But all I come up with is pain—jagged edges digging into my skin, as if the world itself is trying to mark me. Fine. Let it.

The Ringleader's voice keeps circling in my head, soft as silk, sharp as a noose.

"You don't deserve to wake up."

And maybe she's right. Maybe this is where I belong—down on the floor, on my knees, begging a past I can't change to show me some kind of mercy that's never coming.

Jenna's laugh flickers through my mind, bright and weightless, like wind chimes in summer. That crooked grin, the one she'd flash when she knew she was being reckless just to get a rise out of me. The way she used to call me "B" like it was a secret nickname meant only for us.

And now? Just... silence. Gone.

My shoulders start to shake, and this time it's not from the cold. It's something deeper, something cracked wide open inside me. The tears come hot and fast, even as the cold creeps in, numbing my hands, my legs, the parts of me that used to feel like mine. But this chill—deep, bone-sucking cold—it feels deserved. Like a punishment carved from the inside out.

"Maybe I don't deserve to wake up," I murmur. And that thought—it doesn't just sit there. It settles, like dust on a coffin, soft and final.

What right do I have to go back? To live in a world that doesn't include her? The guilt blooms like a bruise across my chest, dark and spreading, and I press my fingers harder against the floor. Nails scraping, breaking. I want it to hurt. I need it to hurt. I want to carve the truth into this place with my bare hands, leave behind a record of my failure that screams I did this.

The shadows lean in close, folding around me like old, familiar arms. They don't threaten. Not anymore. They offer comfort now, a lullaby made of pain and permanence. Stay, they seem to say. Let it end here. Let the guilt swallow you whole.

And I'm tired. I'm so tired.

My body sinks lower, every inch of me sagging under the weight of a single, unrelenting truth: I let her down. And this? This carnival of ghosts and lies and mirrors?

Maybe it's not a punishment at all.

Maybe it's justice.

The air changes. Just like that.

Thicker now—like breathing through wet cotton. Heavy enough to crush ribs, squeeze lungs. Every inhale feels like dragging glass down my throat. I choke on nothing, gag on the weight of it. Something in the walls shifts—groans, moans—and it's not just sound. The Funhouse moves. Pulses like it's got a heartbeat. Like it's watching.

The floor hums beneath me, a low vibration that crawls up through my bones. My knees threaten to give again, but I dig my fingers into the boards, steadying myself like I'm hanging off the edge of a building.

Then come the mirrors.

They ripple like water, like heat rising off pavement on a hell-hot July day. But there's no heat here—only cold, creeping, and sharp. My reflection bleeds into hers—the

CHAPTER 23

Ringleader—and something unholy happens in the glass. My tear-streaked face and that grinning porcelain mask merge, twist, reform. Her mouth stretches across my cheeks. My eyes sink into her sockets. We become this... thing. A monster made of guilt and grief and the unbearable truth that we might not be different after all.

The lights flicker. Then die altogether, sputtering out like birthday candles in a wind tunnel. What's left behind are shadows. Long and thick and alive. They slither across the walls like oil slicks, reaching for me with slow, deliberate fingers. I don't even have the strength to pull away as they wrap around my wrists, my ankles, rooting me in place like I'm a weed and this place is the soil.

The distorted carnival tune falters, notes unraveling into dissonant echoes that mirror my unraveling sanity.

That cheerful, annoying, endless carnival tune—the one that's looped since I stepped into this nightmare—starts to stretch and decay. Notes drag like they're melting off a record that's warped and burning. It turns into something else entirely. Something wrong. Screams. Wails. A choir of agony that harmonizes perfectly with the one inside my skull.

And then the faces come.

They seep from the mirrors, ethereal forms drifting like mist from shattered glass, each bearing a familiar face—people I know, people I used to know, people I helped, people I failed. Some I barely recognize, others hit me like a punch to the gut. Old friends, patients, passing strangers. They all swirl together in the glass, a carousel of pity and disappointment.

But it's Jenna who rips me apart.

Not all at once. No, the Funhouse is smarter than that. It's cruel. It doles her out in pieces. A sliver of her smile. The curve of her brow. Her eyes. They flash in and out, just long enough to shatter me all over again. One tilt of her head and I'm gutted. One hint of her laugh and I'm bleeding.

The ghosts press closer.

Their faces multiply in the mirrors, twisting, warping, stacking on top of each other like a hall of horrors that never ends. They're starving. I can feel it. Drawn to the rot at the center of me. The shame. The guilt. The bottomless ache of being the one who lived. They're here to feed. And I'm the feast.

Every face is a judgment. Every reflection is a sentence. And I?

I'm already halfway to the gallows.

My heart's a jackhammer in my chest, hammering so hard I swear I can feel it cracking bone. The world twists around me like a melting oil painting—colors bleeding, floor bending, air thick as syrup. The Ringleader's laughter—my laughter, twisted and off-kilter—bounces from every surface. It's in the mirrors. In the air. In my skull.

I try to move. Really try. But my limbs? Dead weight. Like they've been poured full of cement. The floor's alive beneath me, gripping like it knows I don't belong anywhere else. Like it's claiming me.

"You're already part of us," the Ringleader coos, and it's my voice. Just wrong.

And the dark. It breathes. It pulses. Shadow-tentacles slither along my skin, cool and damp, like seaweed under black water. Everywhere they touch, I go numb—first, my fingers. Then the edges of my hands blur, fade—turning to glass, to fog, to nothing. I'm disappearing.

Piece by piece.

CHAPTER 23

Panic rises, a scream lodged in my throat, desperate for release. But I can't make it happen. Can't force the air through. If I stop now—if I let this thing take me—I'll be another echo in this freakshow. Another wax figure in the gallery of guilt.

And maybe that's what I deserve.

The thought hits hard. Makes my chest cave a little. Because maybe this place is justice. Maybe it's the exact penance I've been avoiding since that night. For Jenna. For surviving. For not stopping her. For living when she didn't.

The Ringleader leans in close. Too close. Her mask is a mirror, and behind it—my eyes. Cold. Knowing. Done.

"Accept it," she whispers. Almost tender. "Let go. Become what you were always meant to be."

And God help me, I almost do.

The air hums with the promise of it. An end to guilt. A memory end. Just drift. Just vanish. Peace in oblivion.

But somewhere in the mess of rot and sorrow, something flares. Small. Pathetic. But real.

A twitch in my hand. My own. Not hers. Not the Funhouse's.

Me.

A single spark of defiance, stubborn as hell and hotter than the dark wants it to be. My fingers twitch again—just enough to scrape against the floor. I feel it. The grit. The splinters. The realness of it.

And it anchors me.

I'm not gone. Not yet.

Tears blur my vision, and I don't even try to stop them. The choice looms in front of me, heavy as a gravestone: Give in… or get the hell up.

And even though the dark is swallowing me whole, even

though my limbs ache and my guilt is a chain around my throat—I choose.

Summoning the last vestiges of strength, I rise, determined to confront the darkness rather than succumb to it.

Chapter 24

The heartbeat of the carnival now echoes my own, erratic and pounding, akin to a massive beast pressing against my neck. The mirrors tremble on their rusted hooks, rattling with every pulse, like they're barely containing something monstrous just beneath the surface. Me, probably. Or what's left of me.

I stare at my reflection. A dozen versions of me splintered across the funhouse glass, each one twisted, warped, wrong. One's laughing with wide, empty eyes. Another's crying so hard it looks like she'll split in two. And then there's one... just staring. Hollow. Like something behind the eyes gave up a long time ago.

I press my hand to the nearest mirror. Cold. Slick. It vibrates faintly, almost like it's purring, and I get the sickening sense that it likes this—my despair, my fear. It hungers for more. The lights overhead flicker in and out, strobing shadows that crawl across the funhouse walls like spiders with too many legs.

Jenna's face flickers through the reflection—always just behind me, always half-turned, like she's about to say something. Her smile is soft, but it cuts deep. There is an overwhelming amount of kindness in her smile. Too many accusations. My chest tightens, breath hitching like I've been running for miles, lungs full of smoke and memory.

The mirrors start to bend inward. The room folds inward, not just visually but also physically. Corners shouldn't exist like this. The angles defy the laws of physics. It's geometry by way of nightmare. My reflections begin to pile up—stacking, multiplying, each new version of me worse than the last. One is screaming. One is bleeding. One is whispering something I can't quite hear but somehow know is true.

The music—if it can still be referred to as such—transforms into a shrill, grinding sound. Like a calliope being crushed under its weight. Notes stretch and tear, forming a jagged lullaby that coils in my ears and refuses to leave.

The whole place is breathing with me, or maybe through me. I can feel it—the Funhouse feeding off every ounce of guilt I've tried to bury. Every thought I attempt to suppress intensifies its power. The walls pulse. The mirrors twitch. The air thickens.

And still, Jenna's there, in every shard of glass. Her smile. Her voice. Her absence.

I can feel her memory pressing against the skin of this place like it wants in. Or maybe it's already inside and just waiting for me to admit it. The air crackles—static and heat, and something ancient. The carnival's holding its breath now, just like me, and we both know—

This isn't just a reflection anymore.

It's a reckoning.

The moment her voice cut through the noise—clear, steady, real—something in me cracked wide open.

Not broken. Cracked. It resembled the initial crack in a frozen lake, just prior to its thawing. It wasn't loud or dramatic. Just... honest. "It wasn't your fault." The four words were as simple as a breath. But they hit harder than any accusation ever had.

I froze, breath caught halfway between a sob and a prayer, and for the first time in what felt like years, the panic in my chest didn't rise. It stilled. The chaos finally settled like a shaken snow globe, sinking to the bottom. Her voice wasn't twisted or hollow or soaked in blood. It wasn't the version the carnival had tried to puppeteer, either. This voice was Jenna's. Really, Jenna's. The sun shone on her face, Jenna. Laughing-until-you-cry Jenna.

I whispered her name, almost afraid the sound of it would shatter the illusion. "Jenna?"

But she didn't fade. She didn't twist or contort. Her reflection shimmered into view in the mirror nearest me, not the mirror that had been showing me stretched mouths and sunken eyes and screams I couldn't stop. No, this one... it showed her. Whole. Alive. She smiled, as she always did when she saw me spiraling out of control and knew exactly how to pull me back.

"It wasn't your fault, B," she said again, and this time her voice curled around me like a blanket, heavy with warmth and memory and forgiveness I never thought I'd get to feel.

The tears came, but not the kind I'd grown used to—the bitter, shaking kind that left me empty. These tears were different. Softer. They came with breath, not after it. With release. They carried a feeling I had long forgotten.

Hope.

The air in the Funhouse shifted. It still looked the same— shadows crawling, lights flickering like dying stars—but it felt different. Lighter. The mirrors didn't leer anymore;

they waited. Silent. Still. The weight pressing on my chest loosened, like a fist unclenching after too long.

I reached out, fingers trembling, and pressed my hand to the glass. Her reflection didn't flinch. Didn't fade. She gazed back at me, her eyes brimming with vitality, mischief, and love. And for the first time, I didn't pull away from the contact. I leaned into it.

Some long-buried part of me, clenched in grief and guilt for far too long, began to believe her. It didn't happen instantly. Not completely. But enough.

Enough to take a breath that didn't hurt. Enough to feel the beginnings of something shift under all the wreckage.

Enough to keep going.

As Jenna's voice fades, the carnival's bright lights dissolve into darkness. A sudden lurch in my gut signals a shift, and the world around me reshapes. I'm back in the car, the familiar scent of Jenna's vanilla perfume filling my nose.

The radio plays soothing music—that tune we both loved, about summer nights and boundless possibilities. Jenna is laughing at something, and her eyes are shining with excitement as she looks at me. The streetlights created alternating patterns of light and shade across her face.

Then everything changes.

The approaching headlights slice through the darkness and appear unnaturally brilliant. Time appears to slow down, stretching each second into infinity. I see it all with heartbreaking clarity: Jenna's faltering smile, the rapid intake of breath, and the instant strain in my hands as I grip the steering wheel.

The automobile starts to swerve. My body jumps forward against the seatbelt as I attempt to adjust our path. The sound of the tires screeching on the asphalt penetrates the music with a sharp edge. The other car's horn sounds a long, desperate howl that mixes with our own shocked cries.

Then comes the impact.

Metal screams against metal, creating a terrifying grinding sound that drowns out everything else. Glass shatters, splashing us like lethal rain. The world rapidly spins, causing me to feel weightless for a terrifying minute before returning to reality.

The crunch of the collision echoes in my ears, each jolt and violent shake etching the moment into my memory. Jenna's scream cuts off abruptly as the passenger side takes the brunt of the impact, and the terrible silence that follows is worse than any sound I've ever heard.

Yes. This is the shift. The break in the storm. The part where the truth, ugly and overdue, rises up from the wreckage and demands to be seen.

And I see it now.

It doesn't come like a lightning strike—sudden, clean. No, it crawls in. Creeps. Through the fog of trauma and guilt, through the endless replays of "what if I had—" and "why didn't I—" and all the should-have-beens that have eaten away at me for years. It pushes past all of that, dragging something clearer behind it.

The other car.

I see it. Not just the blur of headlights or the crushing sound, but really see it. A tan sedan, paint chipped along the bumper, weaving like it's drunk on the night itself. And behind the wheel? A man. Middle-aged maybe. Hard to tell through the smeared glass and flickering light. But it's him. His head dips forward, jerks up again, nodding in that slow, syrupy way that screams not okay. And then I see the bottle.

And just like that, the narrative I've held only the one where I'm the villain of my own story, starts to crumble.

I watch as he jerks the wheel too hard, his car veering into our lane like it's being pulled by invisible hands. I react in a heartbeat, hands tight on the wheel, eyes wide but focused. I'm not reckless. I'm not careless. I'm trying. But what can you do when chaos barrels toward you with no warning and no room to run?

The tires scream, but now I know—those weren't ours. They were his. That noise, that sharp shriek I've heard in every nightmare? It wasn't a failure. It was a warning. It was the universe crying foul a second too late.

And the crash. It replays in horrifying clarity, but now with context. The sickening crunch of metal. The way our passenger side caves in like foil. His car slams into us, and I see him—his glazed eyes, his loose grip on the wheel, the damn bottle still clutched in his hand as if the laws of physics don't apply to him.

I had believed it was my fault, that I had let her down. But now, the truth stands stark against that belief.

But the truth is, I was never holding the wheel. Not really. None of us were.

We were just two girls in the wrong place at the wrong time, caught in someone else's nightmare. Someone else's mess. And for the first time since that night, I feel the weight of it begin to shift—not vanish, not disappear in some neat, clean epiphany—but move. Reposition. Make room for something else.

Because guilt doesn't just evaporate. But when you finally shine a light on it? It changes.

CHAPTER 24

And that's what this is. Not absolution. Not yet. But the start of something else.

The truth.

The truth hits like a freight train, and all the strength I thought I had just... gives. My knees slam into the floor, hard enough to bruise, but I barely feel it. Everything inside me caves at once, sobs tearing out of my chest like they've been waiting years for permission.

But these tears—they're different. Not the kind born of self-hatred or that gnawing guilt I've worn like a second skin. These are cleaner. Sharper. Like something infected finally lanced and draining.

"Oh God, Jenna..." My voice is a ragged whisper, thick with grief and something dangerously close to relief. I press a hand to my chest, right over that familiar ache—the one that's lived in my bones since the night everything changed. It's still there, but different now. Still raw, but honest. Real.

The air in the Funhouse shifts. Just slightly. That heavy, choking presence—the weight of a thousand ghosts and carnival illusions—eases enough to let me breathe like it matters. Like I'm supposed to.

I see her now—not the specter, not the twisted imitation this place kept throwing at me—but the real Jenna. Laughing with her whole body. Light in her eyes. That sharp, sideways smirk she'd flash before doing something reckless. I'd buried that version under layers of guilt so thick, I forgot she wasn't just the girl who died.

Tears drip off my chin. Hot. Relentless. Cleansing. Not because I'm guilty. But because I miss her.

"I miss you," I choke out, voice hitching on the words. And for the first time in years, I say it without shame, without apology. It's not a confession. It's just the truth.

The grief pours out of me in waves—years of it, maybe. It hurts like hell. But it's a clean hurt that means something's finally healing. Like ripping off a scab that was never going to close right. I cry harder, shoulders shaking, breath hitching, snot and spit and all the ugly things they don't show you in the movies. But I don't care.

This isn't falling apart. This is coming clean.

I push off the floor like I'm rising from a grave, muscles trembling but heart steady. The Ringleader still looms, tall and terrible in her cracked-glass elegance—but she's smaller now. I can see it. The shadows she commands, once thick as tar, now flicker like smoke caught in a dying breeze.

"You can't escape," she hisses, her voice fracturing. "Without your guilt, you're nothing."

And maybe once, I believed that. Maybe I let it build a home in my chest and rot the foundation of everything I used to be. But not anymore.

"You're wrong," I say. My voice doesn't shake this time. It's steady. Solid. Mine. "The guilt was never mine to keep. Not like this."

Something breaks in her—subtle at first. A twitch in her mask. A flicker of light beneath her robe. Her form blurs around the edges like she's made of steam, and I realize she's losing her grip. Not just on me, but on herself.

"You're nothing without your shame!" she shrieks, reaching for me with fingers that look more bone than flesh now. "Nothing without your pain!"

I take a step forward, and she flinches. That's when I see them—my own eyes behind her mask. Not as I am, but as I was: hollowed out by blame, starved on regret. That girl who looked in every mirror and saw only failure. But I'm not her anymore.

"I'm everything Jenna believed I could be," I say. "And I'm done carrying your chains."

The lights above us pulse once, twice—then dim. Not out of menace. But release. Like the carnival itself is exhaling, letting go with me.

The Ringleader falters. A jagged line splits that perpetual smirk in the middle of her mask. With all of its twisted shadows and embroidered illusions, her magnificent coat starts to fall apart, the threads turning to smoke and disappearing with the wind.

"I choose love," I whisper. "I choose to remember her that way."

She lets out a cry—more whimper than scream now—and stumbles backward. Her body fades like mist at sunrise, unraveling into nothing.

Just a shadow.

Just a story I don't have to believe anymore.

The carnival hums around me, a low, contented thrum like a machine finally winding down. The chaos isn't gone—not exactly—but it doesn't bare its teeth anymore. The mirrors still warp my reflection, stretching my features, bending the light… but the fear is gone. They're just glass now. Just memories caught mid-blink.

And I can move again. Not like before—clumsy and frantic, a rabbit dodging shadows—but easy. Each step feels lighter, less like sinking and more like floating. Like the air's thinner here. Like something's finally let go.

Somewhere up ahead, Jenna's voice calls out. Not the broken echo I'd been dragging behind me like a rusted chain, but her voice. Real. Solid. Still full of that soft mischief that always made me smile, even when I didn't want to. "This way, B," she says, and it feels like a hand in mine—warm, grounding. "Come on, slowpoke."

The maze winds on, but it doesn't twist in on itself the way it used to. It leads now. Like it always wanted to, but couldn't until I was ready. The shadows don't clutch at me anymore. They flicker across the walls like childhood memories—harmless, distant, already fading.

"I get it now," I murmur, my voice no longer shaking. It sounds like me again. Feels like me. The guilt still lingers in my chest, but it's different—dulled at the edges, reshaped into something that doesn't cut when I breathe. A scar instead of a wound.

I come to a fork in the path. A dozen ways to go, all veined with flickering light and shifting dark. But for once, I don't hesitate. I don't need to.

What happened that night—our night—will never leave me. It'll live in the folds of my memory, in the quiet moments when I hear her laugh and almost turn to answer. But it won't own me anymore. That's not what she'd want.

Above, the lights blink through the mist—reds, blues, soft gold—casting fractured rainbows on the funhouse floor. They look almost like stained glass.

"I'm ready," I say, louder this time, speaking it into the bones of the place. "You can let me go now."

And the carnival hears me.

The walls breathe. The mirrors are quiet. The music softens to a hum so gentle it could be the wind in the trees—or her, laughing, just out of sight.

I keep walking, not to escape, but to embrace what lies ahead.

CHAPTER 24

With each step, the weight of the past sheds, revealing a self reborn, ready to begin anew.

Chapter 25

The carnival blurs, its once-sharp edges dissolving into a haze, like a long-forgotten dream resurfacing. The air hums with warmth. Familiar. Almost kind.

Above, the lights pulse gently, no longer blinding. They cast halos across the funhouse floor—rainbows smeared like oil on water, blinking and blooming with each flicker. The shadows that used to chase me now hang back, swaying, like they're just waiting for the right beat to join the dance.

The masked performers are still here, gliding past in slow, hypnotic arcs. They move like ribbons in the wind, their costumes gleaming—half-real, half-something else. I can't tell if they're looking at me or right through me, but it doesn't feel hostile anymore. It feels… deliberate. Like they're showing me something if I'd just slow down long enough to see.

The music's changed too. No more broken carousel, no more notes that clawed at my teeth. Now it drips through the air like molasses. Sweet. Thick. Slow. It wraps itself around my chest, not constricting—but cradling, like someone pressing a warm hand just over my heart and saying, you can rest now.

The shadows still twitch at the corners of my vision, but they're gentler now. Not gone—no, they're never really gone—

but softer, like childhood ghosts that only mean to watch from the porch swing. They coil around the dancers like smoke, part of the rhythm, part of the show.

And the air is thick with it. Not dread. Something else. Like sugar and woodsmoke and the faintest trace of her perfume. Jenna's. The one she used to wear when we'd go driving with the windows down and no destination. The scent lingers just long enough to punch a hole through my chest before it's gone again.

It would be easy to stay here. So easy. Let the music sink into my bones, let the lights blur my edges, let the shadows tuck me in like an old friend pulling up the covers.

Everything here whispers stay.

But something in me still remembers. Still aches. Still resists the lull.

As the masked creatures approach, they glide rather than walk, as if their feet never truly touch the ground. They glide elegantly and uncannily in unison, with an elegance that defies physics. With their arms rising slowly in sync and glistening like starlight woven into silk, they make a perfect circle around me. There's a rhythm to it, pulsing just beneath the skin of the world. I can feel it in my chest. My ribs. My teeth.

"Stay here," they whisper, voices layering like wind through trees. "Forget everything. Be with us."

The words slide into me, comforting and familiar. Their tone isn't commanding—it's coaxing. Each syllable smooths down the jagged edges inside me that I've carried for years—maybe decades. Their voices settle into the hollows of my bones, speaking directly to the part of me that's so tired.

"Let go," one of them murmurs, and its mask shifts—just a tilt of the head, a trick of the light—but suddenly it's smiling.

A smile so calm it borders on divine. "There is no pain here. No guilt. Only peace."

And God, it sounds good.

The tightness in my shoulders unwinds, thread by thread. My hands hang loosely at my sides. The fight in me—the scream, the sorrow, the ache—it dims. Just a bit. Like someone turning down the volume on a radio that's been blaring for years.

Overhead lights blur into soft halos, casting amber and violet hues across the masks. I don't know how long I've been standing here. Time's gone soft around the edges, like an old photograph left in the sun.

"Join our eternal dance," a higher, sweeter voice says. "Let the memories slip into dreams."

They extend their hands. Elegant fingers that don't seem real. They invite without coercion, shimmering with that same unattainable brilliance. Like the heat shimmering over asphalt on a summer road, every action causes a ripple to travel through the atmosphere. And I sway. Not out of choice, not entirely—it's like my body remembers a dance I never learned.

The guilt that once clung to me, suffocating and relentless, begins to loosen its grip. A tentative breath fills my lungs—unfamiliar, yet liberating. Their promise isn't just tempting. It's seductive.

Forget.

Let go.

Be still.

Their masks are all smiling now. And something inside me, something deep and weary, leans forward.

But still... somewhere in the distant corner of my mind,

CHAPTER 25

beneath the song and the lights and the velvet-soft lies... something twitches. A spark. A voice. Faint, but not gone.

But just as my knees start to soften—just as I start to sink into their rhythm, ready to slip into that wonderful, honey-thick silence—I hear something.

Not a voice, exactly.

More like a noise.

A hitch in the music.

A slight stutter in the music, similar to a vinyl record skipping a groove. Only once. Barely noticeable. But it slices through the fog as a knife does silk.

I blink.

The masked dancers continue to move in perfect synchronization, their bodies a swirl of color and grace. But now— now that I'm looking, really looking—I notice something off.

My breath hitches.

The sweet air that once tasted like cotton candy and warm summer nights now sticks in my throat like syrup gone rancid. The lights overhead flicker—not softly this time, but in jagged, epileptic bursts. The music falters again. And this time, the skip is longer.

And beneath the melody?

Laughter.

Just a whisper of it. Low and feral. Hidden under the notes like a splinter under skin.

My gaze drifts to the nearest masked figure. They're still swaying, still beckoning—but their hand... it twitches. Once. Twice. A staccato, broken rhythm. And when I look into the face beneath that porcelain mask, I see it.

My own eyes. Glassy. Hollow. Smiling too widely.

A cold shiver slices down my spine.

This isn't peace. It's sedation. This isn't safety—it's erasure.

I take a step back, heart pounding now. The dancers falter in their rhythm, just slightly—but enough. Their arms still extend, hands still offered. But the masks... they've changed. The smiles are too sharp. The teeth are too many.

I look down and realize—my feet are sinking.

The floor beneath me has softened into a dark, viscous ooze. It clings to my ankles like tar, slow but insistent, pulling me downward, inch by inch.

"Stay with us," the masked figures whisper, and now their voices sound less like lullabies and more like buzzing insects. Too sweet. Too close.

I wrench one foot free with a wet squelch, panic flaring like wildfire through my chest. The spell is breaking. The dream is cracking at the edges. And I don't want to see what's behind it.

Not anymore.

Not now that I know what it costs.

The masked figures part like a curtain, moving with eerie grace, and suddenly—I'm not in the Funhouse anymore. I'm back at the cafe. Our cafe. The little place with chipped mugs and that god-awful squeaky ceiling fan, the one that always threatened to fall but never did.

Sunlight pours through the windows like honey, thick and bright. I can smell real coffee—rich and bitter, just the way Jenna enjoyed it. And there she is, sitting across from me, laughing her head off. That laugh. It bubbles up from deep in her chest and spills out like it has a mind of its own, full of light and life and something so heartbreaking that my throat tightens just hearing it.

"Remember this?" one of the masked voices whispers, slick

as oil in my ear.

I do.

It's the afternoon before my big presentation—the first one where I had to pretend like I belonged in a room full of people with sharper suits and louder voices. I was shaking like a leaf, barely keeping it together. And Jenna? She sat there like I was already a CEO, fingers curled around her mug, telling me I was going to knock 'em dead. Her confidence in me felt like armor that day. And sitting here now, it wraps around me all over again.

Another swirl, another memory. We're dancing in our pajamas during finals week, drunk on no sleep and too much caffeine. Then it's midnight again, our headlights cutting through an empty road, no destination in mind, just her hand reaching out to change the song and her voice singing off-key. Then the mall, where we tried on the ugliest dresses we could find just to see who could make the other laugh harder.

And I'm back in the middle of it. Inside it. Not watching these moments, not remembering them—living them. Her scent, her warmth, the sound of her voice curling around my name. It's all so real, it makes my chest ache.

"You could have this forever," the masked figures say, like sirens promising safety to a drowning man. "Each happy moment is kept like amber. No pain. Not to worry. Only joy, endless and pure."

And I want it. I do. To stay here, to feel her hand in mine again, to lose myself in the sweet lull of what was.

Because these aren't just memories—they're anchors. Lifelines back to a time when the world still made sense, when Jenna was still alive, and I was still whole.

But somewhere in the back of my mind, a small, stubborn

voice whispers: It's not real.

And if I stay—if I give in—I may never leave.

I suck in a breath so deep it hurts, like trying to fill lungs that forgot how to work. The air tastes sweet, but I take it anyway. One last drag from the dream before I let it go.

My hands curl into fists, nails biting into my palms until I feel the sting. Good. It grounds me. Reminds me I'm still flesh and blood, still breathing, still me.

The masked figures spin and sway around me, their movements losing fluidity—now jerky, desperate, as if the illusion is unraveling. Their rhythm falters. Their masks twitch like they can sense what's coming—and they don't like it. I hear the whispers still, but they're fading, like voices from a dream you forget the second you open your eyes.

I square my shoulders. My voice is steady, resolute—a sound I haven't heard from myself in a long time.

"No."

They freeze. Or maybe it just feels that way.

"I choose to remember," I say. "All of it."

The carnival reacts like a kicked animal. Lights that once shimmered like stars now flicker like busted bulbs. The colors drain from the walls, bleeding into each other until they look like smeared greasepaint on the side of a clown's face. The illusion cracks. It's still pretty, sure—but not magical. Just smoke and mirrors, ancient tricks with disintegrating edges.

The masked performers stumble in their dance, their motions jerky. Their masks contort, not in terror, but in something near to frustration. Disbelief, perhaps. Like they can't figure out how I slipped through their fingers.

But they don't matter anymore.

I can feel it—something glowing in the center of my chest,

low and hot like an ember that refused to go out. The truth. Ugly. Painful. Real. And that makes it holy.

I lift my chin. Let them glare. Let them beg. I've seen behind the curtain, and there's no going back now. Jenna deserves better than my denial. I deserve better.

"I won't hide in this lie," I say. "Not for you. Not for anyone."

Their arms reach for me, slow and grasping, but I've already turned away. And I swear, as I walk toward whatever waits on the other side of this nightmare, I feel the carnival shrink behind me. Like it knows it's lost. Like it's retreating into the shadows where it belongs.

And me? I keep walking. Into the dark, sure—but not alone.

Chapter 26

The carnival's madness melts around me, all the twisted lights and warbled calliope songs draining into silence so pure it makes my ears ring. A hush that feels… reverent. Like the kind of quiet you get in old churches, just before something holy happens.

And then I see her.

Jenna.

She stood in the mist as if she had never left, as if she had just stepped out for a moment and returned with iced coffees and a sardonic remark about the barista's man bun.

She's so vivid it hurts. She wears that thrifted band tee with faded tour dates and a cigarette hole near the hem—'character,' she used to call it. She's wearing it like she always did, sleeves rolled tight around her shoulders, paired with those busted jeans that were never trendy, just honest. Torn up from actual use. Dirt. Trees. Life.

Her hair's loose, auburn waves catching some light I can't see, moving like it's caught in a breeze that doesn't exist. And those eyes… Jesus. Those eyes lock onto mine, and I feel the ground shift beneath me. They're the same eyes that used to wink at me across classrooms, that lit up when she laughed so hard she snorted. Mischievous. Bright. Alive. None of the weight, none of the blame. Just her.

I almost forgot how to breathe.

She doesn't say anything. Just stands there, hands relaxed at her sides, like she's been waiting for me to catch up. Like she knew I'd get here eventually. And I want to run to her, to throw my arms around her and feel that rib-cracking hug she always gave when I needed it most. I want to ask her all the things I never got the chance to say. I want to apologize and scream and laugh and cry into her shoulder like I used to.

But I don't move. Can't. Because I know that this isn't a second chance. This isn't a resurrection. This is grace.

She's not broken. Not bleeding. Not twisted into a symbol of my guilt. This isn't the Jenna who haunted me in the corners of every mirror. This is my Jenna. Whole. Unburdened. And for the first time in what feels like forever, my memories let me see her that way.

I feel my throat tighten, tears carving hot paths down my cheeks. Not from pain. Not this time. These are tears for everything we had. Everything we were. And for the peace I see in her face. The peace I can finally let live in mine.

She stands there, like a lighthouse in the fog, and for the first time, I don't feel lost.

"You have to go, B."

Her voice hits me like a punch to the gut—that voice. Not the hollow mockery the carnival's thrown at me like knives, not the broken echo that's haunted my dreams. No, this one's warm. Soft. Familiar in the way old hoodies and worn-out playlists are familiar. The kind of voice that used to talk me down from panic attacks or cheer me up after yet another spectacularly bad Tinder date.

I sway on my feet. My knees damn near buckle. I have to lock them in place, clenched so tight it hurts, just to stay upright. My mouth goes dry, and for a second, all I can do is stare. Because it can't be real. I've heard her voice a hundred times in this place, each one laced with knives, designed to carve me up and serve me back my own guilt on a silver platter.

"Jenna?" My voice cracks on her name like it's a spell I'm not sure I'm allowed to say out loud. I want to reach for her—God, do I want to—but I don't. I'm terrified she'll disappear, dissolve into mist like everything else in this twisted funhouse of mirrors and misery.

She smiles.

Not the creepy, too-wide grin the Ringleader wore, or the sneering mockery the ghosts in this place wore like masks. No. This is her. The crooked, lopsided smile that always came right before she said something smart as hell disguised as a joke.

"Remember when we turned your hair purple during sophomore year? That disaster was unforgettable," she says, and just like that, I laugh. Honest-to-God laugh. It bubbles up from somewhere deep, catching me off guard and sounding foreign in my own throat.

Jesus. That night. Us, hunched over the dorm sink at two in the morning, trying to scrub Barney-the-Dinosaur dye out of my scalp while whispering Shh! between fits of hysterical giggles. It was stupid and messy and perfect.

But then her smile fades. That look settles into her eyes—the one she used to get when she was about to say something that mattered.

"But you can't stay here," she says.

I don't want to hear that. My chest tightens. That ache,

sharp and deep, like something's cracking open inside me. After all this—after everything I've crawled through, bled through, broken through—now she's telling me to go?

"I just found you again," I say, and it comes out choked. Weak. Like a kid begging for five more minutes of sleep before school.

She steps closer, not quite touching me, but close enough that I can smell the faint trace of her perfume—the same one she wore for years, the one she swore made her smell like "summer and sass." Her eyes are locked on mine, and they shine with something fierce and true.

"You never lost me," she says, low and steady. "I've been with you this whole time. But not like this, B. Not in this place. You've got to go back."

I swallow hard, the lump in my throat thick as grief. I nod because I know she's right.

I know.

But that doesn't make it any easier.

The truth hits me hard, making me stagger as my legs momentarily forget their purpose. Jenna—my Jenna—is standing there, clear as day. But the weight of what that really means crashes down on me like a falling house.

She's gone.

Really gone.

"No..." The word barely makes it past my lips, like it's trying not to exist. "Please, I can't—"

But I don't get the rest out, because the dam breaks. The tears come fast and brutal, the kind that don't ask permission. They rip their way out of me, each one dredging up a year's worth of everything I buried under work, under distraction, under the thousand tiny lies I told myself just to stay upright.

My knees buckle. I hit the ground hard, no grace to it, just the raw collapse of someone who's been holding too much for too long. I fold into myself like a paper doll, arms locked around my chest like I can physically hold the pieces together. But they're coming apart anyway.

And it hurts. God, it hurts.

"I miss you," I gasp, and it sounds pathetic and broken, but it's the truth. "I miss you so damn much."

The words feel like they're being scraped out of my ribs with a dull knife. I lift my head, barely, just enough to see her through the blur of tears. She's not crying. She's just… there. Calm. Still. The way she used to be when I was falling apart, and she was the only thing holding me together.

"Every day," I whisper. "I wake up, and for half a second, I think you're still here. And then it hits me again, and it's like dying all over."

The guilt—godawful guilt—starts to ease. Just a little. Like a fist unclenching inside my chest. I've held onto it for so long, gripped it so tight, I thought it was the only thing connecting me to her. But now I get it. That's not what she would've wanted. That's not who we were.

"I thought if I punished myself enough," I say, voice wrecked, "if I carried it long enough, maybe it'd mean something. Maybe it'd fix something."

But it doesn't. It never has.

I wipe at my face, but the tears keep coming. "You're gone, aren't you?" I whisper. "Really gone. And no matter how much I hurt, how much I grieve… it's not gonna bring you back."

And the truth of that—it lands like a final note in a sad song. Quiet. Heavy. Unavoidable.

CHAPTER 26

But also... honest.

Through the blur of my tears, something shifts.

A glow begins to bleed out from Jenna—not blinding, not dramatic. Just soft. Warm. Like the kind of sunlight that slants through bedroom curtains on a lazy summer afternoon. The kind we used to chase barefoot through fields, lying on our backs in the grass and making up stories about clouds that looked like dragons and dogs and, once, a burrito (her idea, not mine).

The light reaches for me. Not with force, but with comfort. A thousand invisible arms wrapping around my shoulders, the way she used to when I'd had a hell of a day and didn't want to talk about it. Just her arms. Just her presence. That was always enough.

And then she smiles.

God, that smile. The same one that could pull me back from any edge. It's all there in her face: the dumb inside jokes, the sleepover confessions, the road trip karaoke disasters. Every bit of who we were flickers in that expression like a candle catching its second wind.

My chest cracks open.

Because I know what's coming.

This is goodbye. But not like before. Not like the crash. Not like the hollow days and the screaming nights that came after. This is something else. Something softer. This is goodbye wrapped in love, not trauma.

"I love you," she says. Just like that. No drama, no trembling voice. Just the truth. Clean and whole.

And then—those words. Simple. Sharp.

"Now wake up."

They hit like a wrecking ball. But they land like a lullaby.

There's weight in them—every stupid dance in her apartment, every coffee-fueled pep talk, every quiet moment we never knew to treasure until we ran out of time. It's all in there.

The light around her grows, swallowing the shadows, peeling back the layers of grief and self-blame I'd wrapped around myself like armor. But here's the thing: that armor was never protection. It was a prison. And she's breaking the lock.

This—this—is her final act of love.

Not a haunting. Not a warning. Just a reminder. That I don't have to carry the guilt to keep her memory alive. That what we had wasn't built on pain. It was built on us.

And even now, in this in-between place, it still is.

The world starts to shatter.

Not all at once, no—that would be a mercy. It comes apart the way glass spiderwebs under pressure, little by little, groaning before the snap. At first, I think it's just my eyes. A trick of tears, maybe. But then I feel it in my spine. In my teeth.

A low vibration hums up from the ground like a warning, and I know that this place, this dream, this ghost carnival I've bled in, broken in, healed in… it's collapsing.

"Jenna?" I reach out, but my fingers close on air. My stomach flips, a hot jolt of panic crawling up the back of my neck. The floor rolls under me like it's suddenly made of water, like I've been dropped onto the deck of a ship that's forgotten how to float.

Then—crack—like a bone snapping clean. The air screams. The sky above us splits open, and reality starts to leak in around the edges.

A hospital room. Monitors. Beeping. Sterile light. It

punches through the dream like headlights through fog.

The ground bucks again, and I hit the floor hard, palms scraping against the wood—or whatever this place is pretending to be now. My ears ring. The carousel music, once cheery and warped, stretches out like something dying slowly. The laughter that's haunted me since I got here? Gone. Carried off on the wind like it was never mine to begin with.

Everything is falling apart.

And in the center of it—her.

Jenna stands like the world isn't cracking wide open around her. Calm. Steady. Glowing a little now, as if the light knows better than to desert her. Her hair whips around her face, caught in the vortex of this unraveling place, but she doesn't move. Doesn't even blink.

I drag myself toward her, the floor pulsing beneath my hands like a dying heart.

"Jenna, please!" My voice breaks somewhere between my throat and my chest. "I'm not ready!"

She just looks at me. And in that look, everything. Love. Sadness. Forgiveness.

And the terrible truth.

You never are.

Everything's breaking now.

I find Jenna in the middle of the wreckage—solid, still. She's the only thing that isn't crumbling.

"It's okay, B."

She smiles. God, that smile. Like she's just proud of me for making it this far. Like she never doubted I would.

"You're ready now."

My throat tightens. Not from the smoke or the dust or the stink of endings, but because I know what she's saying. I know. I just don't want to hear it. My heart's beating so loud I can barely stand it, thudding like a fist against a locked door.

"I'm scared," I whisper, and the words taste like blood and salt and every sleepless night I've spent haunted by the weight of her absence.

But then she looks at me—really looks—and I feel it. That warmth. That solid, real love she always had for me. The kind that didn't waver, not even when I broke down. It wraps around my ribs like a brace, holds me up when everything else is trying to drag me under.

She tilts her head, and her eyes shine with something that feels like peace.

"You've got this."

Three little words. Simple. But they hit like thunder.

The ground splits beneath us, but I stay on my feet. My legs are shaking, sure, but I don't fall. I can't. Not now. There's light bleeding in from everywhere, bright and gold and honest—not the fake, flickering crap the carnival offered, but something real. The kind of light you only see at sunrise, when the world is still quiet and full of promise.

Between the shattering mirrors and falling sky, I feel it: the truth of what we were. What we still are. Not just memories, not just pain. Something deeper. Something that even death didn't kill.

Chapter 27

They're closing in now.

The masked ones—those grinning, shifting things—press closer, the fog thickens around their feet, sour and clinging. Their faces shimmer in and out of focus, grotesque caricatures one second, hollow-eyed husks the next. I don't know how many there are anymore. Ten? Twenty? A hundred? It doesn't matter. The walls, pulsing with a wet, meat-slick rhythm like the inside of a throat, are breathing.

"Join us," they whisper, and it's not one voice—it's all of them, speaking at once. Male, female, old, young, blending into one stomach-churning chorus that slithers into my ears and wraps around my spine.

I try to breathe, but the fog clings to me like it's alive. Cold and wet and greedy. It wraps around my ankles first, then creeps higher, a damp lace of ghost-hands pulling me under. The music is now a distorted, unrecognizable cacophony. The cheery carousel tune is stretched thin, warped into a razor-wire lullaby that saws at the inside of my skull. Every off-key note feels like it's being hammered into my temples.

Their masks—Jesus, those masks. Every time I blink, they change. One grins wide enough to split its face in two. Another frowns so hard it looks like its skin's been pulled down by fishhooks. They move like dancers underwater—fluid, unnatural, too smooth to be real. Shadows snake off their feet, dragging behind like spilled oil. They reach for me, and the shadows reach too, stretching toward my face, my chest, my heart.

I say no. Or try to.

It comes out as a gasp.

Like a breath caught in a throat that doesn't want to open.

They don't care.

They move closer, rustling like dead leaves blowing through an alley at midnight. Their robes or coats or whatever-the-hell-they-are brush the floorboards, and I feel it, feel it in my bones—like someone's thumping on the inside of my ribs, asking to come in.

Their eyes burn. Literally burn. Not with fire, but with something worse—something old. Starved. Like they've been watching me since the moment Jenna died, just waiting for me to hit bottom so they can drag me under.

The air gets thicker, the kind of thick that drowns you slowly. Every breath hurts. Every inhale tastes like rust and rot and the kind of cold that settles in you, not on you. Lights flash through the fog, sick colors—infected reds, bile-yellow greens, corpse-blues that remind me of lips left too long in the cold.

They're tightening the circle now.

Closing in.

Feeding on it.

The fear.

The memory.

Me.

I back up until I hit the wall—cold and pulsing like it's got a heartbeat. I can feel them through the floorboards now, every single step. Not heavy, but sure. Like they already know the end of this story, and they're just here to watch me realize it.

Their whispers are louder now.

A wet hiss of promises and threats.

A lullaby sung by monsters.

And the worst part?

Some small, cracked part of me almost wants to listen.

The first hand wraps around my arm, thin, cold, and dry as old rope left out in the frost. My skin goes electric with dread. I yank back on instinct, but it's too late.

Another hand claws at my shoulder. One more coils around my wrist. Then two, three, ten more emerge from the fog like worms from wet earth. They latch onto me—clutching, tugging, claiming.

Each touch burns like dry ice, not fire but the opposite—cold so sharp it screams. My body jerks against them, but they don't let go. They never let go.

"Stay with us," they whisper, and it's not one voice—it's a dozen, a hundred, all speaking in a harmony that has no soul. Like a hymn sung by corpses. "You're one of us now..."

Their faces close in. The masks hover just inches away, their frozen smiles twitching in the strobing light. That smell—Jesus, that smell. Like old popcorn soaked in rainwater. Like cotton candy left to rot in the sun. Sweetness gone bad. Nostalgia left too long in the back of the fridge.

I try to shake free. "Let go," I gasp. "Let me go."

But they tighten. Not hard—no broken bones, no bruises—just firm enough to say we're not finished yet.

And that's worse somehow. The way they cling like something that misses me. Like something that doesn't want to hurt me, just… keep me.

Their faces dance and twist with every pulse, not changing shape so much as revealing things they were trying to hide.

More hands. So many hands. Reaching from the fog, from the cracks in the floorboards, from the corners of the mirrors that shouldn't even be there. Pale fingers that stretch and grasp with the tenderness of lovers and the finality of graves.

The pressure mounts. They don't yank or shove—they hold. That's all. Like being ensnared by grief, its hold is relentless and suffocating. It's not violent, and that's what makes it worse. If they tore at me, I could scream. If they clawed, I could fight.

But they cling.

Like memories you don't want but can't let go of.

Their whispers rise, flooding my head like water in a sinking car.

"Stay… belong… you're one of us now…"

The words worm their way in, coiling around my spine, wrapping tight around the soft spots in my mind. I feel them rooting there, planting something.

And for one long, awful second… I almost believe them.

I break like a dam bursting after years of silent pressure. My throat erupts in a rough, jagged scream. No more faking, hiding, or whispering.

"Get the hell off me!"

Now my body twitches like a live wire, brimming with anger and instinct. I don't think—I react. My elbow drives back into something that gives with a sickening crunch, and one of the masked bastards stumbles away, clutching its face. Its mask hangs crooked, revealing the twitch of something too human—or not human enough—beneath.

CHAPTER 27

I twist violently, my shoulder straining as I break free from another grip. Fingers slip, nails drag across my skin, but I don't stop. Can't stop. My breath comes in heaving gasps, sharp enough to cut. Cold air floods into the spaces they've vacated, stinging like frostbite but making me feel alive for the first time in forever.

"I won't stay here!" I roar, and it echoes. Maybe the Funhouse itself hears me this time. Maybe it finally realizes I'm not its damn plaything anymore.

Another masked figure lunges, arms wide like a lover's embrace gone sour. I kick hard and feel something buckle. It doesn't scream, but the sound it makes is worse: a wheeze, like deflating lungs. It folds in on itself, vanishing into the fog with a hiss.

The whispers change—no longer seductive, no longer sure of themselves. They crack and falter like a scratched record, warbling through static. One voice sobs. Another shrieks. The spell is breaking. I'm breaking it.

Their perfect little circle becomes a mess. Hands still grab for me, but they're clumsy now, frantic. The elegance is gone. The control is gone. All that's left is desperation—and mine is stronger.

"Let. Me. GO!"

Each word lands like a hammer blow. I thrash, sweat stinging my eyes, chest burning like fire's been poured down my throat. Every muscle in my body screams, but I scream louder. They want to drown me in guilt, bury me in pretty lies wrapped in carnival lights?

Not today.

Their grip loosens. One mask hits the floor with a dull clatter, rolling to a stop at my feet. It's empty. Just hollow porcelain. No face behind it. No soul. Just an echo of everything I've tried to be for everyone else. Perfect. Quiet. Guilty.

I grind my heel into it and crush it beneath my boot.

Let them whisper. Let them hiss and cry and beg. I'm not their puppet anymore. I'm done dancing to their tune.

I'm getting out.

"It wasn't my fault."

The words spill from my lips like a secret I've been choking on for years. Not shouted. Not screamed. Just breathed—barely audible beneath the noise—the carnival's warped music, the whispers, the endless rustle of cloth and shadow and rot.

But something shifts.

Inside me, something unlocks. You know the sound—like a deadbolt that hasn't moved in a decade, finally giving way. Not smooth. Not clean. A grind, a snap. Real.

"It wasn't my fault." Again, louder. Stronger. And this time, it doesn't taste like an excuse. Doesn't sting like denial. No, now it tastes like steel. Sharp. Cold. True.

The warmth comes next. Like blood rushing back into frostbitten limbs, angry and alive. My heart pounds—not with fear, not this time—but with something new. Something forgotten. Will.

"IT WASN'T MY FAULT!"

That breaks them.

The masked things jerk back, like puppets pulled too hard on the strings. Their perfect, eerie synchronization shatters like dropped porcelain. Fingers lose their grip, shadows stutter, whispers falter mid-syllable. I breathe deep, and the air hurts, but it's mine again.

I plant my feet. Let them see me. Let them really see me.

CHAPTER 27

The lights overhead strobe in fits, red-green-yellow-pink, like a dying arcade machine having one last seizure. But I don't flinch. Not anymore. Their masks leer, their eyes still glow like dying coals, but now I can see it—they're hollow. Not monsters. Not demons. Just reflections of the worst parts of me. And I'm not feeding them anymore.

"I couldn't have stopped it," I say, and my voice doesn't waver. Doesn't crack. "I couldn't have known."

Every word is a hammer swung straight through the ribs of shame. Their hands slip away. Their heads tilt, confused. The whispers have gone thin, like wind through brittle leaves. All the venom's drained out.

My fists curl. My spine straightens like an iron rod's been welded down the center of it. The tears still come, but they don't weaken me now. They purify. Every drop a release, a letting-go of the poison I've carried.

"Jenna wouldn't blame me."

The Funhouse shakes. Not physically, but deeper than that. At the foundation. That line hits like thunder.

"She wouldn't," I say again, louder. "And I won't either."

And just like that, the air shifts. The masks look smaller now. Dimmer. Like someone turned down their brightness. Their arms hang limp at their sides. Their mouths open, but there's no sound anymore. Nothing to say.

Because I said it all.

I stare them down, every last flickering echo of fear, every specter made from guilt and memory and lies. And they wither.

I'm not their prisoner anymore.

Hell, maybe I never was.

And then—I see it.

Through the chaos of thrashing limbs and leering masks, past the smoke and flicker and god-awful music, there it is: a mirror. But not like the others. Not warped. Not cracked. Not showing a version of me with hollow eyes and blood on her hands. No. This one's clean. Pristine. Standing upright like it doesn't belong here at all. Like it refuses to.

And it pulls me in.

I don't mean physically. It doesn't glow or hum or beckon with some supernatural power. It just is. Silent. Steady. And in this house of madness, that's louder than any scream.

I stare into it.

What I see isn't pretty. My hair's a mess, sweat sticking to my face like spider silk. There's dirt on my cheeks, maybe blood too, and my clothes look like they've been through a war—and maybe they have. But it's the eyes that stop me cold.

They're mine.

Really mine. Not wide and wild with panic. Not deadened by guilt. They burn. With something sharp. Something alive. For the first time in years, I'm looking at a version of myself that isn't bowed under the weight of a thousand could-haves and should-haves. I'm standing straight. Chin up. A little battered, maybe, but unbroken.

The lights flicker above, and this time, they don't look sick. No green-tinged rot, no red smear of horror-film ambiance. Just light. Pure. And it hits the mirror like a blessing, cutting through the thick carnival air, slicing it open like a gutting knife.

I glance back at the masked things still clawing at me. And I see it.

They're fading.

Their grip on my reflection is weak, fingers slipping like

smoke. The mirror doesn't show them as monsters anymore—just shadows. Thin. Cowardly. Frail. Nothing more than the shape my fear used to take when it needed a face.

"I see you," I whisper.

My reflection says it with me. In sync. Fierce. Proud.

The mirror pulses—not with magic, not with mystery. With truth. And, it's more powerful than any illusion this nightmare ever threw at me. Because it's real. Real in the way pain is real. Real in the way healing is real. The kind of real you don't get from running, only from turning around and saying, okay, let's finish this.

My reflection lifts a hand. I lift mine too. We touch the glass together, palm to palm. And it's warm. Solid. Like I'm touching that strength I thought I lost. That I thought died with Jenna.

But it didn't. It was buried. Deep. And now?

Now I remember where I put it.

I reach for the mirror.

My fingers tremble—not from fear, not anymore, but from something deeper. Something like truth rising from the pit of my stomach and clawing its way out. My palm meets the glass. It's cold. Of course, it's cold. But it's also real. Solid. And in this place, that means everything.

The moment I touch it, the floor groans beneath me. A low rumble rolls through the Funhouse—deep and wide, like the earth itself is cracking open. Like a fault line splitting under the weight of every lie I've swallowed since that night. Thunder without lightning. Judgment without warning.

A single crack spiders out from beneath my palm, thin and sharp and fast. It races across the glass like it's alive, splitting my reflection in two. Then three. Then ten. My face fractures, and with it, the world begins to unmake itself.

The masked figures recoil—stumbling, stumbling, stumbling. Their grace collapses like scaffolding in a fire. Their whispers become screams, high-pitched and desperate, like air escaping a dying lung. The floor shakes harder now. Mirrors burst around us like champagne bottles at a wake. Glass flies. Confetti made of failure and memory. It bites at my cheeks, slices my sleeves open. I don't care.

The music wails—no longer a tune, not even noise. Just a stretched-out scream set to a demented rhythm. It coils around my skull and tries to settle behind my eyes, but I push it out. I push.

The Funhouse is falling apart.

Wood groans. Nails scream as they're torn from beams. Walls crumple like they were never real to begin with—just paper, painted over and lit with old bulbs to look like permanence. And the lights, God, the lights—they blink out one by one, dying like stars that were never meant to shine.

The masked figures twitch and shudder, and their movements are no longer smooth. Puppets with cut strings. Their masks are cracked down the middle. One falls to the floor, shattering like china and revealing nothing beneath. It's just black. Empty. Gone.

And me?

I'm standing in the middle of it all, arms trembling, lungs burning, eyes wide but clear. Because I see now. I know now. Everything that held me here—the guilt, the shame, the endless reliving of what I thought I'd done—is coming down with the walls. With the mirrors. With the lie.

The Funhouse collapses, vanishing like a fading memory.

And still, I don't run.

CHAPTER 27

Let it collapse. Let it all go to hell. I've carried the weight long enough.

Now I'm ready to leave it behind.

My legs are screaming. Quads on fire, calves trembling like wet string, but I keep going.

Each step feels like I'm stomping through cement, like the air itself is trying to hold me back. But I push harder. Because ahead, through the chaos, through the roar and panic and flickering lights, is the last mirror. The real one. The one that still shines. The one they don't want me to reach.

They're on me again, the masked ones, hands grabbing at whatever they can—my sleeves, my hair, the hem of my shirt. One of them hisses in my ear, cold breath sliding down the back of my neck like an icicle. "Stay," it pleads. Or maybe it commands. It's hard to tell anymore.

My shirt tears at the shoulder. I hear the fabric rip, feel cold air slap my skin. I don't stop. Not this time. They're like flies now—buzzing, swarming, useless. Desperate shadows, trying to hold on to something that's no longer theirs.

"It wasn't my fault," I grit out, the words cutting through the din like a knife. Each syllable is a hammer blow. With every repetition, they shrink back. I can feel their grip weaken. Like the lie's starting to rot at the roots.

One of them lunges. A last-ditch move. Its hand brushes my wrist—cold, brittle, more echo than flesh. I yank free. Another strobe of light flashes off the mirror and blinds me for a heartbeat, but I don't stop. I can't stop. Not when I'm this close.

The mirror pulses. That's the only word for it—it pulses, like a heartbeat, like it's alive. Or maybe I'm imagining it. But it feels right. Like the world on the other side is just waiting for me to punch through.

"I choose to live," I shout—roar—and I throw my whole body forward.

My hand slams into the mirror.

It doesn't break. Not like the others. This one doesn't need to shatter. This one opens.

Not like a door. Not like a window. More like a breath. A gasp. Like the world on the other side has just exhaled after holding it for far too long.

And everything—everything—starts to change.

The glass is cold. Not just chilly, not refrigerator-door cold, but grave-cold. Like touching the underside of death itself. It pulses under my palm, like it's alive—or dying.

And I shove.

Not gently. Not with hesitation. I shove, like I'm trying to push the entire world away from me.

The mirror gives. It ripples—like black water, like oil disturbed in a shallow grave—and everything shifts. Behind me, the screams of the masked freak show taper into a low, echoing moan. Not human. Not even an animal. Just wrong. But I don't turn around. Not this time.

"I'm not defined by this!" I shout it so hard my throat rips raw, the words barreling out of me like they've been waiting for years—maybe longer—to be said. They split the mirror like an axe to a windshield. The cracks race outward in glowing veins of light, slicing the carnival's reflection into jagged pieces.

It burns, but it's not pain. It's release. It's every heavy thing I've carried burning off in waves. I feel it rushing through me, this heat, this energy, this understanding. Like lightning pumped into my bloodstream. Like someone lit a fire under

CHAPTER 27

my soul and told it to run.

The mirror shatters.

Not like in movies—no slow motion, no gentle tinkle of glass. This is thunder. This is cathedral-crashing-to-the-ground kind of shatter. The shards explode outward in a storm of fire and light, and I move, leaping into the breach before the world can blink.

And just like that—like flipping a switch, like breathing after drowning—I'm out.

Weightless.

Spinning.

Free.

The carnival rips apart behind me in a howl of splintering wood and glass teeth, a thousand screams swallowed by white light. I don't look back. Don't need to. Whatever power it had over me, whatever grip it held, is gone. Unmade. Like it never was.

I'm not falling. I'm not flying. I'm just being. Suspended in this blinding, burning moment. And for the first time in too long, I know exactly who I am.

I'm not the guilt.

I'm not the crash.

I'm not the mask.

I'm me. And I'm still here.

The kaleidoscope of carnival lights shatters around me—colors bleeding into black like watercolors drowned in a thunderstorm. The masked figures are screaming, but it's distant now, like a bad memory trying to claw its way back into relevance. Their voices fade to a whisper. Then nothing. Their fingers slip off me like dead leaves in the wind, powerless now.

I stagger through the dark, legs trembling but moving, every step a defiance. Each breath I drag in tastes cleaner than the last—like I've finally broken the surface after being held underwater far too long. The weight of illusion, of guilt, of them, peels off me like wet fabric, heavy but no longer mine.

Glass twirls in the air—what's left of the mirror. Shards spin through the darkness, catching flickers of light before blinking out for good. With each fragment that disappears, I feel something leave me. A regret. A lie. A tether.

Silence swells around me, thick and calm. Not the heavy silence of dread, but the kind you get just before sunrise. The kind that waits, not stalks.

I lift my hand to my face, bracing for the slick chill of a mask. But all I find is skin, warm, damp with tears I didn't know I was crying. And not the sharp, ugly kind I've cried before. These tears are quiet. Hollowed out. Healing.

The darkness doesn't threaten now. It holds me, gentle and still, like a room emptied of ghosts. I close my eyes and just… breathe. In. Out. Each breath carries something away— another echo of the carnival, another chain I don't need.

When I open them again, the world is coming back to me.

No more neon nightmares. No more warped reflections. Just soft light seeping in around the edges, quiet and natural, like daybreak through a hospital window. Reality bleeding back in. Clean. Honest.

I straighten my spine. Feel the weight of my body. My breath. My heart. I'm here.

The whispers are gone now. Or maybe they're still there, but they can't touch me anymore.

I'm not a reflection.

I'm not what happened.

CHAPTER 27

I'm Brooke Sullivan. And I'm free.

My legs feel like they're made of rusted iron—heavy, stiff, reluctant to carry me forward—but I keep moving anyway, one unsteady step at a time. The night air hits my face like a splash of cold water, shocking in its purity after the suffocating stench of greasepaint and fear. My cheeks are wet, streaked with tears and sweat and maybe a little blood, and the breeze kisses them like something sacred. My heart still hammers, but the rhythm's different now—less like panic, more like... survival. Like living.

I glance back.

What's left of the Funhouse is barely standing, and it looks smaller now. Weaker. The thing that once felt like a monster crouched on my chest is just a sagging, rotting husk in the moonlight. Its garish reds and yellows have faded into washed-out pastels, like a clown costume left to rot in the rain. The mirrors—those awful mirrors—are scattered across the dirt in jagged pieces. They catch the moonlight and throw it back in broken slivers, not menacing anymore, just... quiet.

I ache everywhere. Muscles trembling, knees locking and unlocking like someone else's legs. But there's a strange lightness in my chest. Not weightless, not healed, but lighter. The guilt that once lived there like a snarling thing has changed shape. It's still part of me, but now it feels like scar tissue—something I survived. Something I earned.

A sound bubbles up from my throat—half sob, half laugh—and I let it come. It tears out of me like something wild, something primal, something real. My hands shake as I wipe my face, smearing tears and dirt across my skin, and it feels good. Grounding. Human.

I'm tired. Bone-deep, marrow-rotting tired. But beneath

it, there's something electric, like the air before a storm. Not fear. Not guilt. Something else. Something alive. I've done it. I walked into the belly of the beast and crawled my way out. Not clean. Not whole. But free.

Chapter 28

I stand before the exit, heart rattling like a coin in a tin can. Every inch of me hums with something I can't quite name—terror, maybe, or grief, or just the unbearable weight of almost. The door's right there, a breath away. All I have to do is reach for it. But God, it's not that simple, is it?

The air's turned thick, heavy with something old. Not dust, not rot, but memory. The carnival behind me isn't screaming anymore—it's whispering, soft and sticky, like it's trying to get under my skin one last time. The music plays on, stretched too thin. It's familiar. It's wrong.

The walls pulse around me—alive, maybe. Breathing. They throw shadows that twitch and curl like they've got something to say. I see the masks again in those shadows, just for a moment—those hollow eyes, those awful grins—but now they look like silhouettes of my own doubts, not monsters. Maybe they always were.

The lights flash in seizure-bursts, and with every blink, the room shifts—neon bleeding over rot, beauty covering up decay. It's like the carnival can't make up its mind whether it wants to seduce me or swallow me whole. I clench my fists to keep from shaking. The handle's right there, but my fingers won't move. Not yet.

Because I know the truth now.

The carnival's not just this place—it's everything I've carried. The guilt. The sleepless nights. The could-haves and the should-haves and the what-ifs. This whole twisted place is a mirror, and it's been showing me pieces of myself I didn't want to see. Still don't. But I see them now. And I can't look away.

A shadow slithers across the wall, stretching long and slow toward me like a dying thing. One last reach. One last pull.

I take a step forward anyway.

The air fights me, thick and unyielding, but I keep going. Wading through it like it's made of regret. My breath scrapes in my throat, and I'm crying again, though I didn't realize I'd started. Maybe it's grief. Maybe it's relief. Maybe both.

One step closer.

The carnival groans behind me—"No," it seems to say. "Stay. Stay here where it's safe and familiar. Stay broken, stay haunted, stay ours."

But I've lived with ghosts long enough. I'm done being haunted by what I couldn't change.

I reach for the handle again. This time, my fingers don't tremble.

Not even a little.

I freeze. Not because I want to, but because something primal inside me says: don't move. Like she's a predator, and I'm the weaker thing. But the worst part is—she's not. Not really. Because that thing standing there, that grotesque puppet in my clothes with my voice and my posture? She is me.

Or at least, the part of me I've never wanted to see in daylight.

CHAPTER 28

The Ringleader tilts her head slightly, and that carved smile catches the light just right—mocking, triumphant. Her coat flares as she steps forward, silent as a thought you don't want to have but can't shake. Her heels click against the floor like a metronome counting down to something I'm not ready for.

"Almost made it," she says, voice syrupy and sharp, like honey laced with glass. "But you forgot something, didn't you?"

She taps her temple with one gloved finger. "*Me.*"

I swallow hard. My throat's dry, and I suddenly remember what fear tastes like—metallic, sour, thick on the back of the tongue. I glance toward the door, that glowing promise of escape, but she shifts just enough to block it fully. Of course she does. Of course, she won't let me go without one last performance.

"You think breaking the mirror made it all go away?" she asks, her voice hardening. "That stepping into the light fixed you?"

I don't answer. I can't. Because she's not wrong, not entirely.

"You're still carrying it, Brooke," she says, and now her tone softens—not gentle, exactly, but low and dangerous, like a lullaby with a knife tucked inside. "You're still blaming yourself in the quiet moments. You still wonder if it should've been you. You still need me."

I hate how my body reacts—shoulders curling inward, stomach tightening, pulse skipping like a record that's been played too many times.

"No," I whisper, but my voice cracks. Weak. Like maybe even I don't believe it.

The Ringleader laughs. Low and satisfied. "You can't lie to me, sweetheart. I know the truth even when you don't say it out loud. I am the truth."

And that's when I get it. The terrible, beautiful truth of her existence.

She's not here to scare me.

She's here to see if I'll forgive *her*—or if I'll keep feeding her just enough guilt to keep her alive.

The Ringleader's voice slinks through the space between us like a wet rope, thick and cloying, wrapping around my throat. "If you go," she purrs, "you'll have to live with it. The pain. The guilt."

My stomach clenches. She doesn't yell. She doesn't need to. Her voice is calm, matter-of-fact, like she's just stating something obvious, like gravity or cancer. And maybe that's what worsens it. There's no menace, only certainty. My certainty.

I want to scream at the ringleader to shut up. I want to punch her plastic smile clean off her face. But I don't move. My hands shake. My chest tightens. And in the quiet space between one heartbeat and the next, the guilt creeps in again like it always does—slithering through the cracks, curling up beside my ribs like a loyal dog.

"You don't have to feel it anymore," she says, so sweet and soft it almost sounds kind. "Stay here. Where the pain can't touch you."

For a split second, I want to. I want to slip back into the numbness like a warm bath. I want to forget the funeral, the pitying looks, and the sympathy cards that still sit unopened in a shoebox under my bed. I want to lose myself in this place of mirrors and masks, where nothing hurts and everything is just a little too bright to be real.

But then—

CHAPTER 28

Then I see her.

Not the carnival's version of her, not the twisted thing that's haunted me all this time. *Her.* Jenna. In my head. Barefoot in my bedroom at eighteen, her feet tucked under her, flipping through a catalog of college dorm stuff and laughing at the price of twin XL sheets. Her hair's pulled up in that messy bun she always did when she was focused, and she looks at me like the future is a gift we already own.

My throat tightens. That memory—it hurts. But it's also mine. It's real. I refuse to exchange it for a false smile or a promise of forgetfulness.

I square my shoulders. My legs still shake, but I take a breath and let the air fill my lungs, cold and sharp and full of something new: defiance.

"No," I say, and it comes out low, gravelly. Not a scream. Not a battle cry. Just the truth.

"No," I say again, louder. "You don't get to have her. Not like that. Not anymore."

The Ringleader's smile falters—just for a second. But it's enough.

The moment hovers there, as tense as piano wire. And then, like a blade slipping out of a wound, the tension begins to unwind.

The Ringleader—my mirror, my monster—takes a half step back.

Just one. But it's enough.

Her mask cracks—not loudly, not with some grand shatter, but with a thin, hairline fracture that splits her smile right down the center. It distorts her perfect, twisted version of me. The cruelty in her expression falters, becomes unsure. Afraid, maybe. I can clearly see that she is no longer in control. I am.

The carnival around us seems to groan in response. The floor heaves once beneath my boots, but I don't stumble. Not this time. The lights flicker, frantic now, like a dying heartbeat trying to rally. The scent in the air—burned sugar, wet sawdust, decay—is fading.

"You don't get to decide who I am anymore," I say. My voice is calm. Quiet. But it carries. It slices right through the noise like a scalpel through silk.

I step past the last of the crumbling shadows. My hand reaches out, not with fear, not with hesitation, but with purpose. I touch the exit door and it swings open—not with resistance, not with drama. Just... opens. Like it was always waiting for me to be ready.

And now I am.

The Ringleader flinches. It's subtle, but I catch it. That mask she's worn so smugly—the one that looks too much like me for comfort—cracks just slightly at the corners of her mouth. Not enough to fall apart, not yet. But enough to show she's losing ground.

Her colors bleed out, leaching away like watercolor left out in the rain. The reds dim to rust, the gold tarnishes to dull brass. What once looked regal now looks cheap, threadbare, like a thrift store costume that only ever fooled me because I wanted to believe it was real.

Her eyes—my eyes—widen. And what I see in them is so achingly familiar it hurts: fear. The same fear that's had its fingers wrapped around my spine for years, whispering that maybe I did deserve this. That maybe I belonged in the dark.

But not anymore.

The carnival doesn't roar in protest. It sighs, like something old and tired giving up the ghost. The air lightens. The

CHAPTER 28

music—still warped, still off-key—slows to a lullaby tempo, as if even it knows this charade is over.

And the Ringleader? She's unraveling.

Her stance is off. Her limbs don't move with that graceful menace anymore. She takes a step back, and the floor doesn't seem to make room for her the way it used to. She's shrinking—not physically, but in presence. The mask slips just enough that it looks like it doesn't belong on her face anymore. Like it never did.

That costume she strutted around in—my costume, my guilt, sewn together with the threads of every moment I thought I failed Jenna—it hangs loose on her now. Like it's two sizes too big. Like it was never really hers to wear in the first place.

And me? I'm still standing. Heart pounding, knees shaking, but I'm here. I'm not running anymore. And she knows it.

Oh yeah, she knows it.

The Ringleader moves like smoke—slow and fluid, a stage magician wrapping up her final act. Her arm sweeps out in that overly grand way actors do when they know the show's over and they're just killing time before the curtain drops. It should've looked silly, maybe even sad. But there's a strange, solemn grace in it. A quiet surrender. Not pathetic. Poetic.

She steps aside.

And just like that, the light pours in—real light, not the buzzing neon sickness I've grown used to. This is the kind that breaks through clouds after a long, ugly storm. The kind that makes colors look honest again.

It floods the threshold, spilling onto the warped floor like gold syrup, thick and warm. It creeps toward me, slow but sure, washing over everything it touches. The walls stop twitching. The mirrors stop whispering. The shadows shrink away like they know they're not welcome in this part of the story.

I stand there for a second, blinking like I've never seen daylight. My body buzzes with leftover fear, but it doesn't run the show anymore. My feet start moving, slow at first—testing the weight of this new world—and then quicker, like they remember what forward feels like. Each step is a breath. A heartbeat. A page turned.

The Ringleader doesn't speak. Doesn't try to stop me. She just stands there at the edge of the gloom, half in shadow, half in light. Her costume looks like it's been through a fire—ash-colored, threadbare, barely holding itself together. And that mask? My face? It's not even eerie now. It's empty. Like a photograph of someone I used to be but don't recognize anymore.

She's not my captor anymore.

She's a relic.

And I'm not hers to keep.

I take a step toward the exit, slow and steady, like a man walking out of a dream he's been stuck in for far too long. My chest swells with something wild and heavy—not fear, not exactly, but something close. My throat tightens, and the tears come. Not the kind that claw and choke, but the quiet kind. The kind that says you made it.

They sting a little on the way down, but that's okay. They're honest. Cleansing.

The light ahead is real — not the cheap carnival crap that buzzed like dying insects, but real light. Morning-light. Funeral-light. The kind that doesn't lie to you. It doesn't promise comfort. It promises truth. And strength, maybe, if you've got the guts to stand in it.

CHAPTER 28

Behind me, the carnival lets out a long, low sigh. The whispering starts to fade, like someone slowly turning the volume knob down on an old transistor radio. Static, then silence. The Ringleader — my shadow-self in a costume of pain — doesn't follow. She's shrinking now, folding back into the dark she came from, a figure built on fear that doesn't have anything to feed on anymore.

"Goodbye," I murmur, and it comes out soft and final. It's not dramatic. It's not triumphant. A single word, heavy as a tombstone and light as breath. I'm not sure who I'm saying it to — the carnival, the mask, or maybe just the broken version of myself I've been dragging behind me like a dead limb.

My fingers graze the doorframe. It's solid. Wood, maybe. Or something older. Doesn't matter. It's real. The light swells around me like a tide. I feel it slip under my skin, crawl into the cracks. It doesn't burn. It warms. Fills the hollow places.

I step out of the nightmare and into the light. The past is still with me — the guilt, the grief, the love, the loss. All of it. But I'm not carrying it like a chain anymore.

Chapter 29

My lungs explode with a ragged gasp, like breaking the surface after sinking too deep for too long. Air rushes in—cold, sharp, cruel—and it burns all the way down, as if my body forgot how to breathe and is relearning the hard way.

My heart kicks against my ribcage, wild and erratic, pounding like it's trying to outrun whatever nightmare I just crawled out of. Sound floods in next—machines beeping steadily, the low hum of fluorescent lights, the soft rustle of sterile sheets—and for a second, none of it makes sense.

Where am I?

The darkness clings to me, thick and stubborn. I feel the carnival lingering just behind my eyes—its voices, its mirrors, its twisted light. It hasn't quite let go. Panic claws up my throat, sharp and fast, but I choke it down. I'm here. I'm awake. I think.

I try to sit up, but my body doesn't cooperate. My arms tremble like wet paper, and the effort sends a white-hot pulse of dizziness through my skull. My vision tunnels, the edges curling inward like old film stock catching fire. I collapse back into the pillows, gasping, heart thudding like a war drum.

Everything hurts—not in the sharp, scream-out-loud way, but in that dull, deep, I've-been-somewhere-I-shouldn't-have-

CHAPTER 29

been kind of ache. My legs feel like they're made of cement. My fingers twitch, barely registering the crumpled blanket beneath them.

I close my eyes again, trying to hold still. The world tilts lazily around me, like it's deciding whether to let me stay in it or not. I breathe, slow and shallow. In. Out. The carnival is gone. I think. But something of it-some piece of its weight, of its truth—still lingers in my bones.

My vision swims as I force my eyes open, everything a blur of light and motion. The brightness overhead stabs at my skull, and I blink rapidly, each movement like dragging sandpaper across raw nerves. Nothing makes sense at first— just a kaleidoscope of white, too sharp, too much.

The ceiling comes into focus in hesitant steps. Harsh fluorescent lights hum overhead, washing everything in an antiseptic glow that feels less like illumination and more like exposure. The glare makes my head throb, and I squint, trying to pull the world into something I can hold onto.

White. That's the first thing I register. Not just the ceiling—*everything*. The sheets, the walls, even the silence feels bleached. It's the kind of sterility that scrubs the soul as well as the skin. The walls are a pale, institutional off-white, the color of surrender. No signs of the outside world. Just this quiet box and that smell—sharp, chemical, unmistakably *hospital*.

A steady beeping cuts through the silence to my left. Not urgent. Not comforting either. Just there. Marking time in neat, indifferent intervals. Other sounds drift in—muffled voices, the distant roll of wheels, maybe a TV in another room—but they're wrapped in cotton, dulled by distance and pain meds.

I focus on the sounds, the smells, the flicker of the lights—anything to anchor me. Because the truth is clawing its way up through the haze: I'm in a hospital. I'm alive. The carnival is gone. But something in me hasn't left it entirely.

The silence isn't just silence—it's a presence, thick and clinging, like smoke after a fire. It fills the corners of the room, presses against my chest, curls in my throat like a thing alive. The slow, mechanical beep of the monitor becomes a kind of heartbeat—someone else's, maybe mine, maybe not. Hard to tell. Everything feels like it's happening through glass.

I close my eyes, hoping it'll calm the panic crawling beneath my skin, but all I see is them—them-the shadows, the masks, the mirrors. The carnival hasn't left me. It's just wearing a new costume.

My eyes snap open again, desperate for something—anything—to anchor me. What I get is the mirror.

It's small, tacked to the wall like an afterthought, but the reflection stops me cold. For a second, I don't recognize the woman staring back. Pale as wax. Hair like dried seaweed, clinging to her face in limp strands. The eyes are the worst—hollow and wide, like she's seen something that bent the world out of shape and never quite snapped back.

I want to look away. I should look away. But I can't.

Because that's me.

That's the version of Brooke Sullivan that came crawling out of the wreckage—not the car crash, no, that was just the beginning—but the wreckage of everything that followed. Of grief, and guilt, and the way a person can live inside their own head so long they forget what breathing feels like.

That face isn't screaming, but it might as well be.

And God help me, I know exactly what it's trying to say.

CHAPTER 29

The memories don't drift in—they slam. No warning. Just a full-body, brain-splitting impact. The kind of thing that hits you like a wave you never saw coming, leaves you sputtering for air in its wake. The carnival's laughter still claws at the edges of my mind, high-pitched and grating, like a merry-go-round soundtrack left to rot in the rain. I swear I can still feel those cold fingers on my skin—like frostbite made flesh, grabbing, pulling, always pulling.

And the mirrors—God, the mirrors. Each one worse than the last, like they weren't showing reflections so much as x-rays of my soul, cracked and blackened and bleeding guilt. The masked things that haunted me, danced around me, whispered in that singsong voice that knew just where to dig... they're still there, tucked into the folds of my memory, waiting.

But Jenna's voice slices through the noise.

"Wake up, Brooke."

It's not the echo I've heard in dreams. It's her—the real one. That warm, steady tone she used when I spiraled. When I doubted. When I needed her most. My throat tightens. The guilt slams back in. I'm here. She's not. And that fact hits with the same nauseating twist it always has—survivor's guilt, ugly and relentless.

I stare at my hands—pale things resting on even paler sheets—and will them to move. They twitch. It's pathetic, but it's a movement. I curl my fingers into fists. It's like lifting cinderblocks tied to frayed nerves. Everything inside me screams to stop, to lie down, to forget. But I push.

The sheets are heavy. Not just physically, emotionally. Like they've soaked up every hour of helplessness, every night of silence. My arms shake so hard I think they might give out. My vision goes watery around the edges. I press my palms into the mattress like it's the only thing holding me to this world and force myself up.

Pain. Dizziness. Sweat slicking my brow.

But then I'm sitting. Upright. Barely. Breathing like I've just run a marathon through hell. The room spins like I've had too much to drink, but I hold on.

Somewhere in all that shaking and gasping, I feel it—a flicker. Not strength, not yet. But something. A stubborn little ember down in the wreckage that whispers, You did it. You're not done yet.

And maybe that's enough. For now.

My fingers dig into the edge of the mattress, knuckles pale against wrinkled hospital linen. The thin sheets bunch beneath my grip like damp tissue paper, and I hold on like the bed is the only thing keeping me from sliding back into whatever hell I just clawed my way out of. Every breath feels like a minor miracle—sharp and ragged, but real. My lungs protest, a slow burn catching fire in my chest.

The room around me buzzes faintly—vents whirring, machines pulsing in the corners. Somewhere outside, a cart squeaks along the linoleum, wheels groaning with every turn. It's background noise, but it matters. Because it means I'm here. Not there. Not anymore.

I close my eyes. Just for a second. Not to rest. To feel. And the silence—it's different. Not the cloying, suffocating hush of the carnival. That silence had teeth. This one just… is. It smells like bleach and gauze and maybe a little loneliness, but it's real. Unforgiving, but honest. I'll take it.

My arms quiver under the weight of my own body, muscles jelly from disuse, but I hold the line. The sweat trickling down my temple feels like baptism, not failure. Every ache, every

CHAPTER 29

tremble—they remind me I made it. I bled and screamed and broke, but I came out the other side. A little worse for wear, sure. But breathing.

I can feel something low in my chest, slow and steady, like the first roll of thunder on a distant horizon. Not fear. Not regret. Resolve. That slow thrum of something waking up in my bones. I've stared down nightmares that wore my own face, whispered my own doubts. This? This is just recovery. This is survival.

The path ahead won't be soft. There'll be nights I wake up screaming, days where the weight of remembering feels like too much. But I'm not running anymore. I'm not hiding. I'm here.

Chapter 30

The afternoon sun slipping through half-drawn drapes makes the flicker of the fluorescent lights above almost undetectable. As I move around in my hospital bed, the sheets ruffle and press hard against an unfamiliar sensation on my skin.

Constantly mechanical machines beep next to me. Like a metronome, every noise reverberates off the stark, germ-ridden walls and tiles.

A wilted bouquet sits on the table. Petals curled, edges browned. Someone must've brought them while I was lost in that other place—the Realm of Illusions. The thought tightens my stomach. I pull the blanket closer, seeking warmth that doesn't come.

There is a mix of vitality and decay in the air, with the aroma of antiseptic, and withering flowers. As if attempting to hide the impending doom, hospitals always have that smell.

A glimmer of sunlight peeks through the haze, casting a light on the airborne dust particles. As I return, they continue to drift softly, unconcerned. The walls, which were originally white, now appear slightly gray as they absorb light and reflect weariness.

Amidst the beeps, a hush falls over me. A heavier, more resigned, waiting silence, rather than the stifling noise of the

CHAPTER 30

carnival.

I lie motionless, terrified that any movement could break this delicate illusion. Taking a deep, careful breath at a time. The light streaming in through the window at this late hour makes me look away. The other spot, where the light was misleading, continues to occupy my thoughts.

Memories weigh me down, making my limbs ache. Even now, you can hear the carnival's ghosts—the reflected faces and voices. Understated, but constant.

I swear I see Jenna from time to time. Before I can concentrate, a glimmer at the periphery of my vision disappears. With every repetition, my heart skips a beat as it searches for an intangible recollection.

A ghostly, pallid version of myself appears as I look into the window. A soft ray of sunlight brushes over my cheek, casting a shadow that cannot be fully eliminated.

As a result of the stress and anxiety from the night before, my fingers quiver as I lie in bed. While I want to move and stretch, I also want to stay still. I am not yet prepared to accept the invitation that movement offers.

This sterilized chamber stands in stark contrast to that tumultuous environment. Both seem incompatible to me, and I find myself caught in the middle of them.

Waiting is more like it than recuperation. Still longing for that authentic experience.

Gentle, steady steps are heard in sync with the heart monitor's beat. I feel a shallow gasp. That rhythm is familiar to me.

I freeze, staring intently at the entrance. Echoing in the corridor, the steps intesify in volume. I feel like time is warped.

All footsteps at a hospital have significance. All of them heighten the precariousness of the current situation.

My fingers grip the sheet, anchoring me. The steps stop outside the door. A soft click as the handle turns.

The door opens slowly, light from the hallway spilling in. Shadows stretch across the floor.

With methodical motions, the nurse steps inside the room. As if approaching a holy or perilous object, every step was measured.

My gaze avoids her. As I watch the dust motes silently dance outside my window, I can't take my eyes off of them.

She takes a deep breath in. Her reluctance and the weight of her gaze are palpable to me. Scrunched but clean clean scrubs, dark hair pulled back—that what I see through the mirror. Fearful, she hesitates in the foyer.

She seems taken aback as her hand lingers close to her mouth. As if I were about to disappear, she remains silent and observes me.

Perhaps she sees a miracle. Or a mistake. Someone who shouldn't have returned.

I wonder what she sees—a body alive but barely used, a face slack from sleep and sorrow. Do I look like someone who clawed back from the brink.?

My hands rest atop the blanket, still. Outside, a tree sways in a breeze I can't feel. It appears more alive than I do.

She shifts her weight; her shoes squeak softly. A mundane sound that echoes loudly in the quiet. She want to speak, to ask questions. I could answer, but I'm not sure I know the answers.

So I keep my eyes on the tree, and she stands there, and the machines continue their steady beeping.

CHAPTER 30

The nurse's footsteps falter—a brief pause. Through the window's reflection, I see her expression shift. Shock ripples across her face as her clipboard slips. She catches it quickly, pressing it to her chest.

"Miss Sullivan?"

Her voice is thin, wavering. She probably intended it to be clinical, but there's a crack in it—grief, hope, maybe both.

I don't respond. I just watch her through the reflection as she steps forward, cautiously.

Her scrubs whisper with each movement. She glances for the monitor to me, the back, as if seeking confirmation.

"I... I need to get the doctor."

She doesn't move. Her hand hovers between us, fingers twitching. The clipboard clutched against her ribs feels less like armor now, more like a lifeline.

I see it in her eyes—the disbelief, the hope. How many nights did she sit by this bed, adjusting IVs, smoothing blankets, whispering into the void?

She's been here. Now, so am I.

The beeping continues, steady. I finally shift my gaze from the window and look at her—not fully, just enough. Our eyes meeting in the reflection.

That's when I see it—the truth. She didn't expect me to wake up. Now, she doesn't know what to do with the fact that I have.

I keep my eyes on the wind. Outside, the world moves on. In here, everything feels suspended.

The nurse remains behind me, a blurred presence. Her movements are soft, muted by the silence. I don't turn. I just keep staring at the glass, watching my reflection hover over the branches.

She shifts her weight; I hear the quiet squeak of her shoes. Through the window's reflection, I catch her outline- clipboard clutched tight, fingers twitching, face taut with emotion.

The monitors beep steadily. They're indifferent to my awakening. They just count the seconds.

She has something to say. Her lips barely part and then reseal. Her hand flits up and down, hovers—uncertain. Words might break the spell, she things.

I remain still though. My limbs are immobile on the comforter. I feel a gentle rhythmic rise and fall in my chest. It is too soon for me to speak. I am not ready just yet.

So I savored every second of it.

Chapter 31

The morning light is different today.

It slips in through the thin curtains like an apology, not the harsh slap of fluorescence I've grown used to. No blue-white glare. No sterile sting. Just warmth — gentle and golden — pooling across the stiff folds of my hospital blanket, crawling its way toward me like something alive. I watch it move, inch by inch, until it catches the side of my arm, and I shiver despite the heat.

Dust floats in the beams like tiny ghosts. They spin and drift and tumble with a grace that feels too delicate for this place, and nothing at all like the screaming lights of the carnival — that madness of color and shadow, of mirrors and masks and things that called my name in a voice that didn't belong to anyone living.

My eyes fall to the daisies on the bedside table. My mother's touch, no doubt — bright yellow centers ringed in white, just beginning to droop at the edges but still stubbornly alive. They sit beside the usual fare: a plastic water cup, a paper napkin with a coffee stain, a half-read magazine curled like a dead thing. But the daisies shine. They belong. Somehow, they soften the edges of everything else.

I breathe in. Not shallow, not panicked — in. Deep and full.

The scent of the daisies reaches me, and for the first time in what feels like a lifetime, I don't smell burnt sugar or mildew or old carnival tickets soaked through with blood and regret. Just petals and sun. Simple, clean. Real.

Outside the room, the world hums with life. Footsteps tap and scuff along tile. A gurney squeals on one sticky wheel. Nurses speak in clipped rhythms, voices low and efficient. A cough. Laughter. A door creaks open, and somewhere far off, someone calls for a doctor in a voice that's too tired to panic.

That's the symphony now. Not calliope music or whispering shadows, but real, human sound. The kind of background noise that says the world hasn't ended, that people still eat lunch and change bandages and fall in love and die in rooms just like this one. And somehow, that comfort hums louder than the carnival ever could.

I shift. Slowly. The sheets scratch softly against my skin, clean and stiff. I move like someone learning how to be in a body again. There's soreness, sure. Muscle and bone protesting the effort. But there's no resistance. No grasping hands. No impossible mirrors that show you who you could've become if you'd just stayed asleep a little longer.

The sun keeps crawling across the room. It finds the cracks in the walls, the corners that seemed full of menace in the dark. And in its glow, they're just... corners. Drywall and paint and the faint ghost of a scuff where someone bumped a cart too hard. Nothing to fear.

I let the light touch my face. Let it remind me I'm still here.

And for the first time since I woke, I start to believe that maybe—just maybe—that's a good thing.

I stir.

Not in some dramatic, flailing way. No gasping breath, no

CHAPTER 31

jolting upright like they do in the movies. Just a shift. Subtle. The kind of movement you make when a part of you starts to remember it's alive.

The light finds me first.

It's not harsh. Not the aggressive slap of overhead fluorescents or the flickering white buzz of night shift neglect. This is morning light — the real kind. Golden. Warm. It sneaks in through the curtain seams and lays across the foot of my bed like a dog settling in for a nap.

I breathe.

A slow, deliberate inhale. Not the shallow, hiccuping breaths of sedation, but something deeper. Clean. My ribs expand like creaking floorboards. It doesn't hurt, not exactly — but there's a stiffness, like a house waking up after a long, bitter winter. My chest rises and falls with purpose, and for the first time in a long time, it feels like I'm doing the breathing. Not the machines. Not the drugs. Me.

The sheets rustle under me as I shift. Stiff cotton, starched clean — the kind you only find in hospitals and old motels. They're scratchy against my skin, but I welcome it. It's texture. It's real. Not like the dream-scapes and fog-soaked illusions of that other place — the Realm, the Funhouse, whatever name I give it will never capture the way it wrapped itself around my mind like ivy.

I lift a hand. Slow. Testing.

My fingers tremble as they rise, but they rise. They move. Like old keys turning in locks that haven't been used in years. I flex them once. Twice. They obey, sluggish but sure, like they're learning me again — reacquainting themselves with what it means to be part of this body.

I blink.

The room sharpens by degrees. White walls. Chrome rails. A soft mechanical hiss and the whisper of plastic tubing. A curtain shivers in the breeze, stirred by the ceiling vent above. I follow its motion, track it with eyes that have spent too long staring inward. Everything is dull and bright at once. Too much, too little. But it's all mine.

I'm not in the Funhouse anymore. No warped mirrors. No masks. Just this — a hospital room. Real and plain and unmagical in every way.

And yet... it feels like salvation.

Each breath is a small triumph. Each flutter of fingers, each blink of eyelid, each note from the monitor beside me — it all feels like a *beginning*. Not flashy. Not loud. But rooted. Solid. The kind of beginning you only get after surviving something you weren't entirely sure you'd come back from.

The sun moves across my skin, slow and steady.

And I let it.

Because for the first time since I opened my eyes in this place... I want to be here.

The clock ticks, soft and measured. A metronome for the living. Each second drops into the room like water from a leaking faucet, marking time not with urgency, but with quiet insistence. You're still here, it says. You're still here.

And then—the door creaks.

That's all it takes. One groaning hinge, one note of ordinary sound, and my heart stutters. Not out of fear, not anymore. Out of recognition. Anticipation. A memory stitched into muscle and marrow.

She steps into the room.

My mother's silhouette cuts clean through the soft morning light, and for a moment, she doesn't move. She just stands

CHAPTER 31

there, framed in the doorway like something holy. Her posture is tight with weeks of worry, and her face... God, her face is older. Not in the way time does it, but in the way waiting and not-knowing and hoping can wear a person down to the bone.

But then she sees me.

And just like that, her whole body exhales. The tension unspools from her shoulders, and the cracks in her expression smooth over. What's left is a smile that could knock the air from your lungs — the kind of smile only a mother can manage after nearly losing her child. It's the sun punching through a sky thick with thunderclouds. It's everything I didn't know I needed.

"Brooke," she says, her voice soft and shaking. Like it might fall apart if she says anything more.

She walks toward me slowly, like I'm made of glass. She always did have that look when I was sick — cautious love, steady as the tide. The light catches the streaks of silver in her hair, and for a moment, she glows. Not in the way angels do. In the way survivors do. In the way women who've waited too long for news and kept themselves from breaking because they had to finally get to breathe again.

And then — her scent.

That mix of lavender and something else I could never name. It's not perfume. It's her. It's Sunday pancakes and garden dirt and the hum of her voice while folding laundry. It's home. It hits me like a gut-punch wrapped in comfort, and my throat tightens until I think I might choke on the emotion crawling up from my chest.

She leans in. Doesn't speak. Just brushes her hand against my cheek, and I don't flinch. I let her.

Because this — this quiet, trembling moment — is real.

Not twisted shadows or funhouse lies. Not illusions wrapped in velvet and decay.

Just my mother.

And her love, thick and warm as the sunbeams spilling across my bed.

Mom eases into the chair beside my bed like she's afraid the floor might give way. Her hands hover in the space between her lap and mine, fingers twitching with the urge to do something — straighten a sheet, tuck in a corner, fix something that can't be fixed. I can see the carefulness in her movements. It's the same kind of quiet you bring to a room where someone's sleeping or dying, and you're not entirely sure which it is yet.

"Good morning, sweetheart," she says, her voice soft but practiced, like she's said it every morning since I went under, whether I could hear it or not. "I brought you some flowers."

She sets the vase down like it's sacred. Daisies, of course. Her favorite. Their yellow centers shine like little suns, trying to punch holes in the sterile gloom of the room. It's too bright for the space, too cheerful. But that's her — always trying to beat back the dark with something small and stubborn and alive.

When she pulls her hand back from mine, I catch the tremble. It's tiny. Barely there. But I see it. She smiles anyway — that smile. The one that saw me through fevers and food poisoning and the year I broke my arm and Jenna and I spent Halloween watching horror movies on the couch instead of trick-or-treating. That smile was a promise then. It still is.

"Your Aunt Sarah called this morning," she says, settling into the rhythm of small talk like a lifeline. "Tommy lost another tooth. Right in the middle of picture day." She chuckles, the sound light but stretched thin, like it's working overtime to keep her from crying. "And Mrs. Peterson's damn cat got stuck in our maple tree again. Fire department had to come out. Big scene."

I don't answer, but I don't need to. She keeps going.

She discusses daffodils blooming too early and how the robins are back in the backyard, pecking through the mulch like little feathered thieves. Every word is like a thread pulling me back toward something solid, something real. Not masks. Not mirrors. There are no shadows obscuring my face.

Just home.

She leans forward, and the sunlight hits the silver in her hair just right, making her glow a little, like a lighthouse in a storm. She's still talking — soft, steady, undeterred — and her hand finds mine again. I don't pull away this time.

And maybe I'm not ready to speak just yet, but I listen. Her voice, in this moment, is the only thing that hasn't felt like a dream.

Mom's presence seeps into the room like warmth from an old quilt — not flashy, not loud, just steady, familiar, there. Her hand stays wrapped around mine, thumb tracing those soft, rhythmic circles on my skin, the way she used to when I was five and burning up with fever, and she couldn't do a damn thing about it except be there.

It's stupid how something so small can crack you open.

The silence doesn't need filling. We've shared this kind before — in the backyard with our knees buried in dirt, pruning tomato plants and watching the sky go pink. It's the kind of quiet that says everything without needing to say much at all.

"The daisies are beautiful," I say, and my voice sounds like gravel scraping up through rusted pipes. But I get the words out.

Her whole face lights up, like someone hit a switch. "I remembered they were always your favorite."

I nod, the motion slow, like testing a sore muscle. "You taught me how to split the stems just right."

Her eyes soften, and she gives my hand the gentlest squeeze. I squeeze back — not much, just enough. Like saying I'm here. Still me. Just bruised a bit.

"I was thinking about your old room today," she says, voice low and careful, like she's talking around something sharp. "Those glow-in-the-dark stars you insisted on sticking to the ceiling. They're still there, you know. Still glowing."

That pulls a laugh out of me — rusty and unexpected. "You never took them down?"

She shakes her head, the corners of her eyes glistening. "Never could bring myself to. They reminded me of you — how you always found light in the dark."

I don't answer right away. My throat's thick, my chest tight, but not in the bad way. This isn't panic or grief clawing at my ribs. This is… remembering. The stars. The smell of her lavender hand lotion. Late nights when I used to sneak into her room after nightmares, and she never once turned me away.

Her words hang there between us, gentle and true.

And yeah, maybe I'm still sorting through the wreckage. Maybe I still hear the carnival's music in the corners of my dreams. But in this moment — with my mother's thumb still tracing circles on my hand, and the memory of glow-in-the-dark stars still hanging in the air — I feel something else.

CHAPTER 31

Light. The real kind.

I lift my hand slow, like I'm not sure it's really mine. The weight surprises me — not heavy, but real. Solid. The kind of weight that says you're here. You made it. My fingers find hers, and I thread them together, palm to palm. It feels like home. A thousand Sunday mornings and late-night phone calls packed into one small gesture.

Her skin's warm. Familiar. A little rough around the edges from gardening and years of work that no one thanked her enough for. It grounds me — the texture, the shape, the way her thumb fits naturally in that groove between my knuckles. I didn't know how much I missed this until right now.

Something cracks open inside me. Just a hairline fracture at first, then wider. Like a dam giving way after too many seasons of drought. The tears come hot and quiet, not the kind you choke on, but the kind that run clean and steady, washing out places you forgot were even hurting.

She tightens her grip. Not too much, just enough. Just enough to say I know. I'm here.

And that's all I need. We sit there like that, letting the sun do its slow crawl across the window, painting everything in that golden, forgiving light. The weight of the accident, the guilt, Jenna — it's all still there. But it's not pressing down so hard now. Not when I've got Mom's hand in mine, and her thumb tracing those slow, familiar circles like it did when I was a kid too sick to sleep.

I look over and see the tears on her cheeks. Matching mine. She doesn't wipe them away. Neither do I. There's no need. This is the kind of crying that feels like telling the truth.

The silence sits with us, softer now. Not empty — just full of everything we're not saying out loud. Everything we don't need to. That space between us, the one that used to be filled with fear and not knowing — it's different now. Like maybe it could hold something else too. Something like healing.

And I think — maybe this isn't the end of the story. Maybe it's just the part where we start breathing again.

As Mom rambles about Mrs. Peterson's cat and its latest escapade, something stirs loose in my brain — a flicker of summer sun, the smell of wet grass, and mayonnaise gone warm in the heat.

"Remember that picnic?" I murmur, my voice still gravel-thick from disuse, but stronger now. "The stray cat that swiped your tuna sandwich right off your plate?"

Her eyes catch fire the way they used to when she got punch-drunk on laughter. "Oh Lord, yes! And your father — napkin still tucked into his shirt like he was expecting five-star service — went after it like he had a prayer of catching the thing."

A laugh slips from my throat, honest and unforced. "He tripped over the cooler."

"Face-first into the potato salad," she finishes, tears springing to her eyes — the good kind, the kind that sting a little but don't hurt.

"And then he blamed it on those stupid new loafers," I add, the smile now fully settled on my face, like it remembered how to stay.

One memory uncorks the next. The birthday cake that came out lopsided and gluey because we used salt instead of sugar. Sunday afternoons elbow-deep in dirt, planting daffodils like we were solving the world's problems one bulb at a time. Her voice, always half a note off, singing some old Dusty Springfield song while doing the dishes — and Dad chiming in with lyrics that made no sense but somehow still

CHAPTER 31

worked.

Our laughter fills the room, gentle and cracked around the edges, blending with the steady beep of hospital machinery. It's a weird harmony — grief and joy holding hands like old lovers. The pain is still there, curled up somewhere deep in my chest like a sleeping dog, but these memories... they're something else. Like stones you step on to get across a river — slick with moss, but solid underfoot.

"We've weathered some pretty strange storms, haven't we?" I say, squeezing her hand gently.

She squeezes back. "Yeah. But we always found something to laugh about. Even when everything else went to hell."

And there it is — the heart of it. That quiet, unshakable truth. Even in this sterile box of a hospital room, with shadows still camped out in the corners of my mind, we've managed to find a flicker of light. Not in spite of the pain, but right beside it. Like daffodils pushing up through cold spring dirt — stubborn, and bright, and exactly what I didn't know I needed to remember.

The silence that settles between us isn't empty anymore. It's full—thick with years and memories and the kind of understanding that doesn't need to be spoken aloud. It wraps around us like an old quilt, a little frayed at the edges but still warm, still whole. Mom's hand stays in mine, steady, her thumb tracing those slow circles I've known since childhood. They used to lull me to sleep when the monsters under my bed felt too real. They still do.

Sunlight spills across the floor in soft strips, catching the edges of the blanket and the faint sheen of the IV stand. I watch the dust drift through the beams like it's dancing for us, slow and aimless. It feels strange to find beauty here, in a room that smells like antiseptic and echoes like a chapel. But it's here. And that's enough.

Something's shifted. Not gone—not the carnival, not Jenna, not the guilt that curls like smoke in the corners of my mind—but moved. Repositioned. Made room for something else. Maybe not forgiveness yet, but the possibility of it.

I glance at Mom, catch her profile in the morning light. The silver in her hair gleams like wire thread, and the soft wear of years maps itself in the lines beside her eyes. She's always been this way—constant. My personal lighthouse, even when I sailed straight into the storm. Even when I swore I didn't need saving.

The room hums with small things: the beeping of monitors, the low whoosh of air vents, the whisper of fabric as Mom shifts in her chair. But her presence is louder than any of it. Not in a way that demands space, but in a way that *fills* it. She's here. She's *still* here.

Healing isn't linear. I know that now. It doubles back, it stumbles, it pauses in doorways and sometimes hides under the bed. But it moves. And I'm not walking the path alone—not anymore, maybe not ever.

When she turns to look at me, there's something in her eyes that steadies me more than any pill or therapy session could. No expectation. No forced optimism. Just love. The kind that holds you up when your own legs won't. The kind that waits patiently in hospital chairs and still hums lullabies you don't remember teaching her to sing.

And for the first time in a long while, I don't look away.

The afternoon light has turned amber, the kind of light that softens the world just before it lets go of the day. It stretches long shadows across the room, painting the walls in gold and ash. Mom glances at the clock the way people do when they don't want to leave but know they have to—half-resigned, half-hoping time might stall for a few more minutes if she just wills it hard enough.

She shifts in her chair, adjusting the strap of her purse. It's a practiced gesture, meant to be casual, but I can see the reluctance in it—in her eyes, in the way her hand doesn't quite let go of mine. We've built something in this room today, something small and sacred, and neither of us wants to see it undone by distance or time.

"I should let you rest," she says, barely above a whisper. But her hand stays on mine, thumb brushing across my knuckles like she's memorizing the shape of me again, just in case. There's something raw beneath my ribs, a tenderness I didn't expect, like scar tissue softened into new skin.

She leans in close and the lavender clings to her like it always has—floral, warm, a little earthy. It smells like home. Like safe. Her kiss lands gently on my forehead, and I close my eyes. Let myself fall into that moment. Let myself need it.

"I'll be back tomorrow, okay?" she says. That voice—steady, certain, built from years of midnight fevers and heartbreak and waiting by doors that didn't open when they should have. "We'll keep going. One day at a time."

And somehow, that's enough. More than enough. Her words settle deep, like stones being placed one after the other, building a path forward. Maybe even out of this place.

She straightens, steps back into the light spilling from the hallway. I watch her silhouette pause at the door. Just a second. Long enough to feel like a goodbye without being one. Then she's gone, and the room feels quieter, but not empty.

Something stirs in my chest—not the old grief, not the

weight that once sat like stone. No, this is something gentler. Lighter. Like breath after a long dive. Like the sound of spring just beginning to arrive.

And when I smile, it's not because I'm fine. It's because for the first time in a long time, I believe I could be.

Chapter 32

I lie awake, the ceiling above me stained in that particular shade of hospital gray that never quite disappears, no matter how much light you pour on it. The monitors beside my bed click and beep in their familiar rhythm—steady, predictable. A metronome for the living.

Night has crept in, soft as fog and twice as unsettling. The chaos of the day—doctors murmuring, phones ringing, the gentle invasion of vital checks and polite smiles—has dulled into something else entirely. There is a hush, but it's not a peaceful one. It's the kind of quiet that feels like it's listening.

Through the crack in the door, the hallway stretches out with dim light. The fluorescent lights overhead flicker just frequently enough to prick my nerves. Every stutter of light casts fresh shadows, stretching long and thin across the floor like something trying to crawl inside.

I try to remind myself, *You're not there anymore.* Not in the Funhouse. You are no longer beneath those humming neon arches. But the mind doesn't care for logic in the middle of the night. It cares about shapes it almost recognizes in the shadows. It's about how much a blinking light can look like an eye if you stare long enough.

Every now and then, I catch the soft squeak of nurse

shoes—rubber soles against linoleum, slow and measured. Comforting once. But now, in this stretched-out silence, they sound like something else entirely. Like someone—or something—that doesn't want to be noticed.

A distant machine starts beeping, sharp and regular. It penetrates the atmosphere with the precision of a blade. For a moment, I forget where I am. Then I feel it—pain blooming in my side, the familiar ache that reminds me I'm not floating anymore. I'm tethered. Perhaps I'm still in a state of brokenness. But here.

As I move, the sheets shift loudly, causing me to flinch. I half expect someone to appear in the doorway, silhouetted in the blue light, just watching. Just waiting.

But no one comes.

It's just me and the darkness, and the machines.

And there is something in my bones—something quiet and small—that whispers to me that the carnival isn't quite finished with me yet.

I stand barefoot in the hallway, the cold linoleum biting at my soles like a warning I'm too tired to heed. The hospital gown flutters lightly against my calves, no match for the chill bleeding from the walls. My fingers curl against the plaster behind me, rough and slightly damp. I lean into it anyway—partly for balance, partly to remind myself that this place is real. I'm not in that place anymore.

Across from me, a window runs from floor to ceiling, dark as an unplugged TV screen. It reflects the corridor in that warped way cheap glass always does—flattened and stretched, familiar but wrong. I see myself in it, small and pale, the fluorescent light overhead casting strange ridges across my face. It appears as though someone has excavated me, not

CHAPTER 32

released me.

Behind me, the corridor seems to go on forever in the reflection. Door after door stands closed, and each one may be watching me back. The illusion bends the hallway into something impossible—like those carnival mirrors that make everything just a little too long, a little too narrow. You blink, and the shape of the world jumps a half-inch to the left.

I press my palm against the wall. It's cold enough to sting. The reflection of me in the window mimics my actions but is slightly out of sync. The difference is subtle—my reflection is half a second behind and slightly out of sync with my movements. It's possible that my mind is attempting to catch up. Could be something else.

I keep watching the window, waiting for the reflection to misstep again. For a second I don't blink. I don't make any movement.

The stillness is loud here. So loud I swear I can hear my own heartbeat in my ears—and beneath it, something softer. There is a subtle hum of static in the air. I was unable to take a breath.

The hospital is solid, full of nurses and machines and things that beep in a measured time. But this window—this glass—makes me feel like I'm standing between two floors. Leaning just a bit closer, I perceive a reflection in the mirror that has never left the carnival.

And worse, it might see me back.

I stare into the window and watch the edges of the world begin to unravel.

The sterile corridor behind me bends at strange angles, its clean white walls bleeding into gray, then black, like paper curling in flame. My reflection doesn't follow right away. It lingers—hovering in the glass like something trapped beneath ice. My face floats there, pale and drawn, surrounded by a thickening dark that pulses like a second heartbeat.

I lean in.

The woman staring back at me isn't quite me—not anymore. Her eyes are sunken, ringed with bruises no makeup could hide, carved deep by sleepless nights and carnival screams that never really stopped. The corners of her mouth are pinched, lips tight with secrets she can't even bring herself to whisper. She looks like someone who has seen the end of the world and come back with splinters of it still buried under her skin.

The longer I stare, the less tethered I become. My face begins to ripple, features bending and twisting like wet paint on glass. My eyes grow hollow, until they're nothing but two dark pits sucking the light from the hallway. The shadows beneath them deepen into something cavernous, wide enough to fall into.

The light above me flickers, just once, but the change is instant. My reflection doesn't blink, just watches.

And now I'm not sure who's doing the staring—me, or her.

The corridor fades from the window until all that remains is her face in the dark. No walls. No floor. Just her, suspended in black. A face untethered, a memory with teeth. Her lips part slightly, as if about to speak, and I swear I hear the distant calliope tune of the carousel, just beneath the steady beep of monitors and the hum of hospital lights.

My pulse skips.

I step back, breath caught in my throat, but the image in the glass remains close, as if the space between us never changed.

Behind her eyes, something stirs.

And it remembers me.

CHAPTER 32

My breath fogs the glass, a small bloom of heat in the cold space between us. But the figure doesn't blink. It doesn't breathe. It just stands there in that ghost-window world, watching me with those impossible, hollow eyes.

The mask shifts again.

Not physically—no twitch, no tilt, no gesture. But the feeling of it changes, like watching a face in a dream melt from one emotion to another. The elegant swirls etched across its porcelain skin begin to resemble veins, spiderwebbing outward, as if the mask were growing, alive and feeding on my fear. One of the etched lines traces the exact scar that runs behind my left ear. Another curves just like the slope of Jenna's final smile.

I stagger back, pressing harder into the wall behind me, as if I could disappear into its sterile shell.

The masked figure tilts its head.

And the world stutters.

A flicker—like a reel skipping in an old projector—and for half a second, the hallway around me is gone. No hospital. No fluorescent lights. Only red velvet curtains and twisted carnival mirrors, and that same calliope music, faint and distant, like it's being played underwater.

Then the flicker passes.

The hospital returns. But the figure remains.

Still.

Watching.

I realize, with a chill that scrapes down my spine, that the mask is familiar because it's mine. Not in metaphor. Not in theory. That face—those features twisted in guilt, soaked in grief—it was my face carved into that mask, distorted and frozen at the precise moment I believed I had killed my best friend.

It doesn't move.

It doesn't have to.

It's already inside me.

My pulse thunders in my ears as I take a trembling step back. The lights overhead hum louder. Too loud. The walls breathe. And in the glass, the masked figure lifts a single finger and places it gently against where its lips should be.

Shhh.

It doesn't make a sound.

But I hear it anyway.

The whisper curls into my skull like smoke, coiling around the memory of Jenna's voice.

"You're not done yet."

The corridor groans—an old building sound, plumbing or ductwork—but it startles me like a gunshot. My knees nearly buckle. The masked figure doesn't flinch. It doesn't need to. It has all the time in the world.

Its eyes—if you can call those hollow pits eyes—seem to pulse, just once, like a heartbeat from a heart that doesn't beat anymore. My reflection flickers again, and for a breathless moment, I see a different version of myself in the window. Not just pale and hollow-eyed—but smiling. I blink hard, and it's gone, but the echo lingers, like a bruise on my brain.

The figure tilts its head.

And I feel it in the pit of my stomach. Not like a dream. Not like a memory. Like it's here. In the room. Not in the hallway. Not behind the glass. Not some reflection or ghost. Here.

My mouth opens, but no sound escapes.

Because deep down, I know something awful.

That mask... isn't just staring at me.

CHAPTER 32

It's waiting.

Waiting for something.

Waiting for me.

The humming of the overhead lights shifts pitch—higher, thinner, almost imperceptible, like the sound of a dog whistle but just enough to make your bones itch. My vision tunnels for a split second. I close my eyes, trying to shake it loose. Trying to wake up, though I know I already have.

When I open them again, the mask is closer.

Only by inches.

But closer.

My breath catches in my throat. I haven't moved. I know I haven't. The glass is still intact. There's no door opening, no sound of approaching steps. And yet... it moved. It's still.

But it moved.

Behind the glass, behind that mask, I know there's not a person.

There's a presence.

It doesn't want to kill me. No, that would be too easy. Too kind.

It wants me back.

And if I keep staring, if I keep listening to the silence... I just might go.

My shadow joins the figure's in the glass now—two silhouettes facing off across some invisible chasm. One real, one imagined. Or maybe not. Maybe it's the other way around.

I don't look away.

The mask doesn't blink—because it can't. But it changes.

The shadows around its mouth lengthen, stretching into that same terrible smirk I saw in the Funhouse. Except now, it's not the Ringleader's expression. It's mine. Not a caricature.

Not a twisted mockery. Mine. The smile I wore the day of the accident. The one frozen in time in some forgotten photo Jenna's parents probably keep in a drawer they no longer open.

The edges of the mask shimmer faintly, like heat off pavement. And suddenly, I'm not just seeing the mask—I'm remembering it.

No... not just remembering.

Wearing it.

My throat tightens as the cold realization slithers through me. This mask—this figure—it doesn't belong to something outside me. It's not a monster sent to haunt me.

It's me. Or a version of me. The one who stayed in the carnival. The one who didn't claw her way back to consciousness. The one who gave in to the comfort of illusion and let the real world slip through her fingers like mist.

I stare into its empty eyes, and something like nausea coils in my gut.

Because now I know what it's waiting for.

It's not here to hurt me. It's here to welcome me back.

It wants to trade places.

And the most terrifying part?

Some small, splintered piece of me—the part still lost in the fog of guilt and grief—wants to accept.

I complete the turn.

There's nothing behind me.

Just the hallway. Empty. Silent. A stretch of identical doors and muted overhead lights, humming softly like they're trying to keep a secret. The air is still. Too still.

But that's not the part that makes my skin crawl.

It's the reflection.

Still there.

CHAPTER 32

Still staring.

Still smiling.

I glance over my shoulder again, heart thundering, but the corridor remains bare—white walls, linoleum floor, a faint scuff mark near Room 213 that I hadn't noticed before. No figure. No mask. Nothing but me and the quiet hum of machines and memory.

But in the window?

The masked figure hasn't moved an inch.

It stands right where I should be.

Not beside me.

Not behind me.

Instead of me.

And it's not staring at me anymore. It's staring through me. Like I'm the reflection now.

Something cracks inside my chest—some delicate, protective thing I didn't realize I'd been holding together with duct tape and breath. My knees nearly buckle. I clutch the wall again, nails dragging down the paint, trying to keep myself grounded. Real.

I press my palm to the glass.

The figure doesn't mimic the movement.

It just smiles.

That knowing, patient smile.

Like it's been waiting for me to catch up.

Like it knew I'd turn around and see nothing—because that's how it works, right? You never catch the monster looking back. You just see what it wants you to see. And right now, it wants me to wonder if I ever really left the carnival at all.

And for a split second, I do.

I step away from the wall, one foot in front of the other,

each movement deliberate, cautious—like I'm afraid the floor might give way beneath me. The corridor remains still. Too still. I know hospitals. I know their sounds. The clatter of carts, the rustle of paperwork, the hushed tones of night nurses behind thin curtains. But now, all I hear is the distant wheeze of the ventilation system and the soft squeak of my own footsteps on linoleum.

My gaze drifts back toward the window, almost against my will.

The reflection is empty.

Just me now.

And yet... it isn't. Not really.

There's a residue. Something intangible. The air in the corridor carries the memory of the figure like static electricity clings to skin. I can't explain it, but I feel it—like I've brushed against something vast and ancient that left fingerprints on my soul.

I reach up, touch my chest where my heart is pounding, half expecting to feel something foreign beneath my skin. I don't. Only the rapid thud of panic and breath. But the sense of being watched lingers. A prickle at the base of my neck. A chill along my spine that has nothing to do with hospital air conditioning.

And then I remember something Jenna said once.

"Sometimes absence is scarier than presence. It's what your brain fills the silence with."

My throat tightens. Because I'm starting to wonder if this... thing isn't trying to scare me with what it is.

Maybe it's scaring me with what it isn't.

What it took.

What it left behind.

CHAPTER 32

The corridor hums with fluorescent life, but it's not alive. It's indifferent. Impersonal. It watches without seeing. And me—I'm just another patient in a borrowed gown, shaking in bare feet, held together by tape and stubborn willpower.

I push off from the wall, my knees buckling slightly beneath the weight of adrenaline and confusion. The cool linoleum sends a jolt up my spine with each hesitant step, and I glance behind me. Because even when the figure is gone, the feeling of being *followed* lingers like a bad taste.

Still nothing.

No masked stranger. No impossible shadow stretching toward me. Just sterile geometry—white tiles, beige baseboards, chrome rails polished to a high shine that reflects nothing of value. But something's *off*. Something in the symmetry of the space. My trained eye wants to map it—count the panels between doorways, the pattern of vents, the rhythm of the ceiling tiles. It all adds up.

I pull away from the window, slowly, like peeling a bandage off skin too raw to heal. The breath I didn't realize I was holding escapes in a soft sigh, curling fog against the glass before vanishing.

Behind me, the hallway hums on with its indifferent rhythm. No footsteps. No creaking doors. Just the sterile hush of night and the soft percussion of machines recording my fragile return to life.

I glance down at my hands. Still trembling, but not with fear anymore—not entirely. There's exhaustion there, yes. There's damage. But there's also intent. It lives in the way my fingers flex now, testing strength instead of recoiling. In the way I square my shoulders, just a fraction straighter than before.

My hand lifts without thinking and touches the glass,

fingertips pressing lightly against the surface. It's cold. Impersonal. But it doesn't push back this time. There's no ripple, no cracking sound, no carnival scream just beyond the veil. Just the quiet acknowledgment of reflection—and what's been reflected through.

"I'm not done," I whisper.

Not a threat.

A promise.

The hospital might be real, the lights too bright and the air too clean, but the shadows I carry didn't stay behind. They're here with me—in the circles beneath my eyes, in the hesitation of every step. But I'm here too. And I'm not going to hide from them anymore.

Not when I've already survived their worst.

Chapter 33

It's strange how the body remembers trauma, even as the soul starts to let go. I can still feel the ghost of the mask—the Ringleader's hollow gaze, the way her smirk curled like smoke. But she isn't here. Not now. Not in this room where sunlight now touches even the coldest corners.

I open my eyes again.

The flowers seem to nod at me in the morning breeze leaking through the cracked window. They're so impossibly bright—like they don't know they're in a hospital room. They seem to be devoid of any other emotion except joy.

Maybe that's the kind of rebellion I need.

A nurse passes by in the hallway. I hear her humming softly to herself—something off-key but sweet, like lullabies hummed without thinking. It's the kind of sound that makes me feel tethered again. The kind that says, you're back, and the world kept turning, and now it's your turn to step into it again—when you're ready.

Not yet. But soon.

For now, I let the sun warm my skin, let the scent of daisies carry her memory, and let the beeping monitors remind me, You're here. You made it back. And there's still more story to write.

I draw in a slow breath, steadying myself as I let my feet brush the cool tile floor. The linoleum sends a shiver up my calves, but I welcome it—it reminds me I'm here. Really here. I am not ensnared by mirrors, shadows, or the concealed reflection of my guilt.

I press my palms into the mattress, grounding myself as I rise to my feet.

The tremble is still there, whispering through my knees and fingers, but it doesn't own me the way it did before. I walk two steps toward the window. Just two. It feels like miles.

The city outside is waking up—slow, unaware. Cars pass at regular intervals. A jogger crosses the street below, ponytail bouncing. I wonder what it feels like to move like that without thinking, without having to convince every limb to participate. To just... be.

The thought used to make me angry. Now it just makes me quiet.

The world didn't stop when Jenna did. It kept spinning. People kept jogging. Sunlight still filters through hospital windows and lands on withering petals in borrowed vases.

I place a hand against the glass, the surface cool under my fingertips.

"You'd tell me to move forward," I murmur, eyes scanning the horizon. "You'd roll your eyes and say something like, 'Well, Brooke, the world's not going to wait for you to catch up, so lace your shoes and start walking.'"

I smile despite myself. I can still hear her voice in my head—sarcastic, warm, relentless.

And maybe that's enough for now. Just that voice. Just those two steps. Just this light. Just today.

The second breath settles deeper. Not just in my chest, but

CHAPTER 33

in the places where the pain has lived too long—where I buried guilt so deep it had started to feel like a part of me. But it's not. Not entirely. I feel that now.

I sit back down on the edge of the bed, the mattress dipping slightly beneath me. My hands rest on my thighs, palms open. Not clenched. Not braced. Open.

It's such a small thing, and yet it feels like a decision.

Outside the window, the morning has shifted into late morning. The sky is still pale but warming. I watch a bird land on the windowsill of the building across from mine, its tiny head tilting, surveying the world like it's just waking up too.

I open my eyes slowly, blinking against the light. The room comes back into focus—the walls, the flowers, the faint rustling of nurses passing in the hallway. But Jenna's presence lingers, as if she's still seated beside me, legs tucked beneath her, hands wrapped around a mug she's forgotten to drink from.

I don't want to lose her again.

For so long, I avoided these memories. Locked them away behind walls I built with guilt and grief and the desperate need to survive. I was afraid that if I let myself remember her laughter, it would hurt too much. And it does, but it also feels like breathing again after too long underwater.

Maybe that's what healing really is. Not erasing the pain. Not pretending the loss didn't happen. But learning how to carry it with you—like a photograph in your wallet, a melody that comes back when you least expect it, a laugh that still echoes in your head even after the voice is gone.

I brush a tear from my cheek, not trying to hide it.

"Hey, Jenna," I whisper, my voice raw but steady. "I haven't forgotten."

And I won't.

Because she's part of me. In every cup of coffee, every daisy I pass on the street, every ridiculous sweater I see in a thrift store. She's there. Not gone, not really. Just... different now.

Just memory. And memory, I've come to realize, is a kind of forever.

The hospital room glows gold around the edges, softening the harsh lines of metal bedrails and antiseptic tile. And me? I'm sitting in the middle of it, letting memories of Jenna drift in, one by one, like paper boats on a still lake.

Each one stings in its own way—a thousand tiny cuts I've been too afraid to feel all at once. But underneath the sting, there's a warmth too, and that's the part that gets me. Not the ache, but the fact that it coexists with something good. That even now, with her gone, the echo of her laugh can still crack open the smallest smile.

"B, you're thinking too hard again." God, I can hear her. Clear as a bell and just as sharp. That voice—half teasing, half gospel truth. She always said it when she caught me slipping into my head, retreating like I was a turtle and the world was just too loud to deal with. And she'd pull me out again, like it was the easiest thing in the world.

The sun hits the daisies beside my bed, catching the petals just right, and I swear they glow. Jenna used to bring me flowers when she knew I was struggling. No fanfare, no explanation. "Everyone needs a little sunshine," she'd say, dropping them on my desk with a grin that could melt glaciers.

A tear slips down my cheek—not the kind that chokes you, but the kind that lets something out. Something I've been holding too tight for too long. I can picture her now, plain as

CHAPTER 33

day, rolling her eyes at how long I've stayed shut off from the world. "Life's too short to hide away," she'd say. "You've got to grab it with both hands."

The words land different now. Not like a suggestion, but a truth. A quiet, unshakable truth. Jenna lived like she was burning at both ends, bright and fast and full of grace. She didn't wait. She didn't wall herself off with guilt or sorrow. She dove in, heart first.

And now, I feel it—settling into my bones, curling around my ribs like a second breath. Not a haunting. Not grief's long shadow. Just... her. A whisper. A nudge. A reminder that I don't have to keep living like a ghost just because she's become one.

I close my eyes. Let the sun warm my skin, let it soak into the cracks.

The dust motes swirl in the sunlight, and I watch them dance.

I lift my hand and touch the tear on my cheek. It's gone cool now. But it's real. Just like she was. Just like some part of her still is. Not in some spooky ghost-story way, but in the places she carved out in me, the spaces she filled and left behind like fingerprints.

Some illusions—the good ones, the true ones—they don't fade. They stay, like paint that soaks into the grain of wood, like stardust in the bloodstream. And maybe, just maybe, they're the realest things we ever get.

The memories are still there. Of course they are. But they've settled now, like dust after a storm. They're not gone. They're just... quieter. Less like ghosts, more like books lined up on a shelf—worn, loved, impossible to forget. There's room for new stories now. That feels like a miracle.

The heaviness in my chest doesn't vanish. Grief doesn't do that. But it changes shape. Feels less like something pressing me down and more like something solid under my feet. A weight, sure, but one I can stand on. One I can use.

I rake my fingers through my hair. It's a small thing, but it feels deliberate. Tender, even. Like I'm here, in this body, in this moment, and I care enough to be present in it. There's still work to do, so much work—but for the first time in a long time, I'm not afraid of it.

This isn't the end.

It's the door creaking open.

It's the first step on a long road home.